Acclaim for the authors of
THE BETROTHAL

TERRI BRISBIN
"A welcome new voice…you won't want to miss."
—*USA TODAY* bestselling author Susan Wiggs

JOANNE ROCK
"*The Wedding Knight* is guaranteed to please! Joanne
Rock brings a fresh, vibrant voice to this charming tale."
—*New York Times* bestselling author Teresa Medeiros

MIRANDA JARRETT
"Miranda Jarrett continues to reign
as the queen of historical romance."
—*Romantic Times*

TERRI BRISBIN

is a wife to one, mom of three and dental hygienist to hundreds when not living the life of a glamorous romance author. Born, raised and still living in the southern New Jersey suburbs, Terri is active in several romance writers' organizations, including the RWA and NJRW. Terri's love of history, especially Great Britain's, led her to write historical romances. Readers are invited to contact Terri by e-mail at TerriBrisbin@aol.com or by mail at P.O. Box 41, Berlin, NJ 08009-0041. You can visit her Web site at www.terribrisbin.com.

JOANNE ROCK

Bestselling author Joanne Rock loves writing romances for Harlequin so much that she creates steamy contemporary stories in the Harlequin Blaze and Temptation lines while still indulging her passion for lush medievals with Harlequin Historicals. Joanne graduated from the University of Louisville with a master's degree in English literature and had fun trying on a variety of career hats, including television promotions director, actress and model. Having since discovered that her widespread adventures provided research for her books, Joanne now resides in the scenic Adirondacks with her husband and three sons, content to spend her days penning happy endings. Learn more about Joanne's work by visiting her Web site, www.joannerock.com.

MIRANDA JARRETT

considers herself sublimely fortunate to have a career that combines history and happy endings, even if it's one that's also made her family regular patrons of the local pizzeria. With over three million copies of her books in print, Miranda is the author of twenty-seven historical romances, and her bestselling books are enjoyed by readers around the world. She has won numerous awards for her writing, including two *Romantic Times* Reviewer's Choice Awards, and a Romance Writers of America RITA® Award finalist for best short historical romance. Miranda is a graduate of Brown University with a degree in art history. She loves to hear from readers at P.O. Box 1102, Paoli, PA 19301-1145, or MJarrett21@aol.com. Please visit her Web site at www.Mirandajarrett.com.

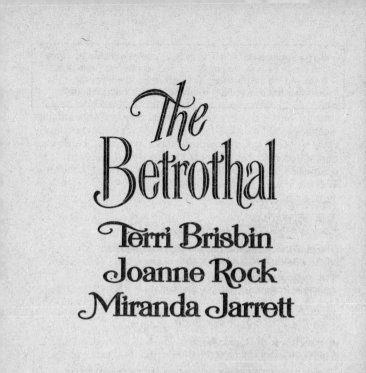

The Betrothal

Terri Brisbin
Joanne Rock
Miranda Jarrett

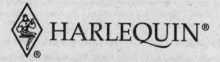

HARLEQUIN®

TORONTO • NEW YORK • LONDON
AMSTERDAM • PARIS • SYDNEY • HAMBURG
STOCKHOLM • ATHENS • TOKYO • MILAN • MADRID
PRAGUE • WARSAW • BUDAPEST • AUCKLAND

ISBN 0-373-29349-6

THE BETROTHAL
Copyright © 2005 by Harlequin Books S.A.

The publisher acknowledges the copyright holders
of the individual works as follows:

THE CLAIMING OF LADY JOANNA
Copyright © 2005 by Theresa S. Brisbin

HIGHLAND HANDFAST
Copyright © 2005 by Joanne Rock

A MARRIAGE IN THREE ACTS
Copyright © 2005 by Miranda Jarrett

CONTENTS

THE CLAIMING
OF LADY JOANNA

Terri Brisbin

Prologue

Canterbury, England
March, in the Year of Our Lord 1201

He was certain his head would split open if he did not clench his jaws together. Such rage filled him that Braden knew nothing good would come from saying any of the things he was thinking.

The damn girl had refused him!

And she'd done so in front of King John's court. The king was highly amused by her antics, as was his court, but the situation simply added to Braden's dark standing among the nobles of England. Most of those who served the king's interest laughed only because they had his protection. Braden's reputation scared them into better behavior when John was not present.

Why had her parents not obtained her consent before making the matter an issue in public view? Her arguments, articulated before a randy king willing to grant his new wife any request, had resulted in John's declaration that the lady must publicly consent to the match.

Although he found her courage before her parents' a

rage and the king's scrutiny somewhat admirable, she needed to be brought to heel quickly and firmly and he was the one who could do it. Even though his plans for her were not as black as some who believed his family's sordid past would suggest, he would not suffer such an insult without retribution and punishment against the one responsible. And Lady Joanna was that guilty soul.

God help her.

When he thought he might be able to speak without revealing the extent of his rage, he turned back to face the unhappy couple who did stand before him. They had the sense to realize how angry he was and what they stood to lose if their daughter did not go through with their arrangements. They wanted this marriage for their own reasons, as did he. They would have to make this right.

"The betrothal is completed, with or without her approval. But, I must have her consent at the wedding ceremony."

"Aye, my lord," Joanna's father stammered out. Everyone there at the king's Easter court knew of his decision now.

"Bring her to me at Wynwydd by the end of the month and make certain that only words of acceptance and consent come out of her mouth. I will handle the matter if you do not, but our agreement will change, as well."

Lord Robert turned to his wife and dismissed her with a wave. When they were alone, Joanna's father spoke again.

"She will give her consent to anything you ask, my lord. I promise you that. Worry not, my lord. She will give it at Wynwydd."

If Braden had misgivings about any harsh treatment his betrothed would receive at the hands of her parents, he banished quickly from his thoughts. The girl could do with some bread and water and a few days on her knees in the most frequent methods of convincing a wayward the wisdom and wishes of her parents.

"At Wynwydd, by month's end," he said, nodding to the other man.

"And the gold, my lord?" Lord Robert's unease at asking was clear; his hands shook, and he would not meet Braden's gaze.

"The agreement was gold for a wife. When I have a wife in name and truth, you will have your gold. And not before."

"She will comply, my lord," Lord Robert answered with confidence now. "Just leave her to me."

Lord Robert bowed and backed out of the room, leaving Braden alone with his anger. He needed a wife and the lord of Blackburn needed gold to rebuild his fortune and his lands. An acceptable trade for both parties. This had to work.

Braden walked to the table and poured a goblet full of the rich, red wine served by the king. Drinking it down without pause, he tried to allow his anger to pass. The girl would be brought to him at his estate near Wales within a few weeks. She would give her consent and they would marry. Her parents would receive their payment. The rumors whispered about the warlock lords of Wynwydd who killed the wives and servants who displeased them would be silenced. And his name, threatened with extinction, would continue.

All would be well.

It had to be.

Chapter One

Welsh Marches
April, in the Year of Our Lord 1201

"Cut it."

"But, my lady…"

"You must do this for me, Enyd. I fear that my hands shake too fiercely and I would take off my ear as well as my hair."

Joanna's attempt to calm her maid through humor did not work. Although Enyd held the shears closer now, the look of refusal on her face did not change.

"'Tis never been cut, my lady. Not since you were a wee one," Enyd said, drifting off into her thoughts. "Is there no other way?"

The waves of pain returned and Joanna fought against the weakness. She had so little time. The journey to Wynwydd would take only a day longer and then her fate was sealed. After finally succumbing to the beatings, she'd given her parents the words they wanted to hear. As the intensity and frequency of the lashings had increased, Joanna knew that her stubbornness and continued refusal to consent to the marriage would get her killed.

Well, if she had to die, at least she would choose the time and place, and it was not in the clutches of a warlock who would lay a curse on her soul even as she went to her death. 'Twould be in Scotland, with her sister.

Her hand slid up to her cheek and she felt the rising heat there. Time was slipping away and the small party of holy brothers traveling north to their home would be leaving just after dawn. The herbal concoction given to her to keep away fever was not working. From the sticky feeling that trickled down her leg, she knew that one or more of the wounds had reopened and were bleeding again.

"Enyd, if you love me, you will do this now, and then be gone. If you know not of my plans, my parents cannot hold you responsible." Or torture it out of her.

Tears poured down the old woman's cheeks as she raised the shears and cut off ten-and-eight years of growth that lay over her shoulder in one braid. Joanna closed her eyes as the sharp blades chopped through her hair. Swallowing against the pain, she waited for the servant to finish. Enyd stood with the long, dark braid in her hands and shook her head.

"A lady's crowning glory," she murmured sadly as she held it out to Joanna.

That glory was difficult to mask and her disguise would be the difference between escape and death. After a moment of mourning for all that should have been otherwise in her life, Joanna nodded to the woman who had cared for her for as long as she could remember a caring face and voice.

Enyd threw her arms around Joanna and the searing pain of the embrace made her hiss. Not willing to miss the moment, she held on tightly and breathed in the woman's comfort for as long as she could endure it. Then, releasing her, Joanna stepped back and nodded at the door of the chamber. Without another word, Enyd left and Joanna struggled to gather what she needed for the journey ahead.

She had bartered a bracelet for clothing and some small coins that would draw less attention. Pulling the bundle out from under the bedcovers, she made quick work of removing her gown and tunic. She tugged up the longer stockings over her own and tied them to the belt for that purpose. Joanna took her extra chemise from her traveling trunk and tore it into strips. Then she bound her breasts down as flat as she could manage. For once, not being well-endowed was a blessing.

Replacing the bandages on the back of her legs took a few minutes and she also listened while she worked, worrying that the rest of her party was rousing for the day. Balancing herself on one foot then the other, she tied on the leather shoes. Finally, she tossed whatever additional pieces of clothing and jewelry she could find into the sack she'd obtained in her trade and pulled the hood that lay around her neck up as far as she could to cover her face.

Looking around the room for anything left behind or anything that would give away her plans, she realized that she had nothing here. Joanna knew that she should feel some guilt over what she was doing—any God-fearing woman would. But the thought of escaping the imminent death her marriage would mean and making a life with her sister in Scotland gave her a moment of hope. Her parents, who had left her on her own so much, would have to fend off the warlock of Wynwydd by themselves.

Now more servant than lady in appearance, Joanna hunched down and walked toward the back stairs of the inn. Passing a few serving women already beginning their tasks for the day, she mumbled greetings in return for theirs. A few minutes of wending through the darkened corridors of the building and she pushed the door open and stepped out into the yard.

Spring was truly progressing through the English countryside. The smells of the blossoming trees that surrounded the inn and the roads filled the air with their sweet aromas. The warbling of the birds of dawn—sparrow, robin and lark—greeted her as she made her way through the crowded work area toward the resting place of the monks of Holme Cultram Abbey. Sweat beaded Joanna's upper lip and trickled down her neck and face.

She must make it to them before the fever took control. Whispering a prayer to the Almighty that they would take an ill stranger on their journey, she found them already preparing for the road ahead.

"Good brother," she said, greeting the apparent leader of the group in a voice as deep as she could force it. "I was told that travelers could seek safe passage with you on your journey north?" She fought the urge to adjust her hood as she felt the scrutiny of the monk passing over her.

"We welcome the company of anyone sent to us by the good Lord, my son. Join us and may the miles ahead pass quickly as prayers to His Glory." The monk pointed to a place among the others.

Joanna mumbled a reply and followed the gesture until she was behind one of the other monks in the party. In a few minutes, the whole group was making its way along the well-rutted road, walking a few paces behind a cart that carried the oldest and ill disposed of their group. Large enough to offer some protection, but not large enough to draw undue attention, she allowed herself to dream of success.

The road and the trees blurred together and she soon struggled for every step she took. Chills passed in waves over her, making her shiver in spite of the layers of clothing and the exertion of the pace. Then, heat grew in her head and limbs and threatened to overwhelm her. When one of the older monks approached her with questions about her condition, the world around her grew dark and she felt herself falling to the ground.

* * *

The days and nights melded together and she had no idea
of how many had passed when she returned to herself at last.
In spite of the layers of padding beneath her body, she ached
as the small wagon in which she lay hit every bump and rut
in the rough road. Her groans brought the attention of the
cart's driver, a wizened old man whose blue eyes still blazed
with life's forces.

"Ye are still with us? I feared we'd be digging yer grave
on our arrival at the abbey."

Joanna felt her clothes and found her hood around her
neck. Pulling it up on her head, she leaned up on her elbows
to look around. She tried to speak, but her throat was sore from
being ill and lack of water. The driver held out a skin to her
and she took it, anxious to ease the burning.

"Here now, have a care. Too much and ye will just heave
it up."

Joanna nodded and took a smaller amount than she wanted.
After it slid down her throat and settled in her stomach, she
took another sip. The man smiled a near-toothless grin as she
heeded his warning. She handed it back to him and tried to
sit up. The rocking motion of the cart and the soreness of her
body kept her from doing it.

"Rest a bit more. The good brother who has cared for ye
said ye are lucky to be among the living after that fever nearly
took ye."

So, the fever had gotten worse. And the monks had taken
over her care. Had they discovered her secrets, as well? When
she would have pursued the matter, exhaustion struck her and
she found herself drifting off to sleep again. She needed to
know so much—where they were, when they would arrive at
the abbey, where she could seek safe haven.

None of that mattered as sleep overtook her once more.

Chapter Two

Joanna of Blackburn had best be dead when he caught up to her.

Braden rubbed the rain from his face for the tenth time in only a few minutes and searched through the torrents for some sign of the promised haven. His men slowed with him as they cautiously followed the muddy path. Surely the monks' directions were accurate? They should have reached Silloth Keep hours ago.

One of his men called out and pointed in the distance. A large, dark stone fortress stood to the west of them, and only a flash of lightning had revealed its presence and now led the way. They reached it and approached the gates. Guards called out from one of the towers to challenge their entry.

"Who goes there? State your name and your business," called one of the guards.

"I am Lord Braden of Wynwydd and seek the hospitality of Lord Orrick for the night," he answered. "Brother Lawrence sent me."

The brother's name eased his way, for the gates began to open in spite of the hour and the growing darkness. A soldier walked forward to meet them and directed them to the entrance to the hall. A few boys took their mounts and Braden climbed the steps to where the guard said the great hall of the keep, and his lord, was. As he entered the large room, he noticed a guard had gone ahead of them to inform his lord of their arrival. Braden and his men waited for a sign of their welcome here.

"Lord Braden, come and join us in our meal," a man he assumed was Lord Orrick called out. "Warm yourself here before the fire."

Braden nodded and strode to the dais and around the high table to where Lord Orrick stood. He noticed his men being directed by a servant to a table just in front of the steps. They would remain in his sight and close enough to come to his aid if needed. As he stopped before Lord Orrick, his stomach let out a loud growl, probably encouraged by the aromas of a steaming pot of stew and the hot loaves of bread on the table.

"Share our meal first, my lord, then we can see to your other comforts," the woman to Lord Orrick's right said. His wife?

"I am Orrick of Silloth and this is my ladywife, Margaret."

"I am Braden of Wynwydd," he replied, holding out his hand in greeting. Orrick grasped his forearm and Braden returned the gesture. Both men were unarmed. "My thanks for your offer of hospitality this night."

He moved to the chair indicated at Lady Margaret's side and was impressed by the prompt and thorough attention he received. A servant helped him remove his dripping wet cloak and gloves. In spite of the meal already being in progress, a laver bowl appeared to his right as soon as he was seated and then a towel so that he could wash.

The fare was hearty, well-cooked and seasoned and Braden listened to the banter between Lord Orrick and his retainers. The ease of exchange and conversation told him much about the way that Orrick managed his manor and his people.

"So, tell us, Lord Braden, what is the news from court?"

Lady Margaret asked him as honey-coated cakes and other treats were served along with cheeses and wafers as the last course.

"The king held his Easter court at Canterbury and the queen joined him there." All of England knew about the scandalous marriage of John to Isabella of Angouleme. "Their plans to leave for Normandy were in place even before the holy day was observed."

"Is there trouble in Normandy?" the lady asked. "I would have expected them to stay in England through the summer."

"None that was the subject of open discussion, but some old wounds have not healed."

He probably should have guarded his words. The Lusignans' claim to prior betrothal was known throughout the continent and England. However, the ties to that family were not so strong here. From the comments overheard at the abbey, Lord Orrick kept to himself and had not ventured to court in over a score of years.

The lord and lady exchanged knowing glances. So, their lack of attendance on the king did not mean a lack of knowledge of the maneuverings of the Plantagenet kings.

"What brings you to this part of England, Lord Braden?" Lord Orrick asked in a quiet voice that managed not to draw the attention of anyone except his wife. The lady missed nothing that happened between them.

"I would speak to you in private, if I may. 'Tis a personal matter," Braden answered as he fought the urge to grit his teeth again.

He hated that he would have to reveal, to this stranger, his betrothed's refusal to marry. He despised showing weakness, but Joanna's actions necessitated this and many other humiliations to him. Before he could say anything else, Lady Margaret intervened.

"My lord, our guest has still not shaken off the chill of the road. Can this not wait until morn?"

"Of course, my lady." Orrick nodded to his wife first, then to him. "Join me after you break your fast in the morn, Lord Braden." Orrick stood and held out his hand to his wife. "My steward will see to your comfort and to that of your men."

If the haste with which the lord and lady left the hall was unseemly, no one but he took notice of it. Within moments, Orrick and his very fair wife were gone. Orrick's steward approached him with instructions on the sleeping arrangements and surprised Braden with the offer of a private chamber. Grabbing up a few of the apples, he took them with him as he left the dais to speak to his men.

Remembering the cautious steps of his horse on their approach to the keep, he decided to check it in the stables before retiring. His men, assured of food and ale and a challenging dice game, were well cared for. As he walked through the hall and out into the yard, a pang of wanting, so strong that it took his breath away, struck him. Looking around he knew that this was what he wanted—a well-ordered, successful estate, his people well fed, and a family to enjoy it with him. Pushing away such sentimental thoughts, Braden focused on his problem.

First he needed to find his betrothed and take her to Wynwydd. Then he needed to show his people that he could keep a wife and gain an heir. The wise-woman of his village had assured him that a spring bride, a woman of black she said, would be fruitful.

At first he'd scoffed at the instructions she'd given him; any logical man would have. The ceremony should take place outside the walls of his castle, away from any place of death or fear and under a bower of fresh flowers and blossoms and vines. He should plant his seed during the time of the earth's own fertility, in that same bower, and the dew of his wife's release should mix with the morning dew. Gwanwyn promised that his seed would grow and produce a son and end the curse that had haunted their family for the past five generations.

So, after years of not believing the stories and living in a sort of cowardly refusal to seek a wife and sons, Braden had finally faced the need for an heir. And he did not want to follow in the steps of the other Wynwydds before him—he wanted to live and see his sons. The wise-woman, raised in the ancient Cymric traditions, had been his last hope.

Braden strode down the path that led to the stables. Shaking his head, he laughed under his breath at the speculation and rumors about his family and the powers they supposedly had. Although they were suspected of being warlocks and able to lay curses on others, it was someone else's words that had seemed to damn the Wynwydd males to never living long enough to see their sons.

All the deaths or injuries seemed to be natural, no foul play evident, but none of his male relatives or ancestors back to his great-great-great-grandfather had ever looked on a living son. Even wives were not immune from it—many had died while birthing sons who did not survive. The birth of daughters had saved many a Wynwydd life, but sons had been costly to produce and never enjoyed. By the time a son was born, his father had either died or gone mad or was blind. A terrible legacy and one which he prayed he'd found a way to end.

Braden arrived at the stables and knew, from the quiet surrounding it, that all grooming and care was done for the night. Seeking the door, he opened it slowly and quietly so as to not disturb the animals inside and let his eyes adjust to the darkness. His horses stood in the stalls closest to this doorway and he found and quieted his own mount with a few soft whispers and an apple from Orrick's table.

It took but a few moments to check the horse's back leg and determine that there was no injury. As he closed the gate of the stall behind him, a soft sound caught his attention. Turning around and peering down the shadowed line of stalls, he realized it came from the back of the stables. Following the enchanting sound, he walked softly on the packed dirt so as to not disturb the maker of it. A few yards from the back wall, he found the source.

A lantern burned low, giving light to a small circle of the stables. Behind the last stall was an area where someone slept. A few blankets tossed in the corner made up a sleeping pallet, and the lantern and a cup and an empty bowl sat on a wooden crate. Then the crooning began again and he found the person making it, leaning over a colt that lay unmoving in the nearest stall.

He froze as he recognized the voice. He'd stood behind her at the Mass at court, knowing she was meant for him before she did and wanting no surprises when she was presented to him. Her voice, then raised in the singing of a hymn, was clear and strong and its purity had sent chills through him. Those same chills moved through him now as he listened in wonder as she sang softly to the ill horse. Though softer, there was no mistaking the voice of his betrothed.

Lady Joanna of Blackburn was here in Silloth.

Braden's fists clenched, even as his jaws did, while he watched her tender care for the unfortunate horse. Dressed as a boy with her ankle-length black hair under some filthy hood and her womanly curves beneath a loose tunic and cloak, she soothed the animal. Tempted to step forward and end her farce, he knew he must make plans before claiming her. 'Twould be better, now that he'd found her alive and well, to gather his men, take her and leave this keep just before dawn. Once the gates opened, he could be gone from Silloth and Orrick's lands without ever having to explain his reasons for being here and without risking interference from this local lord.

Convinced of his plan, he waited for her own movements to cover his own and, with a care for silence, Braden walked down the aisle and slipped out of the stables. He returned to the keep and spoke to his men, preparing them to meet him at the stables. The comfortable chamber, with its rope-strung bed and soft mattress, was a waste, for he slept not at all while waiting to spring his trap and catch his bride. When the first rays of light crept into the dark clouds of dawn, he was already dressed and standing next to the stables.

Two of his men soundlessly guided their horses from the stalls and readied them for a quick escape. Another two stood guard at both of the doorways to the stables and one more protected his back as he crept nearer and nearer to the woman who had thwarted him. As everyone took their positions, Braden knelt down at her side and thought on how best to accomplish this without alerting Silloth's lord and guards to his actions.

"Joanna," he whispered into her ear as he straddled her sleeping form. When her eyes flew open and focused on him, he covered her mouth with one hand and encircled her neck with the other. "Say not a word. Make not a sound and you might live through this."

Her quickly indrawn breath and immediate thrashing about told him that she recognized him even in the darkened stables. He grasped her neck tighter and hoped she would realize that her struggles were useless. Fearing that he would hurt her, he leaned closer.

"Cease!" he said harshly. "Come, we must leave now."

One of his men whispered a warning about the village waking for the day and his attention strayed from the woman beneath him for a brief moment. When he turned back to pull her to her feet, he was met with the sharp end of a deadly looking dagger. Before he could stop her, she had shoved the dagger through his tunic and stopped just before reaching the part of him that would be needed to make sons.

"Truly, lady, you task my patience. Once we arrive in Wynwydd, I will show you what such behavior will cost you."

Their stalemate surely lasted for an eternity—he did not move his hands, or any other part of him, and she kept a firm pressure against the blade. Finally, he gathered his thoughts together and squeezed her throat harder for a second. As she reacted to it, he rolled quickly from her, letting go of her mouth and neck and grabbing for the dagger. Twisting her arm and hand until she released her grasp on it, he flung it as far as he could. Climbing to his feet, Braden dragged her with him. When they stood, his man retrieved the dagger and held it out to him.

"I wish not to gag you and truss you up like a goose for the table, but will if need be." He watched as she staggered to her feet, leaned over and braced her hands on her knees and gasped for breath. "If Lord Orrick's people are alerted, some may be harmed. I certainly need no more sins marking my black soul. Do you wish to add to your burden?"

Her dark eyes widened once more and he thought she would answer. Her mouth, now swollen from his hand, worked, but no sounds came out. She touched her throat and neck and he saw the bruises under the layer of dirt she wore now. When she stopped gasping, and when Braden was certain he had her compliance, he wrapped his hand around her arm and led her from the stables.

"Lord Braden? Would you like to explain why you abuse my hospitality and seem intent on stealing my stable boy?" Lord Orrick stood blocking his path and a large number of heavily armed soldiers surrounded the stables.

Braden would never know what made him do what he did next. He could blame it on desperation or a need to avenge his humiliation or just simple rage, but some devil sat on his shoulder goading him. Lifting the dagger still in his hand, he turned Joanna toward him, placed the tip of the blade under her tunic and, with one powerful stroke upward, sliced through the layers of clothing on her. He tossed the dagger to one of his men and took her by the shoulders and turned her to face Lord Orrick.

"This, my lord, is not one of your stable *boys*. This is my betrothed, Lady Joanna of Blackburn."

Chapter Three

Lord Orrick looked away from her disgrace. His face was like granite as he nodded to his soldiers and they followed his lead. The hood she wore to cover her hair and most of her face had slid down onto her shoulders and the strips of linen that bound her breasts fell loose to her waist. She could hear the anger in each breath taken by the man holding her.

Braden of Wynwydd. Her betrothed husband. Master of enchantments and killer of women.

A noise drew her attention and broke the mad spell that held them motionless. The lady of the keep pushed her way through the men in the yard and to her husband's side. After a moment of hesitation to take in the scene before her, Lady Margaret walked directly to Lord Braden, pulled the ties of his cloak and began tugging it from his shoulders.

The lady's actions must have surprised him into reaction, for he stepped back, removed his cloak and tossed it over Joanna's shoulders to cover what he had exposed to all.

"Lord Braden, if would you join me in the solar, mayhap we can sort through this confusion?" Lord Orrick said in a voice that was tinged in anger. When Lord Orrick's soldiers moved to surround them, she knew it was no polite invitation.

Braden nodded and held out his hand to her, but Lord Orrick stopped him. "If you would allow Lady Joanna some time with my wife, she can make herself presentable."

Lord Braden moved closer to her and wrapped his hand once more around her arm so that she could not escape. "With all respect, my lord. I have searched many weeks to find the lady. I do not wish her out of my sight right now."

Her escapade was over. As soon as he took her from these walls, Joanna suspected her life would be ended, too. The fury on her betrothed's face made him fearsome to behold and, in that moment, she believed every wicked and dangerous thing she'd ever heard about him. Joanna could not stop the shudders that moved through her nor the fear that she was sure covered her face as he met her gaze.

Lady Margaret came to her side and spoke to Lord Braden in a soft voice. "My lord, let me see to the lady's condition. She has lived as you see her since she sought sanctuary here nigh on to a fortnight ago."

The rest of the words blurred in her thoughts, the only one that she heard, that repeated over and over was *sanctuary*. She'd found it here in Silloth. Lord Orrick had accepted her story and given her a place to heal and to rest. She knew that it had been a temporary one and that she could not stay here, but for the few nights, she'd felt safe here.

Now, Lord Braden's arrival had crushed her plans.

"...sanctuary," Lady Margaret said.

Shaking her head, Joanna realized she'd missed the rest of the lady's words, but the searching look in the lady's eyes told her that it was a message. Confused and frightened, Joanna listened more carefully. She began to walk again and felt the soft touch of the lady at her side. Meeting her eyes, Joanna watched her mouth the word again—*sanctuary*.

The meaning finally struck her and she stumbled as she realized it. The family chapel had just been enlarged and rededicated, and it was a short distance away. A man could claim sanctuary in a church for forty days, more if supported by the bishop. Did she dare? Could she gain sanctuary and then wait out Lord Braden and his interest in her? Could she dare not to try?

His grip loosened as she stumbled again trying to keep up with his long strides. Taking advantage of his inattention, as she had in the stables, Joanna tore free and sprinted down the path that led to the stone building some yards´away. It must have been shock that held everyone else in their places as the distance between her and her betrothed increased. The loud roar signaled an end to that period of grace.

Any advantage her knowledge of the layout of Silloth gave her, the slippery mud left after the storms of the last day took away. Sliding around one corner and then almost losing her balance, Joanna saw the stone chapel surrounded by the low fence ahead. Dropping Lord Braden's cloak as she labored to keep up her pace, she could hear him and his men catching up to her. Jumping the fence, she pushed open the door and ran to the altar. Father Bernard was preparing for Mass and, tugging her hood back up and her disheveled clothing back together, she grabbed for the edge of his robes.

"Sanctuary, Father," she choked out. "I beg sanctuary."

He looked bewildered and then nodded, a serious expression on his face. "Of course, my son. Sanctuary is granted. What matter can be so grievous that you must seek refuge in God's house?"

The crash of the door behind her, the loud swearing and entrance of Lord Braden, Lord Orrick and the others gave him an answer.

"The evil lord of Wynwydd, Father," she whispered without looking at his approach, hesitant to call him a warlock in his hearing. "My life, my very soul, is in danger if he takes me from here."

The priest stuttered and stumbled back as Joanna found herself lifted from her knees and thrown over Lord Braden's shoulder. She pounded on his back as he walked to the door of the chapel, obviously intent on taking her. Then, when she thought all was lost, their progress was halted.

"Father, did you grant sanctuary?" Lord Orrick called out. Twisting around, she could see that he blocked the doorway, backed by a full contingent of his guards.

Father Bernard ran to the door and sidestepped to get around Lord Braden. Glad that she could not see Lord Braden's face, she was nonetheless certain it was darkened by rage. 'Twas then that she realized she'd never seen him smile. What would his face look like if it was lightened by a smile? It must be hanging upside down over a warlock's back that caused such strange and wayward thoughts in her.

"I did, Lord Orrick. This man—"

"This *woman*. This is a woman, Father," Braden growled as he slid her to her feet. Pulling the hood from her head, he repeated his claim, "This is my betrothed wife, Lady Joanna of Blackburn, and you cannot grant her sanctuary here. I speak for her and she will accompany me back to my estates now. Besides, women are not entitled to seek refuge in a church."

Still dizzy from being carried in such a manner, she swore she saw a look of pity on Lord Orrick's face. Strange. It seemed to be directed at Lord Braden and not at her.

"You would interfere with me taking custody of the woman given in betrothal to me before the king himself? Lord Orrick, you draw yourself into a battle in which you need not participate." Lord Braden's voice bristled with frustration.

The lord of Silloth seemed to hesitate at the mention of the king, but only until his wife reached his side. Her presence appeared to give him a stronger resolve in his actions. Lady Margaret slipped her smaller hand into her husband's larger one. Could Joanna be safe?

"The *soul* before us has asked for refuge in God's house, my lord. Unless Father Bernard rescinds his words, sanctuary has been declared and we have no choice but to honor it."

"If I cannot take her from this place, then neither can she leave until we resolve this matter. My men will stand guard at the door to insure the lady's safety," Braden said.

Joanna nearly smiled at the blatant insult to Lord Orrick. She watched the two noblemen parley in low voices as to the arrangements for who would stand guard. Within a few minutes, she was left alone inside the chapel while everyone else, save two guards, followed Lord Orrick back to the keep.

She turned around and around, looking at the interior of the building and realized that, but for the raised wooden altar and a few benches along the back wall, it was empty. Pulling the rough edges of her tunic together and wrapping her arms around her waist, she tried to plan her next step.

Joanna felt his presence once more before even a word was spoken. She backed away with each step he took toward her, finally stopping when her legs met one of the benches along the wall. He grabbed the tunic she wore and pressed his hard body against hers until she could feel the heat of him seeping into her. With but one finger under her chin, he forced her head back so that her eyes met his.

His eyes were the color of the greens of spring. Deep and clear, they reminded her of the creeping ivy that clung to the side of this very building and of the newly sprouted leaves on the tall oak trees of the forest. But if his eyes were of spring, his mouth and the kiss he gave were of the summer's scorching heat.

Nothing in her life until this time prepared her for the claiming of his mouth on hers. The polite kiss exchanged during their betrothal was nothing, nothing, when compared to this one. The fury he felt was there, as was something else she could not identify. He pressed his lips to hers and she felt the message he gave. She gasped as his hand slid to her waist and inside her torn tunic and he used her surprise to enter her mouth with his tongue.

Over and over he tasted her and he pushed inside with his tongue again and again until she offered hers to him. A grunt answered her surrender and he suckled on hers even as his fingers teased the sensitive undersides of her now-unbound breasts. When she would have protested, he delved deeper into her mouth and now held her head in one of his hands, not allowing her to pull away.

If she could.

If she wanted to, which she doubted at that moment.

"This is God's house, my lord," the priest said with a cough.

Lord Braden did lift his head now and their gazes met and held. He dipped lower once more and this kiss was more devastating and confusing than the ones given, or taken, before. The barest of touches, a soft moving of his lips on hers, and it was over.

"You are mine, Joanna, by word and pledge, before God and king. And you will be mine, body and soul. Think not that it ends here. This is only the beginning."

His voice was deep and spoke to something within her that she could not understand. In her life, no one had ever wanted her before, so this public claiming of her, even as a possession, made her wonder about things she'd never thought of before. Why did he not simply wash his hands of her? He would lose nothing; her parents, and she, stood to lose everything.

Lord Braden stepped back and she could only watch him leave, the actions and emotions of the past half hour's time finally catching up with her and making her excessively weary and sore. As he strode out the door, she realized that he had once again wrapped her in his cloak.

Gathering it around her, she sought out one of the benches and sat on it. Pulling her legs up within the cloak's thick layers and turning so that most of her weight was not on the backs of her thighs, she leaned back against the wall and sank into the exhaustion that threatened.

Giving up on any comfort to be gained with sitting, she slid down and pulled the wrap around and over her so that only her face was open to the chill of the stone chapel. Sleep claimed her even as she thought on the possessive kiss given, or taken, by the lord of Wynwydd.

"My lord, I appreciate not your interference in this private matter," Braden told the lord of Silloth straightaway. "'Tis a lawful betrothal and I have the papers to prove it."

Braden reached inside his tunic and pulled out the packet of parchments. Orrick took the packet, walked to a table in the room and unfolded them. As the agreements and sworn statements were being examined, Braden tried not to think on his two errors in judgment and actions earlier.

The rage inside him drove him to do such stupid things. He'd been told that it was part of his legacy. All the Wynwydd males were hot tempered...and hot-blooded. What good did it do them to rage against their fate? The futility of the anger forced his hand in situations when calm and coolheadedness would be advantageous.

And what good was the drive to procreate when it meant your own death? Even if he followed the somewhat ludicrous instructions given him by Gwanwyn, there was no guarantee that he would be any more successful in his quest to end the curse that plagued his family. The kiss, and her passionate yet innocent response, just made it worse. Now the need to possess her was greater than before. He wanted to taste her mouth as she screamed out her satisfaction. He wanted to peel off...

Orrick finished reading the documents, stood back from the table and nodded to his wife, who sat in a tall-backed chair near the hearth. So, he was convinced of the legalities. Now

Braden could take Joanna and get out of here. Braden cleared his throat.

"You see that I have the right to her?" He placed his fists on his hips. "She is my betrothed and she gave her consent before witnesses to the marriage."

"So it would appear," Orrick said as he rolled the parchments and held them out. "But there is still the matter of sanctuary asked and given in my chapel. 'Tis a serious issue."

"Now that you are content in my rights to the lady, simply give leave to your priest to rescind it."

Father Bernard harrumphed behind him and Braden turned to face him. "Obviously, good Father, you granted the request without knowing the details. Now that you do, you can see that no sanctuary is needed. The lady's lawfully betrothed husband has arrived to escort her home."

"I am bound by the Church's rules on this, my lord. I granted sanctuary before witnesses. To rescind it, I would need the permission of my bishop." The priest stepped closer to Orrick and then spoke again. "If 'tis your will, Lord Orrick, I will begin my petition now to the bishop of Carlisle to release the bond of sanctuary given."

The priest was dismissed with one look from Orrick and no one spoke until the door closed behind them, leaving only the three of them to talk.

"Lord Braden, I would prefer not to involve the bishop in this, for the bishop's attention might gain the king's, as well. Can we not handle this quietly?" Orrick walked to where his wife sat and touched her shoulder. "Allow my wife to speak to Joanna and mayhap this can be worked out with little further trouble?"

Obviously, the lord of Silloth did not want the attention of the king? What was at work here in this seemingly sleepy corner of England? Well, if he spoke the truth, he wanted no more scrutiny of any kind on this matter—the humiliation of her refusal at court still stung and even the document citing her consent given before witnesses did not lessen that. Bringing in the bishop would complicate this and make him a laughingstock in the north as well as the south. He reached up and rubbed his forehead trying to ease the pain that throbbed there.

"Fine. I also do not wish this private matter to draw more attention than it already has. Lady Margaret, please speak to Joanna and discover her requirements for leaving the chapel without resistance."

"Do you know why she is here, my lord? Have you knowledge of her reasons for seeking a safe haven far from home?"

The lady's voice was soft, but the accusing tone in it gave him pause. Other than exchanging their vows at the betrothal, he'd not spoken directly to her…ever. All correspondence, arrangements and discussions went through her father, as was appropriate.

"No explanation was given to me, my lady. She disappeared from her parents' care on their journey to my home and they contacted me to aid their efforts in finding her. 'Tis all I know."

A look given by the lady to her lord made him think. Why had she refused him? Why had she run? Did the reasons make it right? Should she not have come to him? A creeping sense of discomfort filled him. Although his family's history was never mentioned, he knew that Lord Robert was aware of the rumors. If nothing else, the amount of gold offered for the shrewd man's daughter would have been a clue. He'd never given it a thought and had allowed his anger and desperation to direct his efforts in tracking and finding her.

"I would see to her comfort, as well, my lord." The lady's words were to her husband and Orrick looked to him for an answer.

"With your permission, Lord Braden."

"'Tis well. But I would advise not expending too much effort, for my plan is to leave here by midday. I will see to her needs on our journey."

"My lord, would you send Wenda to me?" Lady Margaret stood and approached the doorway.

Braden was confused and intrigued. "Who is this Wenda? A seamstress?" Joanna was wearing the rags of a peasant when he'd found her and the need for proper clothing should be seen to immediately. The smell of the stables permeated her tunic.

"Wenda is a healer, my lord. The lady was just recovering from some illness when the brothers brought her here," Orrick explained. Orrick nodded in answer to his wife and she left.

"Ill?" he asked. The pain in his head increased as he thought of a sick noblewoman in disguise traveling the length of England with no protection. *His* noblewoman. "What was the cause of her illness?" He turned back to face Orrick.

"I am sure that between Wenda and my ladywife, they will find out the details."

With a nod from her husband, Lady Margaret was gone. 'Twas then that Braden realized that Orrick had known the stableboy was no boy.

"You knew from the time she arrived, did you not?"

"I knew she was not the role she played. The brothers who brought her here told me that much. When she said she sought work in the stables, I assigned her there."

"You did not think to interrogate her? To discover the truth about her?" Braden fought against clenching his teeth.

"'Tis not my way, Lord Braden. The brothers who brought her knew that she would be safe here until her truth was revealed."

Braden shook his head in disbelief. His betrothed had been allowed to keep her identity secret and work in the stables, all the while the lord of the keep stood aside uninterested in the truth.

"Not your way? Your pardon, Lord Orrick, but how would you know if you were harboring a criminal or a runaway serf? Is it your practice to offer haven to anyone who asks for it?"

"If they come by way of the good brothers, yes. If I think that a short respite here will give them the strength to continue their journey, yes. If they…" Orrick hesitated as though thinking over his answer now. "Yes." He crossed his arms over his chest. "Yes, I do."

Braden stopped the angry retort that tried to escape. What a strange place this was and what a peculiar lord who would admit to such a thing! Somehow, though, Braden knew that this place was safe. That if his betrothed had ended up elsewhere, many dire things could have happened to her. That other noblemen would have closed their gates to strangers regardless of the cost of that refusal.

"My thanks."

The words escaped without warning for 'twas not what he wanted to say. Well, mayhap he did? His life had been turned upside down since he let himself believe that Gwanwyn had the answer. He'd bartered for a bride, faced embarrassment before the king and court and ridden the breadth and length of England. With less than a month left in the spring, he knew he must conclude this or it could be the end of his name.

Joanna fit the descriptions given by the Welshwoman— both her coloring and her name were "of black." Something deep inside him spoke of the rightness of this match. Not of the ease of accomplishing it or the difficulty. But, in that place deep within where he allowed himself a measure of ridiculous hope, Braden knew that he needed and wanted Joanna of Blackburn for his wife.

'Twas simply too bad if she did not want the same thing. Too many lives had been lost and generations had perished for a thing like her virginal fears or fancies to matter.

"We could break our fast in the hall while waiting for Margaret's return," Orrick said.

His stomach rumbled its own answer. Braden nodded and waited for Orrick to lead. With his own men guarding the chapel, he knew there was time to eat.

Chapter Four

"Lady Joanna?"

The sound persisted, but she tried to pay no heed to it. She was so tired and cold and she simply wanted to sleep.

"Lady?"

Now a shake of her shoulder accompanied the voice, making it impossible to ignore. Without loosening the tight cocoon she'd finally made of the overlarge cloak, she opened her eyes and looked around. Lady Margaret stood before her, along with a maid and an old woman who Joanna had seen in the village before.

"So, 'tis true then? You are Joanna of Blackburn?"

"Aye, Lady Margaret," she said, pushing the cloak away and sitting up. Wincing against the pain, she sat upright and faced the lady of Silloth. When she tried to stand, dizziness forced her back down to the bench. "Forgive me, my lady. I am not feeling well."

Lady Margaret clucked her tongue and moved aside for the old woman. The woman reached for the cloak and Joanna instinctively clutched it. Shaking her head, she realized that her disguise, effective for weeks, was useless to her now.

"This is Wenda, our healer. If you will allow her to see to your injuries, she can ease your pain."

Joanna nodded and permitted the old woman to poke and prod her face and neck, shoulders and arms, even stomach and knees. So many places hurt now, she could not pick them out.

"Did he beat you in the stables?"

"Beat me? Nay. But he pounced on me while I was sleeping, twisted my arm to take my dagger and threw me over his shoulders. I ache in so many places from just that."

Lady Margaret and the healer exchanged looks of horror and Joanna realized that her description of Lord Braden's treatment of her sounded very bad indeed. His actions in subduing her did not come close to the cruelty of her parents' so she tried to explain. "And he kissed me."

An expression she could only describe as "stunned" filled their faces and Lady Margaret waved her maid over closer as she and Wenda stepped away. Without a word, the servant poured hot water out of a jug she carried and into a bowl. Producing a small bar of soap and cloth, she proceeded to help Joanna wash her face and neck and hands.

The feel of the heat after so long without washing soothed her and being able to cleanse herself of the layers of dirt was a relief. The whispering between the other two continued until she finished her ablutions, and then they turned back to her. The maid was dismissed with a look and the chapel was silent until they were alone and the door closed.

"I hesitate to ask you this, Lady Joanna, but I think I must." Lady Margaret's tone was soft and her eyes were filled with concern. She took Joanna's hand in hers and patted it. "Did Lord Braden take you…your virginity…in the stables before my lord Orrick arrived?"

She thought Lord Braden had attacked her and taken her virtue? Joanna shook her head. "No, my lady. He did not… do that."

Another glance between them. Wenda spoke this time. "I think the pain is from some bruises and being roughly handled, my lady. I do not think there are any serious injuries." Wenda stepped away. "Some rest should be all that is needed for that."

"Before you leave, Wenda," the lady began. "Joanna, the brothers who sent you here said that you had been ill through the whole journey. Do you know what caused the fever you suffered?"

So, the good brothers had not examined her during the journey from the south? They had simply treated the fever? Still she hesitated to discuss her parents' treatment of her and their attempts to gain her consent for the marriage. She really did not want to talk about all that had transpired before she'd run away.

"I know not, my lady. Did the brothers have any hint of the reason?" She looked at the lady and waited.

"None that they shared with me, I fear." When it appeared that she would say something else, the lady shook her head instead. "Wenda, we will call you if we have need."

And then they were alone.

"Lord Braden is demanding that you be turned over to him."

Joanna could not help her reaction—the shudder tore through her, making her shake and tremble. Pushing her hair out of her face, she tried to stand once more. This time she gained her feet. "But, I have been granted sanctuary here. Will he ignore the priest's words?"

"Lord Braden is not willing to recognize that, Joanna. He wants to take you from here this day." The lady walked closer to her. "Mayhap if you can tell me the basis for your flight and your hiding here, I can convince him otherwise."

"He paid my father a large amount of gold for my hand in marriage," she said. "Enough that my father would look no further."

"'Tis the way of things."

"My father would not accept my refusal and took all measures he thought necessary to gain my consent." She looked at Lady Margaret. "All measures." The skin on the back of her thighs and her lower back pulsed with its own memory of the punishments she'd endured.

It did not take the lady very long to realize what she meant. Recalcitrant daughters were dealt with swiftly when a marriage that was advantageous to her family was involved. For certain, Joanna was not the first, nor would she be the last, daughter treated as she had been.

"Did Lord Braden order such things to be done to you? Although he seems brutish, he does not seem cruel," the lady said.

"I do not know if he did or not," Joanna said as she paced the back of the chapel. "I know only that he wanted me to wife and wanted me now. My father redoubled his efforts after I spoke out about the betrothal at court. He swore he would not take the chance of losing such wealth over my concerns."

She had not realized how terrible her words of refusal were until the repercussions spread through King John's court. Then the king's attention and involvement simply guaranteed the treatment she'd received.

"Is it that you do not want to marry the lord of Wynwydd because you fear more beatings?"

She had guessed part of it. But the physical pain, as bad as it had been, was not the worst. She feared dying unloved even more than she feared dying. As so far, in this life, she had been loved by no one but her sister.

"The truth about Lord Braden was discussed almost openly at the king's court, my lady. I fear losing my soul more than I fear losing my life. His true nature will rob me of that before he kills me." Her hands and knees shook as she forced the words out. "He is a sorcerer who will curse me even as his family is cursed. 'Tis widely known that Wynwydd wives do not survive."

Silence filled the stone building. 'Twas the first time she'd voiced the fear to anyone save her maid Enyd, but she'd heard the stories every day at court. The fates of Lord Braden's father and grandfather and most male relatives were well-known— they died under mysterious circumstances or went mad. Some said it was caused by trying to control the unworldly powers they'd been given. Some said the Wynwydd males were simply evil incarnate—one only had to look into their eyes to feel the malevolence. Anyone who knew anything agreed she would never live to see the next anniversary of her birth.

"Is this the reason you ran from him and the betrothal? Where will you go if not with him?"

"My sister lives in Scotland. I was trying to reach her when I…became ill. I confess, I was using my time here to regain my strength to make the rest of the journey." Joanna walked closer to the lady. "I am sorry to have brought you into this. Your lord offered me a haven and I have brought the very devil to his doorstep."

Lady Margaret said nothing in reply. Instead she stared off toward the altar and shook her head. "And now? How would you have this standoff end?"

"If Lord Braden takes me from this keep, he will kill me. I saw it in his eyes when he first took me in the stables. He means to avenge the insult to his honor that he blames on me. Do you think that Lord Orrick will support his priest in this or will he comply? Will he allow Lord Braden to take me from here?"

"'Tis not Lord Orrick's decision, lady." His deep voice broke into the discussion and shook her to her core. He walked across the small chamber and, in spite of her resolve to face him, Joanna found herself shrinking back, preparing for the worst. "Lord Orrick has no standing in this and neither does his priest. You," he said as he stalked her on the last few steps to the church's wall and pinned her with his nearness and his intense glare, "answer to me and only to me."

He towered over her and she felt the fear flood back into her soul. Mayhap he would kill her quickly if she acquiesced now and caused no more delays. Then, some spark within her flared and she pushed her chin up and met his terrifying countenance. She did not want to die and did not think that the good Lord had watched over her this long to let her perish in His own house.

"My lord, the lady needs some rest. Can you not delay your decision for a day to allow her that?" Lady Margaret actually positioned herself between them, forcing Lord Braden to back away a few steps from her. "I am certain her outlook will improve with rest."

Her betrothed looked from one to the other before replying. A suspicious glint entered his eyes. Did he remember that 'twas Lady Margaret's words that had spurred Joanna to run here?

"Another day will allow the roads to dry from the rains. I think it a good idea to remain for one more day."

He stressed the last words, unknowingly giving her both an ultimatum and another chance to escape his grasp. If Lady Margaret would assist her, she could sneak out during the night and be miles ahead of him. Lord Braden nodded to Lady Margaret and then began to leave. He paused near the door. "I will escort you back to your husband."

"Is there another way out of here?" Joanna whispered to Lady Margaret when she came closer. "If you can distract his men, I will try to get out of the gates before he knows. I have some food, a few coins and my bag hidden in the stables. It can only be a few more days' journey to my sister's."

"I would urge you to careful consideration of any action you plan, Joanna. Such a move could be more dangerous than you know."

But before Lady Margaret could agree to help her or not, Lord Braden interrupted. "I visited a cathedral in London once that had the most amazing architectural feature." He turned to face them and continued with an ill-timed explanation of his travels. "The church had been built in such a way that all sounds moved up the walls, across the ceiling and down the wall on the other side. 'Twas called a *whispering* dome."

His focus followed the curve of the roof overhead, and the look of triumph told her the meaning of his words—he'd heard her plea to Lady Margaret for help. Could it be so? He opened the door and called out to his men who surrounded the chapel to double the guard and be prepared for her attempt to escape. He *had* heard her words.

When he held out his hand for Lady Margaret, Joanna felt some small measure of desperation creeping into her. What could she do now? Lady Margaret nodded to him and left Joanna's side.

"Rest now, Joanna. I will return as soon as I've spoken with my lord husband."

Braden followed Lady Margaret and spoke as he pulled the door closed behind them. "As will I."

His voice was filled with both menace and some kind of promise and made her quiver from head to toe. Deserted once again, Joanna sought the meager comfort that her makeshift pallet offered and tried to pray for a safe outcome.

He was the kind of man who would have drawn women to his side with but an inviting glance. Even at her age, two score and one, his fine figure, dark hair and chiseled features stirred an admiration that might have caused problems were she not completely in love with her husband…and nearly old enough to be Lord Braden's mother. Margaret walked at his side trying to sort out her assessment before they reached Orrick.

A few things had become apparent rather quickly in this

perplexing situation. Lord Braden was a man accustomed to getting his own way and he used his sordid reputation to scare and bully people around to do his bidding. His reputation was well-known by most of England and feared enough to terrify a young woman into running away from the only security and family she'd known. She was not completely convinced that he deserved the reputation he carried.

Or mayhap he did?

A few times she had caught him watching Joanna when he did not know he was being observed. Anger bordering on rage was clear in his features and his tense stance, but there was something else, a desperate longing for Joanna or what she offered, deep in his expression. He hid it quickly as though he feared someone else seeing it. As though it undermined him in some way. As though the desire for her was dangerous to him.

They walked in silence toward the keep. Then, as if he knew she was judging him and his actions, he stopped and turned to face her. One look at his face, his very handsome face, told her that he did not desire her involvement.

"I would advise you to stay out of what is between Lady Joanna and me." He crossed his arms over his chest and looked down at her. "Pardon my candor, Lady Margaret, but I do not appreciate your interference."

She fought the urge to smile as she felt it tug at the corners of her mouth. She had faced down men more powerful than him in her life and relished the challenge his insult offered. Margaret knew 'twas probably not a good idea to incite him to more anger, but the memory of the terror that controlled Joanna gave her any permission she sought.

"And I do not appreciate stubborn, thick-skulled men who seek to terrorize young women under my protection."

She crossed her arms in the same manner he had and raised her chin. 'Twasn't a fair argument for she knew all but six people in the keep would leap to her defense if need be. That complete support and sense of safety gave her any courage she needed to speak to him boldly.

"Your behavior and insults are unseemly, lady. Surely your husband would counsel you to a more modest demeanor."

She did laugh then. His words would have hurt a woman who was uncertain of her worth. "'Tis at my lord husband's request that I am here. 'Tis through his tutelage and at his urging that I have learned to be forthright in my words and manners. Mayhap a similar attitude on your part toward your betrothed would have prevented the lady from seeking a safe haven from you?"

She would give him some credit—the grimace that crossed his face as she answered his insult with one of her own spoke of the words being considered in his mind. 'Twas a step at least.

His attention moved over her, and he examined her from the top of her head to the slippers on her feet. This frank and open assessment should have embarrassed her, but she recognized it as one opponent for another. Another step on his part.

Was there any hope for these two?

Margaret did know that Joanna was utterly terrified by Lord Braden. She also recognized that part of that terror was due to the effects of her physical condition and part was due to the outrageous rumors she'd heard, ones she suspected he had partly spread himself to keep his life as private as possible.

Sorcerer? Warlock? The devil incarnate?

Although she could believe that women would whisper it of him in certain situations, Margaret did not believe such tales. When there was ignorance about someone, the courtiers who toadied to royalty created whatever they needed to keep themselves amused. There was probably some seed of truth within the words shared by Joanna, but it had been embellished and had grown beyond any semblance of reality.

Until Joanna saw Braden of Wynwydd as a man, she would

never leave the chapel and the sanctuary willingly. Until she could separate the reputation from the man beneath it, there was no hope of happiness. And until Braden could shed the myths that he used to protect his secrets, he would never offer Joanna or any woman what they truly wanted.

With a grunt, Lord Braden offered her his arm again and they walked up the stairs into the keep. Surely Orrick would have words of wisdom to offer in this matter.

"No."

"But, Lord Braden, surely you must agree that some accommodations must be made in this situation."

"No," he repeated. The lady wanted clothing and a set of bedding and even a brazier delivered to the chapel so that Joanna would be comfortable while she stayed there.

"Father Bernard decided that it would be inappropriate for him to remain in his chamber while Lady Joanna is…in residence so he will stay here in the keep," Lord Orrick announced.

"Then a maid must attend her," Lady Margaret began.

"No!" he shouted as he clenched his fists and teeth. "These arrangements are unnecessary. The lady will leave with me on the morrow."

Braden suspected that the lord and lady of Silloth were in league with his betrothed to prevent him from taking her. Why else would they become so involved over the plight of a stranger.

"And food? Would you deny her sustenance while she is there?" Lady Margaret challenged.

He did not mean to starve her, truly he did not. Braden struggled to control his temper as he faced his adversaries.

"Please, my lady. I only wish to get back to my own lands and people as soon as is possible. Cozening her in this foolhardy course will only prolong her resistance. Feed her, certainly, but leave the rest and let me deal with her."

He'd thought on the lady's earlier words to him and knew she was correct—he was using fear to try to force Joanna to his will. 'Twas the only way he knew to deal with problems like those she presented. For too long his reputation had protected him and his from the prying eyes and greed of nobles and neighbors. He'd even been responsible for some of the tales told, or rather embellished, about his powers. All in an effort to keep away those who would gawk at his family's misfortunes.

Now, when he needed a bride, his own deeds came back and prevented what should have been a normal occurrence for a nobleman—the procurement of a wife. Braden did terrify Lady Joanna. He had seen it in her eyes and felt it in her uneven breathing as he had held her down in the stables. The trembling of her hands and her chin as she looked on him had told him, also.

"This is all most difficult for me," he admitted without thinking on his words. "I will have her to wife and it seems that her actions leave me no other course but to force her from the chapel and take her to Wynwydd."

"There is always a choice, my lord," the lady said in a soft voice. "'Tis never the easiest one to see, but it is the one that holds the most promise."

Concerned about the doubts that were creeping into his thoughts about Joanna, he knew he must control any sign of weakness over his plans for her. Crossing his arms over his chest, he shook his head at them.

"She is mine and she leaves with me in the morn."

When both looked as though they would argue with his declaration, he turned and left the chamber.

Chapter Five

The sun's rays danced lightly over her features, revealing freckles he'd not noticed before. The dirt that had obscured her pale cheeks was gone, too. The most striking change was her hair. Where it once had fallen to her ankles in ebony waves, now it barely passed her chin and neck and, without the weight of its previous length, it curled and swirled around her face.

Braden watched from the path as Joanna leaned as far as she could out the door of the chapel without taking the step that would remove her from her haven. She stood with her eyes closed and inhaled deeply, looking so much at peace that it made his chest tighten. One of his men called out to him and the moment was disturbed. Now, a look of fear dropped like a veil over her face and she backed quickly into church and away from him, slamming the door as though it would stop him.

He walked to the men who served as guards and discovered that, although alone now, many people had visited Lady Joanna since he'd left. Lady Margaret and the healer had returned, as well as an assortment of both ladies and maids. Other than the food he'd given permission for, nothing else had been brought into the chapel.

Braden nodded and walked to the now-closed door and felt the absurd need to knock. He did, but entered without waiting for a response. Joanna retreated even farther into the shadows of the chapel. She stopped next to the bench where his cloak lay.

"What were you doing at the door?" he asked. Seeing her reaction to his approach, he stopped and waited for her answer.

"There are no windows in the chapel, my lord," she said, nodding her head in the direction of the walls. Her curls moved as she did it and one fell over her forehead. She shook her head to fling it out of the way. "No way to let the sun in."

Braden turned his head to look around the chamber. True, the only light was from burning candles and a small lantern on the altar. Without a word, he walked back to the door and pulled it open. The midday light flooded in, but the direct rays fell only on the doorstep, where Joanna had stood before he came in.

"And you like the sunshine?" He had always favored the shadows.

"Spring is my favorite season of all, my lord. The sun grows stronger and warms the earth. I like the feel of its light on my face." Her voice softened as she spoke and, as her words echoed those of Gwanwyn's, he felt something in his soul soften toward her.

"It has caused your skin to freckle," he said.

She touched her face and nodded, looking away from his gaze. "My mother informed me how unappealing it is to see them on a lady's skin, my lord."

Unappealing? Far from it. The urge to find out where else she had them grew and he fisted his hands to keep from reaching for her. Those things would have to wait until she was truly his.

"You can enjoy being out in the sunshine during our journey to Wynwydd. Once we travel away from the coast, the rains should lessen a bit." He watched as a shudder moved through her. But he would not relent in this. They would leave on the morrow. He took a step closer and crossed his arms. "And we leave in the morn."

She began to shake her head at him, but he stopped her with a wave of his hand. "Do not think to naysay my order on this, lady. You have reached the end of your disobedience in this matter. On the morrow, you shall leave with me and travel to my home as befits the lady of Wynwydd. I will accept no more arguments from you."

"What do you plan to do to me, my lord? Will your punishments wait until we reach your keep or will I not see that?" Her voice was stronger but still trembled as she asked the impertinent question.

"Punishments?"

"Aye, my lord. You have been quite clear to so many about what you will do to me once you take me from here." She touched her neck where the imprints of his fingers stood out against her pale skin. "Do you really wonder why I would not want the *honor* of being your wife?"

Lashed by the insult, he felt the blood pulsing in his temples. Control warred with the instinct to strike out at her, to make her realize that she did not have the protection of someone to keep her from the consequences of her actions and words. Not like Lady Margaret's husband, Orrick, whose lack of supervision encouraged his wife's poor example.

"Do you really wonder why I am angry over your behavior? Every action you have taken since your father agreed to our betrothal has held me up to ridicule and embarrassment. Before the church, before the king and his court, before even these strangers. If I seek retribution against you for it, none will object. 'Tis my right as your betrothed husband to correct your wayward tendencies."

Something flared in her eyes and it startled him. For the first time since they'd met, it was not fear. He watched as the anger he felt was reflected back at him by her stance and by the set of her chin. And by her infinitely kissable lips as she pressed them together in some attempt not to speak out her thoughts.

Anger meant her fear was lessening. Anger was something he was familiar with and with which he could deal. Much better for her to be angry than to be afraid.

"Why did you not simply let me go? Why did you have to find me?" she asked.

"I chose you and you were declared mine. I would have followed you all the way to Scotland and brought you back, Joanna." Her eyes widened at his referral to her flight from him to supposed safety in Scotland and he stepped closer. This time, she stood her ground.

"If you returned and announced to my parents that you found and buried my dead body, you would still have your gold and could find another wife. No one would be the wiser for my escape."

Joanna matched his stance by folding her arms over her chest. The slit edges of her shift and tunic gapped and granted him an enticing glance at the curves of her breasts. He really did want to see if the freckles continued down onto them and so Braden took the last step between them and slid his hands into her hair as he'd been longing to do since he saw her at the door.

"I would. I am not willing to give you up," he said, meeting her gaze. "You are mine."

Braden brought her closer and touched his lips to hers. Joanna's hands covered his, but did not stop them as he moved them through her silky locks. As he deepened the kiss and turned her face to meet his, he felt her breathing begin to quicken. When she tentatively touched his tongue with hers, he possessed her mouth as he would soon possess her body.

Easing back from her lips, he nuzzled his way down her

chin, over to her ear and then onto her neck. Her soft sighs as he touched the sensitive skin there urged him on to bolder deeds. He touched his tongue to the place where the slope of her breasts began and followed the soft skin down to the now-exposed nipple. Braden felt Joanna's hands move to his chest and grasp at his tunic, but she did not stop him.

Sliding his hands down to her waist, he knelt before her and took one of the tightened buds in his mouth, licking and sucking at it until he felt her legs tremble. Then he moved to the other and soon, her ragged breath echoed through the chamber. Braden kissed the line down the center of her stomach and slid his hands around to caress her bottom when she tensed and pulled from his embrace.

"No," she said, shaking her head. "No."

He stood and watched as she tugged the edges of the tunic together and held them tightly. Her breaths were still uneven and he was pleased that she had been affected by his kisses and by his touch. She might be a virgin and not know the ways of physical love yet, but her body was ready for his as much as his was for hers.

"Consummation is all that is left for us, Joanna. The final step in making you my wife. Our last step." He adjusted his belted hose and tunic to ease the tension against the part of him that urged for that act more than any other at this moment.

"I will not say the words at the church door, my lord. I will recant my consent." She stepped away from him and walked a few paces in the direction of the altar. "I still claim sanctuary here."

Her fear of him had lessened and he had tasted of her innocent passion again, but nothing had changed between them. In the morning, it would take force to remove her from this chapel and that sin would be added to his long list of previous ones.

"So be it, lady. I will take you from here if need be."

"I will not come willingly, my lord."

Nodding at her, Braden turned to leave. Mayhap the loneliness and darkness of the church for the rest of the day and night would give her time to relent. If not, he knew what he had to do.

He had no idea about what to do.

Lord Orrick's invitation to dinner had surprised him. He expected to be seated in the back of the hall, but instead found himself at the lord's table. His men were offered every comfort again as was he. The only strange thing was that the women were missing. Lady Margaret and her ladies were gone from the table. No explanation was offered until the meal was finished and then he knew that his mission was in trouble.

"My ladywife is eating her evening meal in the chapel, Lord Braden," Lord Orrick began.

"As is mine," said Sir Royce, Orrick's chief knight and castellan.

"As is mine," added Sir Richard, the knight who oversaw Orrick's interests in the salt lathes and monastery properties.

"And mine, I fear," said Sir Hugh, captain of Orrick's guards.

"And mine." The words continued down the length of the womanless table as each of Orrick's knights and retainers reported the same occurrence—all the women were in the chapel.

With Joanna.

This could not be a good thing.

Braden did not realize he'd said the words aloud until the men grunted and nodded in agreement. Two pitchers of wine were placed on the table and quickly shared by all. The men ranged in age from young knights about one score in years to Lord Orrick at just past two score and even older.

"What is their purpose there, my lord?"

"Companionship for Lady Joanna, I am certain," Orrick replied but his expression did not look as though he was certain at all.

"Mischief and mayhem," answered another of the men farther down the table. When all the others nodded or grunted in agreement, he could not tell who had spoken the words.

"I do not understand, Lord Orrick. How is it that you allow your wife such behavior? Should you not exert more control and guidance over her? I tell you candidly that she is not setting a good example of wifely behavior for my betrothed."

Every man to a one at the table stopped and stared at him. Had he gone too far and offered too great an insult to his host? Braden swallowed deeply from his cup before looking at Orrick. When he did meet Orrick's gaze, there was amusement there as well as the benevolence of a teacher for his student.

"My ladywife is my partner, Braden. I trust her implicitly as she trusts me. She strives always for my health and happiness as I strive for hers. Margaret knows that any actions she takes on my behalf, any words spoken by her in my name, any protection extended will be supported by me, as she supports all that I do. It has taken us years and many, many mistakes to come to this point, but it has given me all I could want in life."

Braden could hear the conviction in his words and watched as each of the men at the table nodded in agreement. He shook his head trying to clear his thoughts—this was not the way of things. It sounded as though the wives ruled here and the husbands gave way for them.

"Do not misunderstand my words, Braden," Lord Orrick said to him more quietly. "If the need is there for me to give an order, my ladywife will obey me. In all things. But there are better ways to accomplish what you need to do than by making a battle of it."

"You think this is a battle? One I cannot win?"

Braden had fought many enemies in the past. Strategy and planning were his strengths. One mere woman would be no challenge.

Hell.

This woman was more than a challenge—she was a formidable adversary. She'd already begun to undermine his plans by being something, someone, very different from what he had expected.

Still, any softening in his feelings about her did not change his pressing need. Spring was full upon England and his time was limited. If Gwanwyn was correct, he had only a few more weeks in which to return to his lands with his wife. Braden knew he needed to resolve this quickly. He did not have the luxury of time.

"Do not make it one." Orrick stood. "I must check out the battlements of the keep. Join me."

Braden finished the rest of his wine and stood. He followed Orrick through the keep, up several flights of steps until they reached the roof and battlements of the keep. The strong ocean winds buffeted him as they walked to the edge and looked out over the yard and village. They stood in silence for several minutes and Braden thought about how to answer the questions he knew would be asked.

"I can see the anger and the urgency in your actions. Will you share with me the reason?"

Braden let out a breath of exhaustion and frustration. He'd had no one in his life who could understand his burden. His father had never spoken two coherent words to him before his death. No uncle or male cousin had survived long enough to guide him in the quest to protect the family name. Could Orrick help?

"Do you know my lands, Lord Orrick?"

"Please use my given name. 'Tis another of my eccentric

ways." Orrick laughed even as he admitted to it. "Wynwydd sounds Welsh."

"It is. My lands lie at the foot of the mountains that separate England from Wales. I am the last of my line, Orrick."

"Ah, the pressure to marry. I understand that well enough."

"I have my reasons, but I cannot disclose them to you." He was simply not ready to trust a stranger with the story of his family's weaknesses.

"More importantly, have you disclosed them to the lady?"

Braden walked a few paces away and looked over the stone wall to the yard. The chapel where the lady in question sat at this moment was below him.

"Her fears are real, Braden. And they've given her a strange strength to be bold and daring. More than most women, and most men, in her situation. Think on it—she came up with a plan to disguise herself and make her own way to her sister's village in Scotland. And, in spite of an unplanned illness, she nearly made it."

Orrick's tone irritated him.

"She disobeyed her parents. She ran from a legal betrothal. She lied before witnesses. And she has drawn you into it. I would not think to hear such admiration in your voice when you realize the problems she could cause for you."

Orrick's amusement quieted for a moment and then he smiled. "I do admire her, Braden, as I am certain you do if you would only admit it to yourself. I would think that she is exactly the kind of wife that the 'warlock of Wynwydd' would want. One filled with spirit and daring and passion."

He'd heard the rumors. Braden had hoped that they had not traveled this far north. "I am not a warlock, Orrick. Surely you know that." Braden faced the lord of Silloth now and shook his head.

"I know that, you know that, but the lady believes it. And she believed it so strongly that it gave her the courage to run from everyone and everything she knew. Breaking through that fear and gaining her trust will be a formidable task."

"I care not if she fears or trusts me, Orrick. I want only her compliance and obedience." Orrick laughed out now and smacked Braden on the shoulder. He felt no such humor.

"Think on your words this night and mine. If you force her to your side, you will gain a wife. If you ease her fears and bring her willingly to your side, you gain a partner. Which would you rather have?"

"If it were only that easy. There is much you do not know."

"Aye, there always is more to any story. But that is between you and the lady. I would urge you to remember that honey draws more flies than vinegar and cats come to cream."

"I have heard those sayings before, Orrick."

"And you must swear never to tell Margaret that I used them in speaking about how to treat women. But, man to man, you must learn to choose the battles you fight, especially with women. And never risk more than you can afford to lose."

Noisy chatter rose from the yard and Braden looked over the wall to see women spilling from the chapel. The evening meal and womanly talks must be at an end. He needed to seek his rest, as well, for he did not relish what the morrow held for him.

Orrick picked up the lantern he'd brought with them and began walking back to the doorway. When they reached it, Orrick looked back at him before opening it.

"I cannot allow you to force her from the chapel tomorrow." When Braden would have argued with him, Orrick held up his hand to stop him. "I think you will see the wisdom of making it seem to be your choice to stay."

The soft scuffling of feet on the stone floor woke her just as the light of dawn crept over the walls of Silloth. Father Bernard walked to the altar to prepare for daily Mass. Nodding to her, he went to the small chamber behind the altar and brought out the linens he needed. He set about covering the altar and putting out the crucifix and chalice and plate.

There was still time before he would ring the bell and call the faithful to church. The door was ajar and she lay quietly on the bench and watched as the light grew stronger and stronger. Outside.

Outside, where spring would be bursting forth again today.

Outside, where the people of the village would be preparing their fields and planting the seeds that would become food for them.

Outside, where the sun could warm her skin and the wind could ease her spirit.

Joanna stretched and tried to remember all the words of encouragement from Lady Margaret and her women. Never in her life had she been included in such a gathering. Her mother could never stand her presence, so Joanna spent most of her time with her maid and her sister, until her sister left for her own marriage. To be included in the chatter and gossip of the women of the keep had been a wonderful gift.

Every muscle in her body ached and she took a moment and tried to stretch each one to loosen them before trying to sit or stand. Her ribs were the worst, having borne most of the weight when Lord Braden jumped on her in the stables. Wenda had checked her again before leaving last evening and told her, though bruised, nothing was broken.

As she rubbed against the ache, her body remembered the other ache, the one caused by Lord Braden's hot mouth on her skin and her breasts. The tips of them tingled now as she thought on his strange caresses and kisses and the heat they caused in her. When Lady Rosamunde mentioned something later in the evening about her husband, Sir Gautier, doing something that caused her toes to curl, Joanna feared that her blush gave away that she knew something that could do that.

Lord Braden had done that to her. When his tongue had touched her, Joanna swore her toes had curled. Now, her body pulsed with an awareness that had never been there before. Not before he'd kissed her and touched her and… She must stop these thoughts. Surely they were sinful and not appropriate in this place.

"My lady?" Father Bernard whispered. "'Tis time now."

The priest went to the front corner of the chapel and tugged hard on the rope that hung there. The bell above chimed loudly enough to call those in the keep and the village to church.

Joanna sat up and then stood, still wobbling and not steady on her feet. As she stumbled, someone grasped her arm to help her.

Lord Braden.

"My lady, allow me to be of assistance." He brought his arm around her waist and waited while she gained her balance.

"You come to Mass?" she asked in a whisper as they made their way toward the altar. Did not the devil fear the cross and chalice?

"I admit that I am not as religious as I should be, but I do attend whenever I have the opportunity. There is a small but lovely chapel at Wynwydd."

Stunned by his admission, Joanna stared at him and watched for any signs that he was struggling against the Lord's presence here. A few minutes of close scrutiny revealed nothing save his habit of clenching his jaws.

They took places to one side of the altar and waited for the Mass to start. Joanna remembered that her head was uncovered and felt for the hood that she'd worn these past weeks. "My lord, I must cover my head before Mass begins. Let me get my hood at least," she said, slipping from his side. As she searched the bench where she'd slept, she felt him at her side.

"Wear this, Joanna," he said, placing a hooded cloak over

her shoulders. It hid her inappropriate attire completely from view and covered her head at the same time. And it fit perfectly.

"Where did you get this?" she whispered as they walked back to their places.

"I brought it with me. A gift for my betrothed. One I did not have the opportunity to present to you upon your arrival at my home."

The priest rang small gold bells that announced the beginning of the Mass so Joanna could not ask him any more questions. She knew that once the Mass was over, he would try to take her from here and she must collect her thoughts and be ready. He stood close to her and she could smell the scent of the soap he must have used recently. A fresh herbal smell, one probably concocted by Lady Margaret for her guests. Taking in a deep breath of it, she realized how badly she must smell.

Braden caught her and gave her a look of puzzlement. He nodded his head at the altar and she comprehended that he was telling her to turn her attention to the priest. Her breath caught as she watched the dimple appear in his chin. His green eyes sparkled with the merriment of one involved in a prank. For a moment she could almost forget that he meant to force her to his will.

Just as she'd forgotten last evening when his mouth caused such magical feelings in her body and her heart. She had nearly surrendered to him, until he touched the still-new wounds on her bottom and her thighs. It would cost her too much to allow simple lust to break her now. Shifting on her feet, she strengthened her resolve to fight his evil plans for her.

Pulling the cloak more tightly around her shoulders, she moved away from him so that his scent and his nearness and his heat would tempt her no longer. Father Bernard said the final blessing and Mass was over. Although most left the chapel, many stood just outside the fence waiting to see what would happen between them.

Lord Orrick appeared at her side and Lady Margaret stood at his. Joanna held her breath about what was to come. She was not strong enough to fight him physically. Only Lord Orrick could do that and she was not certain that he would. They all looked at Lord Braden.

"I will ask you once more, Lady Joanna, to relinquish your claim of sanctuary and come peacefully from this place with me." His deep voice echoed through the chapel. The calm tone surprised her, for she assumed that he would yell out his demand at her. Lord Braden did touch her hand and she jumped at the contact.

Joanna looked at his face and, for a moment, she believed the words he spoke. She heard some promise, some enticement, buried deep within them and she wanted to take his hand. But, the stories and the terror grew inside of her until she could not bear it.

"Nay," she whispered. "Nay, I will not leave this place willingly to go with you."

She drew back her hand inside the cloak and wrapped her arms around her to await his response. Expecting an immediate and angry retort, she was amazed at the silence. And when she finally scraped enough courage together to dare a look at his face, she found him scrutinizing hers with a blank expression.

Lord Braden simply nodded at her and stepped back away. Turning, he walked swiftly to the door of the church and called to one of his men. After giving some quiet instructions, he faced her again.

"I do not understand your need to seek sanctuary here, Lady Joanna, but I have decided that I will not break the bond given by the priest. I will not interfere with your need to examine your conscience in this matter and make your peace with God and your confessor before coming with me." He smiled then, a wicked smile, and bowed to her and the lord and lady of Silloth. "Take whatever time you need, my lady."

Lord Braden waited at the door until his man returned. With her sack. He placed it on the bench and spoke. "My lord, if you will see to the lady's comforts as you offered, I would consider myself in your debt."

Stunned by his easy agreement, Joanna watched as Orrick and Margaret followed him out of the chapel. She could hear his words as he spoke of breaking their fast in the hall. Letting out her breath, she realized that she had lived through the worst moment of her life and that she was safe. When everyone was gone and the chapel returned to its quiet state and the sun shone outside the doorway, the truth of the situation struck her.

She had not gained a safe haven, she'd set up her own prison and Lord Braden, warlock of Wynwydd, held the key.

Chapter Six

The next three days passed in a blur. Items for her comfort were delivered to the chapel, all by Lord Braden's order. He did not present himself during that time, but she spied him walking by the chapel a few times when she tried to enjoy the sun's warmth. Now, there was a wooden folding screen to give her a measure of privacy. A mattress overstuffed with feathers to use on top of the benches that formed her pallet. A chair and embroidering frame to keep her occupied through the day.

Her company increased as well in numbers and frequency. There were always several of Lady Margaret's women to share her meals and more in the evenings when the gossip and chatter turned to their favorite subject—their husbands.

The best things were the clean clothes and the bath. Two chemises, two gowns with matching tunics and new stockings. Soft leather slippers and even some veils to cover her unruly hair. Each time a servant arrived, it was all with the compliments of the lord of Wynwydd.

The bath was one she would never forget. The weeks of being in the same clothes, sleeping on pallets on the floor and not washing off the dirt that offered her some disguise were horrible. Then, the bumps and bruises she'd gained on the journey and while here still hurt. And the backs of her thighs still stung and pulled when she moved. The evening of the day he said he'd not interfere, that first bath arrived.

One appeared each evening now and as she slid into the steaming water it was both pleasure and pain. However, Joanna would not have given it up for anything. Lady Margaret's own maid helped her through it. Her hair was washed and rinsed twice in a separate bucket and she soaked until the water cooled before getting out. Her body, now cleaned and soothed from its injuries, wanted only sleep.

Wearing a new chemise and covered with thick, warm blankets, Joanna could feel the pull of sleep on her. Even the thought that she was not alone could not keep her from it. In the shadows she noticed Lord Braden's cloak still hanging on a peg by the door. Then, the dream began and she was lost in it.

She traveled on a horse, down a road in a dark forest. The trees were so thick that no light broke through to show her the way ahead. Someone was behind her and she knew she must escape. The sounds of a horse and demonic laughter made her urge her mount to greater speeds. Then, the forest ended and she was trapped before a huge black castle. The walls grew as she watched and her pursuer stopped before her, blocking the way.

Joanna climbed down from the horse and tried to run around the other rider. He controlled the massive destrier without effort and her attempts were stopped. When he flew off the horse toward her, she backed against the wall and covered her face.

There was no way out.

Then the voices began, first whispers she could not hear and then accusations made louder and louder until they wailed like the wind around her.

"His father was mad."

"He killed his mother."

"The devil's own."

"Evil."

"Madness."

"He will not let you live knowing his secrets."

"You will die giving him a son or for not giving him one."

She turned and turned, looking for the source of the voices, but no one was there. Only him. In the shadows now where his face did not show. His cloak flowed around him like the clouds in a storm—dark, swirling, uncontrolled.

Then he stepped closer to her.

The scream caught in her throat as she saw his gleaming eyes and evil intent. Forced back as far as she could, her voice finally escaped and she let out a long, keening scream. On and on, with no one answering her plea for help....

Strong hands held her and shook her from the dream. When she forced her eyes open, the object of her nightmare sat next to her. She pushed him away, forced her way out of his grasp and slid back until she hit the cold stone wall. Even the protesting of her legs and bottom did not stop her from putting as much distance between them as she could.

"Joanna? Are you well?" he asked as he leaned over her. "You were screaming."

Images from the dream flooded her thoughts again and she saw the menacing look in his eyes. Blinking over and over, she watched as his face took shape. His eyes were filled with concern, not evil. His face no longer looked demonic, but just like a man. She tried to speak, tried to breathe, but her chest would not take any air in. Gasping, she tore at the blankets.

"Here now. Your thrashing has tied you up in these," he said as he grabbed the blankets and pulled them free. "Come away from the wall and sit on the edge." He took her hands to help her move forward and she dangled her legs over the side of the benches. Then, with one hand on her back and one on the top of her chest, he straightened her up. "Breathe now. Force my hands apart with your breaths."

The heat from his hands spread and soon Joanna was able to expand her chest and take in air. He quietly urged her on as she struggled with each inhalation and exhalation. After a few minutes, he released her and stepped away.

"Were you dreaming of me?" he asked from across the chamber. His voice was soft again, but his expression was heated. 'Twas as though he could look through her with his intense eyes. Then she realized that the light from the candles and the burning brazier exposed her in just her shift.

"Yes," she answered. Fearing to say more, she looked away from him and pulled one of the blankets around her shoulders.

"The fear is back in your gaze, my lady. I had hoped it was gone."

"Fear, my lord?"

"Aye, fear. I could see it there in every move you made and hear it in every word you spoke to me until just yesterday. I had hoped that it was gone."

Joanna did not answer him. The dream had simply reinforced all the terrible things she knew about him. 'Twould take more than a gift or two or a show of kindness to rid her of her fears about him.

"Will you answer me truthfully if I ask you some questions?" She decided it was time to face some of it.

"About my reputation?" He sounded tired, his voice flat now.

"Aye, my lord." She clenched her hands together and waited. Even if he said yes, how would she know if it was the truth?

"Go ahead, lady, give me your questions." He walked to the wall nearest her little alcove and leaned against it, crossing his arms over his chest. Lord Braden closed his eyes for a moment and then looked over at her. "Well?"

"Did you father truly go mad?" This one was known across the land, so it was more for her use in gauging his replies.

"Aye, lady. My father was overcome by madness before my birth and died when I was a small boy." He shifted against the wall. "Next?"

"Did your grandfather throw himself and your grandmother off the tower of your castle to their deaths?"

He lifted his hand now and placed the heel of his palm against his forehead before answering. Lord Braden stood like that for several minutes before saying a word.

"'Tis true but not in the way you described, lady. My grandmother died giving birth to my father and my grandfather carried her to the tower and killed himself."

Part of her wanted to comfort him. To live with such a history, to have to live with such sadness. But, the next question was the one she feared the most for its subject was close to her own story but for the ending...at least so far. She hesitated to ask, but he nodded to her.

"I have been told that your previous betrothed begged her father to gain her release and that he offered you gold to release her." She paused now, for the rest was worse than that. Taking a breath, she blurted it out, "And when you refused to release her, she took her own life."

Joanna expected him to give some explanation to the accusation, but his reaction frightened her even more. He stood to his full height and turned his intensity to her. She shuddered at his approach and found herself held up against the wall by his harsh grasp.

"Damn them for speaking of it!" he growled at her. He shook her once and leaned in closer. "And damn you for listening!"

With another shake, he released her and she slid down until she touched the floor. She dared not move for his fury was a living thing. He swung his fist back, knocking down the wooden partition. Stomping on it until it broke, he kicked at the pieces and they scattered across the floor. Finished with that, he looked around as though searching for something else to destroy.

Joanna curled up into a ball and tried to protect her head and face, much as she'd done when her father did his worst. She heard his heavy footfalls and knew he stood before her. Saying a prayer in what she thought would be her last minute, she held her breath and hoped it would be over quickly. His panting was right next to her and she waited for the first blow to fall.

"Damn you," he whispered in a choking voice and then his steps moved away.

She dared a peek from behind her arms and watched him stumble from the chapel. The door stood no chance against his anger. It was pulled from its frame and, with a loud crash, fell to the floor. When his guard stepped forward, Lord Braden shoved him back and ran down the path.

In these past weeks, she'd never given in to the urge to cry. Now, the tears burned her eyes and rolled down her cheeks as any hopes she might have had of living through this crumbled. The anger inside of him was so great and so dangerous that she knew, with the wrong word or action, she could be its target.

Daylight crept in a few hours later and so did the servants. Without a word, the splintered partition was removed and a new one installed. A quiet unease reigned over the chapel, even through the Mass and later. All the gossip in the world could not lighten her mood. Now confronted with the truth of his character, Joanna knew she must escape the lord of Wynwydd.

But how?

He kept guards around the chapel and another near the front gates. Anything pertaining to her care was asked of him first. His scrutiny missed nothing.

For two days it rained and the weather made Joanna long for a walk outside this stone prison. Left on her own, most of her time over these past few years had been spent at the one remaining family estate in the woodlands of eastern England.

With no one to tell her otherwise, she'd walk for miles, enjoying the sound of the birds and wildlife around her. Her own gardens were fruitful with herbs and plants and flowering bushes.

She would never see those gardens again. Never choose seedlings again. Never harvest the bounty of herbs her garden produced. The winds outside whipped around the buildings and wailed down the pathways of the yard. The mournful sounds matched her feelings. Now, she could only pace the forty steps front to back and twenty paces side to side that this church offered.

And walk them she did. She tried to exhaust herself so that she could sleep, but the dreams and worries kept rest from her. The leaky roof of the church did not help, for the rain dripped in several places with such force and regularity that it almost sounded like music to a song. A discordant song, though.

The thunderstorms woke her in the night and the heavy rain kept most away from her side. A servant would scurry in with her meal and then race through the raindrops back to the keep. Then on the third day of rain, things changed. Instead of just a meal, the servants brought out a table in pieces and assembled it in one corner. More arrived with linens and platters and goblets and pitchers of wine and ale and then all manner of foods. 'Twas much more than one or even two could eat.

Lord Orrick led the way, followed by Lady Margaret and then Lord Braden. Her betrothed appeared uncomfortable as he approached her. Joanna tried not to back away or shake as he took her hand and lifted it to his lips. Not usually the one for reticence, he would not meet her gaze as Lord Orrick began.

"My ladywife thought it might be worthwhile for the four of us to dine together. As the caretakers, or future caretakers, of a large number of souls and many acres of land and crops, there may be topics of mutual interest to us all."

The servants had finished their work and a square table,

surrounded by four chairs and covered with linen cloths and platters of mouthwatering food, awaited them. Lord Orrick took her hand and led her to one of the chairs and she watched over her shoulder while Lord Braden did the same. Lady Margaret nodded to the servants and the meal proceeded.

Joanna ate silently as the two men exchanged ideas about the practice of crop rotation and the weather patterns of the past two growing seasons. When Lady Margaret brought up her own garden on the other side of the keep, Joanna joined in the talk.

"I would like your opinion on the layout of my newest herb garden, Joanna. I think it is the best place for it, but you can tell me what you think when you see it."

Silence spread as they each realized that Joanna would not see it as long as she stayed here.

"Actually, my lady, I have seen it. I delivered a cartful of…manure to it the first week I worked in your stables." She felt their scrutiny and smiled. "'Twas my job then."

Orrick laughed at the situation and they all joined in. "And what think you of the layout? Is it like your own?"

"Nay, Lord Orrick," she began before he stopped her.

"As I explained to Braden, one of my eccentricities is my permission to use given names and not stand on 'lord this' or 'lady that.' If you have no objections?"

Such freedom existed here. The lord moved and lived among his people, his wife was forthright and outspoken, and all seemed right with it. Joanna's weeks at court had been exhausting for her as she tried to remember the correct titles and order of precedence that one lord had over another. With little else but the pomp to cling to, her parents would never have allowed this familiarity among their servants and serfs.

"None, my…none, Orrick." He smiled at her with such kindness that she wanted to cry once more. Joanna swallowed the tears and answered the questions about the gardens. "My own is evenly split between cooking and healing herbs. But with your other estates pooling their resources, you may not need to do that here."

"And Wenda's adds to ours, as well," Margaret explained.

"As Gwanwyn will do at Wynwydd," Braden said. "She is known in both Wales and England for her healing abilities."

He still would not look at her as he spoke. The practice continued as the meal progressed and they talked on a range of topics including the king's recent second marriage, the possibility of being called to fight for their liege lord and the past glories of the Plantagenet kings.

Finally they finished the meal and Orrick offered to show her an intriguing family secret about the altar's design. She walked at his side to the front of the church as he explained the intricate pattern carved into the main stone of the altar.

"He feared that he had ruined any chance with you," Orrick whispered. "He asked for our assistance in taking this first step."

"Braden is afraid?" she asked, shaking her head. "He is angry and frightening and stubborn and…"

"Afraid, Joanna. This marriage to you means more to him than simply a wife and possible heirs. Whatever has happened to his family in the past has scarred him. His anger hides much of the real person inside him." Orrick outlined the carvings of his, his wife's and his children's names. "Something deep drives him and all he will tell me is that you are the one he must wed. And it must be accomplished soon."

"Do you know of his family, Orrick? Did he tell you of them?"

Orrick shook his head. "Nay, he would not. He would only say that there is more to know."

Joanna thought on his words. What did he hide? Could she bear it? Would she live through it?

"You were still ill when you came here. I know that now. I think your illness made you believe things that you otherwise would not have. I think it was the fever that made you run away. If you had been thinking clearly, none of this, or most of this, would not have happened." Orrick took her hand and clasped it in his. "He is not a warlock, Joanna. I think you know that somewhere inside of you, but the fear built by that fever's distortions is keeping its hold on you."

"But, is he evil, Orrick? Are the stories true?"

He was correct—a part of her recognized that the magical powers attributed to Braden were fabrications of scared minds.

"All men are both good and evil, Joanna. And so much of the balance depends on those around him."

"Orrick?" Margaret called out to him. "I wish to retire."

"Joanna, these old eyes see a man molded by his family's misfortunes, surrounded by rumors and tales, who is searching for a way for his name and family to survive. He has pinned his hopes on you. Are you strong enough to be the woman he needs?"

Orrick held out his arm and Joanna placed her hand on top of his. "Think on my words, Joanna."

Joanna watched as Orrick and Margaret took their leave and then she stood aside as the servants efficiently removed all traces of the meal from the chapel. It was soon only the two of them.

Braden was not certain that the meal had been an effective first step, but she was not backing away from him. A good sign, surely. Now, the difficult part. He cleared his throat and coughed a few times.

"May I stay a while longer, Joanna?"

She walked to one of the remaining chairs and sat down. "If you wish, my lord."

"Please. Can we not follow the example of our host and use our given names?" At her nod, he sat facing her in the other chair. "I would like to apologize for hurting you. I truly did not mean to, not the other night or when I found you in the stables. And yet, I know that I have."

Her hand strayed to her neck and the bruises that were now a mix of blues, greens and purples. In truth, he wanted to soothe those and all the others she must carry from the rough journey she made. Margaret reported that she was quite battered and only now was moving without pain.

"And I would ask your pardon for terrifying you with such behavior as you saw here. Sometimes…sometimes…"

He searched for a way to tell her that she was not the cause. The catalyst mayhap, but not the cause. He had worn himself out in the yard these past days trying to drain the rage from him. One after another of Orrick's knights had challenged him and he had exhausted his strength there so that he would have none with her.

"My father always told me that I had the most annoying way of angering him, too. His reaction was much the same as yours."

Her focus drifted into the shadows with her matter-of-fact words, but he heard more in them than she probably realized she was saying. Her hands opened and closed as he watched, like fists being formed. Whose fists?

"I will not strike you, Joanna. I have never struck a woman in my life and will not begin now."

She looked at him now and he saw her chin tilt out just a bit. "Why do you want me, Braden? Why did you choose me?"

He smiled at her. Just as she might be beginning to believe he was only a man, and a flawed one at that, his words would make him sound mad.

"'Tis apparent that some kind of affliction has beset the last generations of my family. I sought relief from it and finally a wise-woman in my village told me to seek out a woman 'of black' and to marry her in the fullness of spring. She said that my son—" Braden stared at her as he continued "—*our* son would end this affliction."

He waited for her reaction. Only her hands trembled. Then

she searched his face and must have read the seriousness of his intentions there.

"You want me because of my name?"

"Your name was the first thing that gained my attention. Joanna of Blackburn. Then when you were pointed out to me, your black hair seemed a confirmation of it."

Her hand went to her hair, or what was left of it. "And I cut it off to elude you. Will it nullify the prophesy if I cut it?"

She gifted him with a smile that lit up her face the way it had been when she stood in the sun at the doorway. Her laughter, full and generous, touched his soul and he felt something other than despair for the first time in such a long time.

"I know this sounds foolish, Joanna, but I've lived with the prospect of going mad since my father did. And back through five generations, the lords of Wynwydd have been cur—afflicted with this tendency. The only hope in all of my searching is Gwanwyn's words."

He stood and approached her chair. Going down onto one knee at her side, Braden took her hand in his. "Even if none of this is true, even if it is only cruel coincidence that afflicts my family, I still need a bride and find that I want you in spite of our less-than-fortuitous beginning."

"Your mother died birthing you?" she asked in a soft voice.

He would not lie now. "Yes."

"And no male relatives survive? You are the only one left?"

"Yes." He would not turn away.

"You have no…powers?"

"Nay. I know the gossip, Joanna. The lords of Wynwydd are not evil wizards or mages. We do not lay curses on others. Indeed, 'twould appear that due to some long-ago wrong, we are the ones cursed. I confess though, to encouraging some of the gossip, for it gave us some measure of privacy against the greedy or curious when we were feared."

"I have one more question, but I hesitate to ask it of you."

"Is it about Cecily? The woman I was betrothed to?" He knew this was her test of him, of his control, but he worried over his reaction. She nodded her head. "Ask your question."

She slid her hand from his and clasped her hands together in her lap. Well, 'twas better than holding them in front of her face as he'd last seen her do.

"Did you cause her death?"

Braden stood and walked to the door. He feared the results of failing her test, but did not have the strength of heart to speak of Cecily with her. Nor with anyone. He pulled the now-repaired door open and stepped outside. Turning and seeing the surprise on her face, he nodded to her.

"Aye, Joanna. Her death was at my hands and marked against my soul, but I cannot, will not, speak of it with you."

Closing the door, he walked back to his chambers and fell onto the bed. Defeat was pressing in on him. When he wanted to give her words that would have convinced her of the rightness of his course, he could not. When he wanted to explain his part in Cecily's horrifying end, he could not.

Sleep did not come easily that night. Even as the storms outside dissipated, the ones in his heart and in his soul strengthened. There were but a few weeks left of spring and he knew that his chances of getting Joanna to leave the church had lessened with tonight's frankness.

If he believed in Gwanwyn's words, she was his one chance.

As seemed to be the pattern over the past week, the sun shone brightly on the morning after the three days of storms. He woke just as confused over his future as he'd felt when he'd finally drifted off to sleep. The warmer winds signaled that spring was gaining control over the days of winter. But his own life spun out of control.

Orrick's man Royce had invited Braden to train again this

morn and he was on the way there now. His feet however took the long way to the yard, the one that passed the church.

As certain as he was that the days were growing longer, he was more certain that he would find her there, stretching as far as she could to feel the sun on her face. Braden turned onto the path and looked at the low stone building on his right. Joanna was exactly where he knew she would be. Although every part of her was legitimately in the church with her toes on the end of the stone doorstep, she somehow managed to balance herself without falling out.

Braden stopped and watched her for a moment. She wore a gown now, and the soft material of it flowed over her womanly curves, enhancing not hiding them from him. A scarf of some kind wrapped loosely around her shoulders hid most of the damage he'd done to her when he'd captured her in the stables.

She would be the perfect wife for him for all of the reasons that Orrick had mentioned and several others of his own. She was bold and there was a passion in her that he wanted to taste. She was intelligent. And, from the expression on her face as he had told of his mother's death and father's madness, she was compassionate. She knew when she was wrong and could accept her errors, and she fought valiantly when she thought she was right.

She was his.

Braden recognized the feeling that was becoming stronger within him for Joanna, but worried that the outcome would be the same as for the last woman he loved. He had driven Cecily from his side with words of hate, and she had met her death because of him. No matter that his intentions had been to save her from his fate. No matter that her father had agreed. No matter that he had loved her more than anyone in his life. Cecily was dead and he was still trying to cheat his fate.

He did not plan to love Joanna as he had Cecily, though.

The death of another loved one would surely send him to the brink of the same madness that had claimed his father. Was that the cause, then? The loss of so many loved ones and family members and the failure to somehow make it stop. If he followed this foolhardy plan and it did not work, was that his fate, as well?

Braden walked up to the stone fence and stood by the gate. The sun warmed the morning air and all it touched. The breezes moved over the yard, and he watched as they lifted and teased her now-clipped hair. She laughed and the sound of it warmed him. Then she opened her eyes and saw him.

He held his breath and waited to see if she would turn and run inside as she had the last time. Or would she simply turn away with disdain over his admissions last evening?

"Good morning, my lord," she said quietly.

"I thought we had decided to use our given names, Joanna."

She leaned her head in the direction of the guard as though his presence was the cause. "Your people will surely think it unseemly, my lord."

Braden nodded to the guard and stepped closer, using care not to block the sun's rays from her. "My people would think that most of what I do is unseemly. But, while here in Orrick's domain, we can follow his example."

She nodded and stood quietly as he watched. Within minutes, the doorway would be in the shade and any warmth would be lost to her until the next morn. He'd noticed the dampness and chill inside the building last evening during the meal and now realized that it must be a terrible loss to someone who loved the out-of-doors as much as she did.

She must be very serious about her objections to him to willingly deprive herself of the spring breezes and blossoms and all the other signs of the earth's renewing. Joanna was not being frivolous in claiming sanctuary if it resulted in the loss of her favorite season and most likely her only pleasurable memories.

He held out his hand to her without much more thought on it. "Come, Joanna, step into the spring's fullness."

Joanna stepped back and shook her head. "I cannot."

So, her fears were not yet gone or managed. He must give her some sign, some way for her to know him better and to put those fears behind her.

"As I see it, the stones in this pathway touch those of the church's doorway so they are part of the chapel building and part of the place where you claim sanctuary. You would be safe from…interference while on those stones."

He watched the hesitation in her eyes war with the desire to take that step, not only out into the spring but also with him. Braden moved closer and reached for her.

"I give my word that I consider the path to be part of the church."

Joanna looked from his face to his hand to the flat stones at their feet and back to his face. He held his breath as he waited to see if she would take this step in trust.

Chapter Seven

Joanna stared at Braden with his hand outstretched to her and thought he had never looked more like an enchanter than at that moment. His long dark hair hung to his shoulders and threw shadows onto his chiseled features. His green eyes glimmered in the sun's light and his smile was pure temptation. His offer, though only for a step into the gorgeous spring morning, spoke of much, much more when she looked into those eyes.

He was asking for her trust.

Could she give it? Could she not?

Braden gave his word and she would love to escape from the dismal confines of the church and feel the sun and smell the flowers she could see from her perch on the doorstep. She wanted to see the green grass filling in around the yard and see how far the ivy crept on the walls of the church.

Joanna looked at his hand and grasped it for the chance it was. His fingers curled around hers and she stepped down onto the path, out of the church for the first time in over a sennight. Then, with another step, she was fully engulfed in the warmth of the sun and the breezes that moved through the yard.

"My lord," the guard said, approaching them. "You have her now! We can go."

Joanna felt Braden's grasp tighten as he shook his head and held out his other hand to stop the guard's approach. "Nay, Raymund, I gave the lady my word. Her sanctuary extends on these stones to yonder gate. Let her be."

Daring one step then another, Joanna walked down the path to the stone fence and its bounty of flowers. Irises, eglantine, even monkshood and wild roses, all displayed their blossoms and, as she moved closer, their scents. After watching them opening over this past week and not being able to enjoy them, Joanna breathed in deeply now.

When he dropped her hand, Joanna turned around and around trying to capture all the images of the newly alive season—flowers, the sound of birds in the trees outside the keep's walls, newly sprouted grass that filled in many empty spots in the yard's dirt and along the keep's walls and buildings.

'Twas spring in earnest in Silloth.

Her gardens in the south of England must be past full bloom. Who would look after them now?

"Why are you sad? I thought it would please you to be free of the church for a time?" he asked as he walked to where she stood.

"It does please me, greatly, Braden. I just thought of my own gardens and how there will be no one to tend them now."

"You will have new challenges as lady of Wynwydd, Joanna. I assure you that you will not find my lands wanting as a place to grow your plants and herbs."

They stood together at the fence and Joanna pointed out and named the various flowers and plants that grew there. Many passersby stopped and stared at her appearance outside the church. She knew they must think her turmoil over and her decision made, but she did still fear the punishments he would mete out for her disobediences and humiliations.

"You have that worried look again, Joanna. Tell me why."

He offered his hand and she took it. He led her to a wooden bench inside the gate and they sat.

"I wish not to ruin this wonderful moment, Braden."

"If 'tis some worry that I can soothe, tell me." He lifted her hand to his lips and kissed the back of it, sending shivers through her. "I would clear up any misunderstandings between us as soon as possible."

She needed to discover if her beatings and mistreatments were at his order. If he had done so before, he would do so again, especially if he were in his home and answered to no one. Joanna moved a bit over from him so she could look at his face when she asked.

"Would you consider the beatings I have already received to be sufficient punishment for my misdeeds or do you plan to order more?"

"Beatings?" he asked in a soft voice. "What do you mean?"

"My parents made certain that I knew they were carrying out your wishes with every blow and with every lash. I just wonder if you consider that enough or if you will seek more."

"Beatings?" he asked louder now. "My orders?" He stood and shouted now. "I ordered no such thing!"

"But I heard your words to my father. You demanded my consent at any cost."

His face was red with anger and he clenched his teeth as he took a few steps away and returned. He towered over her and she began to back away when she realized that any steps away from him would take her off the stone path. Joanna gathered up her skirts and ran back inside the chapel. Once inside, she knew there was nowhere to run from him.

"Tell me of these beatings," he whispered. She could tell he was trying to control his rage. "Tell me what was done in my name."

Joanna did not want to face him when she spoke of her shame, so she looked away instead. "My father has a servant who he uses for just such things. This man can punish and leave little trace. When I would not agree to the marriage, they began by withholding my food and then he was sent to me."

She tried to keep the images from her thoughts, but she could not. Her father had watched as she was pummeled with fists and open hands. She'd managed to pick herself up the first few times she'd fallen, but the rest was a blur.

"When did this happen?" He was closer now, but off to one side.

"Right after I spoke in front of the king. My father threatened me with everything he could, including your reputation. He said only my swift compliance would save my life and my soul."

"And you would not. What was it that frightened you the most and caused your refusal?"

"The story about your ability to curse souls. And the one about the fate of your betrothed." She dared a glance at him now. "I did not want to die, Braden. I do not, but somehow any fate that ended with me as your wife seemed to involve my death."

He would not meet her eyes. How much was false and how much was truth?

"A few nights later, just after you demanded that I be brought to your lands, my father began in earnest to force my compliance. First with the cane and then with the lash. I remember not ever giving my consent, but I admit to those next days and nights blurring together."

She shivered as the memories of the sting and then burning of the cane's touch came once more. She thought she had held her tongue during that. Not until the lash tore her skin and she was weak from the loss of blood did she think she uttered the words of her surrender. Then the fear for her immortal soul rather than her life took over and she formed the ill-advised plan to run to her sister's home for refuge.

"I think Orrick correct when he said that the fever drove

me here. I only know that my thoughts turned to running from you and whatever else you had planned. If I could not save my life, I would save my soul from your evil purposes."

The expression on his face was one she'd not seen before. Horror filled his face. His mouth and eyes strained with it.

"I hurt you when I touched your back that night?"

Remembering the kiss and the caresses that had touched her bottom and back, she nodded. "Wenda said they will not stop hurting until they are completely healed."

"I would look on them," he said, approaching her now.

"No!" she said, retreating. "There is no need."

Never would she have thought that would be his reaction. But her objections did nothing to slow him. He reached for her and pulled her behind the screen to the pallet. Sitting down, he grasped her arms and placed her over his lap facedown.

"Please, my lord," she argued, trying to hold her skirts in place. "Do not do this."

"I do not wish to hurt you more, Joanna. If you lie quietly, this will be over quickly. Struggle and it will take longer, but I mean to look on the results of the words I spoke in anger."

He was so much stronger that fighting him was useless, and she acquiesced in this. Trying not to imagine what he would see, she felt the heat of embarrassment growing in her face as he lifted her tunic and gown to her waist. Only her shift hid the rest of her from his view. With a soft touch, he slid his hand along her thighs, over her bottom to her waist taking the layer of linen with it.

His indrawn breath told her more than words would. She could not see what they looked like, but she was sure that the scars would be ugly even when healed. As a warrior he must have seen the like before. And, if she did become his wife, any physical relations they had would be in the dark so he would never look on them again.

He placed his hand, large and warm, on the small of her

back and she could hear only the faintest whisper under his breath. Then, he replaced her clothing and helped her to stand next to him. When she finally tamped down the terrible embarrassment she felt at this exposure and could finally meet his gaze, she was unprepared for the pain she saw there.

"I…" he began. "I…"

His words came out in an indistinguishable stutter until he stopped and shook his head. Then without another word, he walked past her and out of the chapel. Joanna raced to the door but dared no farther. He disappeared from her view a moment later.

Braden took the sword from one of his men and climbed over the fence into the training yard. Although more dangerous than practicing with wooden ones or with quarterstaffs, both he and Royce were experienced enough to do it without killing each other. Since this was not warfare and the day was getting hotter, they stripped down to their breeches and, at the call of the weapon master, they began.

Braden lost himself in the steps of the fight that came without thought after so many years. Royce was more than competent and Braden had the feeling that he had seen the man fight before. With the practiced moves of a champion, his opponent blocked Braden's usually successful thrusts and parries.

Soon, those gathered to watch began betting on the outcome of the fight and he felt the intensity of the weapons play rise. 'Twas at the worst possible time, as he struggled to keep ahead of Royce, that his thoughts turned back to Joanna.

He was no stranger to cruelty and had seen any number of examples of it across England, but none had turned his stomach so thoroughly as the marks and scars on her body. No wonder she flinched at his touch and feared his actions. If she thought him the cause—and she did—he had no chance of her coming willingly to his side. Inviting certain death was not only madness, it was stupidity, and Joanna suffered from neither.

Even if he had calmed her fears over the rumors of supernatural powers, she would be a fool to put herself in the hands of a man who would have the power of life and death and the infliction of such punishments over her. And she was not a fool.

The shouts brought him back to the fight and he felt the tip of the blade as it sliced the skin on his chest. Blood trickled down his stomach, but it was a mere scratch. He motioned to Royce to continue and he went on the attack. He forced Royce backward from his onslaught and laughed as he finally took control. He managed to nick Royce's arm and now his opponent's blood mixed with his in the dirt of the yard.

Had hers left a trail across England? Was that the source of her illness and fever? Every mark on her spoke of deep, bleeding wounds, wounds that would have been painful and would have drained her strength and life as she ran away.

From him.

From being his wife.

From tying her fate to the lords of Wynwydd.

He stumbled and his sword barely deflected Royce's swing. Regaining his balance, sweat dripped into his eyes and he swiped at it with his hand. Too late he spied Royce approaching from his side and, as he tried to move out of the reach of his sword, he felt it cut into his side and down onto his thigh. Startled at the pain, Braden fell back, never seeing the rock tucked into the dirt of the yard.

Oblivion reached up and claimed him.

The voices reached into the tranquility of the chapel and gained her attention. She walked to the door and crouched down to see the source of it. A crowd, mostly men, from the look and sound of it, was running to the keep from the yards where Orrick trained his men. She recognized a few of Braden's men in the lead as they came closer. They did not pause, but she could see that they carried someone on a plank of wood between them.

Braden.

All she could see was his dark hair and his blood-covered body as they ran past her. Then, she could see nothing of them. Loud voices called out orders. Her guard walked to the end of the path and watched as they carried his lord.

"Raymund, you must go and discover what has happened to your lord!" she called to him. "Go now!"

He hesitated, torn between his duty to his lord and his duty to stay there, but after a few moments, he ran off to the keep.

Was Braden dead? How had it happened? Joanna knew he'd been training with Orrick's men, but they were not supposed to be real battles. She shivered as she remembered the moment that the crowd had moved and she saw the blood pouring from his head. Would he die?

Turning around, she realized that no one was in the yard. No one between the chapel and the keep. And from the silence that covered the area, no one between the chapel and the gates.

Her stomach clenched. Joanna knew that this was the best time to get away. She was healed and well rested and stood her best chance of completing her journey north. She noticed the sack of clothing she'd pushed under her pallet.

She could escape.

Grabbing the sack and the scraps of bread and cheese from her morning meal, she stepped outside and peered around the yard. Convinced that the way was clear, she ran from the chapel, through the gate and toward the walls of the keep. Still not seeing anyone paying attention to her, she crept nearer the open gates that led to the village and freedom.

A few more paces was all that stood between her and escape from Braden. Then, her chest tightened and she realized that she no longer feared him as she had before. Was he still alive in the keep? She did not want him to die.

The urge to run dissolved.

She wanted to have the chance to talk with him, to come to some agreement with him about his plans and her place in them. She needed to hear the truth about his family from him. They might have a future together once he explained his past.

She might give up her claim to sanctuary if she understood.

Joanna turned now and ran to the keep, up the stairs that led to the great hall. Following the clamor, she found what she was looking for. Lady Margaret and Wenda were at his side, washing the blood and repairing some damage. Most stood back a bit watching the women work, so she had no difficulty reaching his side.

"How can I help, my lady?" she asked.

"Joanna, what are you doing here?" the lady asked. Pointing something out to Wenda, Margaret met her gaze. "You should not be here."

"I had to find out if Braden lived. What happened?"

"He took a deep slash in his side," Wenda said as she probed the wounds. "At least two ribs are broken and this will take cauterizing to stop the bleeding."

"Why is he not awake?"

"He hit his head on a rock as he fell, my lady," the knight called Royce said.

"Will he…die?"

"If he wakes soon, I think he will recover," Wenda said. "He is strong, with a reason to heal."

Joanna knew the old woman spoke of her.

Then, with a loud groan, Braden opened his eyes. At first his focus moved from person to person and then it settled on her. She smiled at him, pleased that he was not seriously hurt.

"Joanna," he whispered.

He held out his hand to her and she took it. Moving closer

so she could hear his words over the work of those who cared for him, she leaned down. "How do you fare?"

"You are mine."

He'd said that several times before, but there was a strangeness to it now. His grasp tightened. Joanna tried to retreat and found his hold was like an iron cage on her hand. She looked at him and noticed that his eyes were clear, as was his intent. His words merely confirmed it.

"Miles. Take her until I can see to her. In my chambers, tied if need be to keep her here."

"Braden," she whispered, shaking her head in disbelief. "No. I have sanctuary."

"Once you stepped out of the church, you lost that claim, Joanna."

Sick to her stomach, she looked around at those closest and saw the truth of his words. In coming to him, she'd surrendered herself, and before she had any assurances. She'd trusted him earlier but 'twas evident now that it was simply a ploy to lull her to his side.

Joanna did not struggle or fight back as Braden's men surrounded her and took her from the hall. Up the stairs they went, to the chambers assigned to Braden during his stay here. Miles held her wrist firmly all the way and entered the room with her.

"Must I restrain you here, my lady?"

She ignored his question and walked to the window in the room. Lifting the leather flap, she peered out. The chapel sat squarely in view below, taunting her for her stupidity.

"My lady?" Miles repeated, waiting for her compliance.

She would not say the words he wanted. She looked at him and then sought the only chair in the room. Leaning her head back, she closed her eyes.

The guard stepped out of the room and gave orders to the others. Just as the door closed, she heard the words that broke her heart.

"My lord said he would get her out of that church however he could. I will not doubt him again."

The mocking laughter of his men tore into her and Joanna put her face in her hands and cried for all that she'd lost.

He'd not expected her to surrender gracefully after all she'd risked in her attempt to escape him. Indeed, the warrior in him respected the efforts it had taken her to do what she had done. But the change in her was completely unforeseen.

Other than the two broken ribs, Braden's injuries were more flesh wounds and he'd spent two days healing before leaving for his home. In those two days and in the two days that they'd been on the road, she'd spoken not a word to him. The worst thing was that she was not sulking. She did not cast him angry looks. She did not whisper under her breath.

She was not the same.

When he asked her questions about the trees and plants around them, she did not respond. When he tried to tell her of his home, she said nothing. When he tried to explain that he could not have ignored the opportunity in the hall that morning, she looked through him. In place of the woman who had angered and intrigued and interested him was an empty shell of a person.

The fight was gone from her. The spirit was gone. The passion was gone. He had regained the woman and would have a wife but, as Orrick warned, he would not have a partner.

Braden tried to convince himself that she knew more about him now and would not fear him as she had at first. He had been as patient as he could in giving her time to learn about the man he truly was and he tried to persuade himself that she would come around once they settled at Wynwydd. The arguments and his answers rang hollow even to his ears.

He had betrayed her trust. She had come to him when she could have run and he had handed her over to his men. After three days on the road south, he realized what he must do.

Chapter Eight

Braden assisted Joanna out of the tent and to a place where she could take care of her personal needs. They broke their fast with the plain fare of travelers—bread, cheese and ale. As his men readied their horses according to his orders, Braden took her aside to explain the change in plans.

"I have asked four of my men to escort you to your sister's home in Scotland. Miles will make any arrangements necessary along the way."

She looked at him for the first time in many days.

"I will send word to your father that I found your dead body and that our agreement is at an end."

The words tore him apart, but he knew it was the only way. In searching his thoughts and his intentions, he finally realized that the true curse of his family was in believing that anyone was expendable in their quest for release from their situation. He'd taken her against her desire and was willing to sacrifice her life and future to protect his own.

"My lord?" Her eyes searched his face as she tried to understand.

"My family has been cursed somehow for the last five generations. No male lives to see his heir or is sane enough to recognize him. Our women, our wives, seem not to be immune either. Many die in childbirth. 'Twould appear that I am the last of the lords of Wynwydd."

He turned and peered off into the forest around them. Spring's fullness had reached northern England and taunted him for his failure.

"Each generation has sought answers and relief from what seemed to be happening, but we have failed. When I realized the fruitlessness, 'twas too late." He pressed the heel of his palm against his forehead.

"I loved Cecily with all my heart and soul and wanted nothing so much as to have her as my wife," he began. He must explain this to her.

"Then my last uncle died and my cousin's wife died giving birth to a son. I realized that marrying her would simply make her suffer from the curse as the rest of us. Death and madness was all that lay before us."

He swallowed and tried to continue. Cecily's face as he ended their betrothal swam before him. "She would not agree to end it, so I paid her father to do so. She ranted, raved and begged me not to end it so, but it was the only way I had to protect her. When the dispensation was granted and a new match arranged for her, she came to Wynwydd and we argued. Thinking it would be easier for her to bear if she hated me, I said terrible things to her."

The sounds of that night, the words of anger, and the look on her face would haunt him until the end of his days. Even worse, finding her broken body after her horse had thrown her and knowing she had died hating him.

"Her horse threw her as she rode out of Wynwydd and she died that night."

He took Joanna's hand and led her to her horse. "I will not watch another woman I love die because of my family. I will not take a wife when I know now that I want a partner, like Orrick of Silloth has."

Braden lifted her up onto the horse's back and handed her the reins. "I release you from our betrothal, Joanna. Go now and I hope you find some measure of happiness in your life and a husband who will not betray your trust as I did."

If he thought or hoped that she might say something, he was disappointed. As Miles led the way north out of their camp, she simply stared at him as they rode away.

As he'd told her, he had learned so much from Orrick and Margaret of Silloth. And from all of their people. But, all that he had learned about himself and about what he truly wanted was for naught.

Joanna watched the backs of two of Braden's men as they rode back the way they'd come from Silloth. Miles told her they would travel to Carlisle and then on to Scotland. With so many traveling to and from that city, their appearance would not gain the attention of anyone. No need for a disguise this time.

Try as she might, she was not able to wipe the sight and sound of Braden from her memory or from her heart. When he had ordered her held, she was prepared to hate him. She wanted to come to him after her questions were answered and after she knew what to expect from him.

Now, she had all the answers but no Braden.

No wonder he was angry at fate for dealing such a horrible burden to his family. He watched as everyone he cared for perished in unspeakable ways. And not by his hand as the gossips reported.

What would be her fate as his wife? Would he go mad as his father had? Would she die in childbirth, trying to give him a son? Or was she the one chance to change the fate of his family as Gwanwyn had foretold?

As she thought on his words, she remembered the reason he'd given in sending her away and finally understood that, if he could send her away to protect her, he was the man she wanted to marry. The kind of man she would be safe with. The kind of man who would be her husband and her partner in the challenges that life had to offer.

The kind of man she could love.

"Miles!"

She would always remember the look on his face as she and his men caught up with him on the road.

Shock.

Confusion.

Love.

And such hope that she cried as she saw it in his eyes. Joanna slid down from her horse and rushed into his arms. He caught her and held her as though he'd never let her go. Then, the stupid man began to try to talk her out of her decision.

"I may go mad."

"As might I, Braden, if you force me away."

He kissed her for that comment, his hands ruffling her hair and his tongue tasting her mouth.

"You might die in childbirth," he whispered, his voice filled with the fear of losing her.

"Aye, I may. All women might. But, with Gwanwyn's help, it should work out."

Braden held her closely and nuzzled her head with his chin.

"'Twas only after you let me go that I knew you were not the man I believed you to be. Or should I say you are the man I hoped you would be."

"Are you certain about this, Joanna? I could not bear it if you ran from me again."

"As certain as any woman can be, Braden. Unless there is something you have not shared with me that I need to know?"

He leaned back and looked into her eyes and she saw amusement within his. "Only a few surprises that I would not want to spoil for you, love."

Epilogue

The first of the surprises was Wynwydd itself.

Somehow she'd expected dark brooding forests and shadowed landscapes to match the reputation of the lords of Wynwydd. As they crossed the last stream and entered his lands, Joanna was astonished to find green, rolling hills, lush forests, clear blue lakes and farmlands that looked as plentiful as any she'd seen.

Any hint that his people lived in fear of him vanished as they entered the village outside his walled manor house. He called out her name to them and they cheered her arrival. His people crowded around as they said their vows twice—once at the doors of the church and once under a bower of the most beautiful blossoms and vines she'd ever seen.

The second surprise was Gwanwyn.

For some reason, she had the image of an older woman, one of an age such as Lady Margaret or Wenda, in mind whenever Braden mentioned the wise-woman of his village. Instead, Gwanwyn was a well-endowed young woman of not more than a score of years with a lithesome figure, bright blue eyes and shimmering locks of blond hair, hair that would have rivaled her own, before she cut it off.

Joanna's attempts to tamp down the jealous feelings when she saw this woman talking in a familiar manner with Braden did not go unnoticed. Indeed, she was so surprised by Gwanwyn's true appearance that he had to reach over and close her mouth when he introduced them.

But the biggest surprise happened after their wedding.

After Braden claimed her and made her his own, she had drifted off to sleep. Sometime later, he roused her from her sleep and carried her outside. Wrapped in only a cloak, she huddled in his arms as the guards opened the gate and he walked back to the same bower where they had spoken their vows earlier.

"Braden, why are we here?" she asked in a whisper as he placed her back on her feet. "Someone could hear us or see us."

"'Tis the part of Gwanwyn's words that I did not tell you about, Joanna. A surprise. Fear not, love, no one will approach this place until after dawn."

He slipped his hands inside the cloak and touched her breasts. The chill of the air and the heat of his hands made for an enticing feeling and she leaned into him. Knowing now what was to come, Joanna leaned her head back and accepted his kiss. His tongue swirled around hers and he traced circles around the tightened buds of her nipples with his thumbs. Arching into his hands, she kissed him back, sucking on his tongue and lifting his tunic to reach inside.

Before she could stop him, he tore off his tunic and untied the laces of her cloak, dropping it on the ground behind her. Gooseflesh rose on her skin and she started to pull away. Instead, Braden rubbed his hands down her back, onto her bottom and pulled her closer to him so that his heated skin touched hers. And warmed her.

The pulsing heat spread through her as he touched and teased her body. Still new at this part of it, Joanna wrapped her hands around his neck and held on tightly as he took her once more on this journey of love. She felt his hardness against her belly and knew that he would claim her soon.

Braden knelt before her and kissed all the way down from her breasts to her stomach and then even onto the curls that shielded that most private part of her. When he spread her legs and tried to put his mouth there, she startled.

"Braden?"

"Too soon then, love? We can try that in our bed. For now…" he said, his words trailing off into a whispered promise.

He sat back on his knees and guided her to straddle his legs, bringing the place that now throbbed onto his hardness. When she hesitated, he teased the aching folds between her thighs with his hands and eased her down. As he filled her, her head fell back and Joanna moaned out the wonderful feelings within her. Then, shifting once more, he laid her on her back and thrust as deeply as he could.

Surrounded by the soft green grass, the scent of nearby honeysuckles and the sounds of the approaching dawn, she felt everything within her tighten as she met his thrusts with her own. Her toes curled and she drew her legs up so that he could enter more deeply into her body. Aching, she welcomed his hardness against the core of her. Moving together and apart, together and apart, she could feel the tension within her growing and growing until, with a last thrust, he spilled his seed inside of her.

Her own release welled up from the core of her, through her heart and soul, and out until her cries mingled with his. Their essences spilled out on the grass, now covered with the morning dew.

They stayed joined, until they could breathe again and then he eased from her. Although her body had begun to notice the morning's chill air, she was still too caught up in the throes of their joining to complain.

"Did you feel it?" he asked, turning on his side and gazing on her. He slid his hand down and rested it on her belly.

"I felt much." She smiled at him and reached out to entwine her fingers with his.

"Gwanwyn said the curse would be lifted if we joined in such a manner."

Shaking her head, she wondered if she should be fearful of the power of Gwanwyn over her husband. Then, realizing what the wise-woman's words had done, she decided not.

"And do you believe it, Braden? Is it gone?"

"I hope so, love. I hope so."

They were not completely alone.

'Twas Gwanwyn's practice to gather certain herbs at dawn when they were just opening and most potent. She skirted the bower not wanting to intrude, but the sound of a woman's keening release and a man's deep groan of satisfaction could be heard throughout the valley.

The lord of Wynwydd had found his life mate and brought her back to his home.

Her words, her prophecies as Lord Braden called them, were not really a magic spell or enchantment. They were the simple words of someone who recognized the danger of hopelessness. For once a man lost hope, he lost all and could hold nothing.

Her own family had lived on this land and served the lords of Wynwydd for generations as ill fortune met disaster and the family was nearly destroyed—first by untimely deaths and then by the growing gossip and rumors about them.

Lord Braden's father did not heed the words of her mother, nor his grandfather before him. 'Twas only when Braden came to manhood and showed the spark of knowledge and the willingness to listen that she could fulfill her family's calling and help him lift the true curse that plagued them.

And it was only through a woman like Joanna that it could work. Only with Joanna's demand for him to change, and her love and support for him, could he learn to hope again.

And hope was the answer he sought.

Even as the light of dawn crept over the horizon, the laughter of the lord and lady spilled down the valley and across the meadows. Gwanwyn smiled and entered the forest assured that the curse was gone and, in nine months' time, the lord of Wynwydd would look upon his heir.

* * * * *

*If you enjoyed THE CLAIMING OF LADY JOANNA,
look for Terri Brisbin's new book,
THE DUCHESS'S NEXT HUSBAND,
available in May 2005,
only from Harlequin Historicals.*

HIGHLAND HANDFAST

Joanne Rock

With thanks and humble gratitude to my three sons,
Taylor, Camden and Maxim, for providing me with
the most profound experience of my life...motherhood.

Chapter One

Scotland, 1310

There had been a time when Countess Brenna Douglas Kirk-patrick would have never paid a visit to Blackburn Keep without brushing and perfuming her hair, cloaking her brown mane in the best silken veils her father's moderate riches could obtain. She would have pleaded and wheedled with her sister to borrow her best gown, a taffeta and velvet surcoat dyed in the deepest shade of purple, because Brenna fancied the rich hue complimented her dark hair more than her sibling's blond tresses.

Once upon a time, Brenna's heart would have pounded with feminine anticipation the whole way to Blackburn Keep, her pulse unsteady as she indulged in girlish hopes for a future with the strong and silent Scot whose legendary sword had kept invading English forces at bay when he was a mere nineteen summers.

Yet today Brenna rode hard through desolate moors and dense thickets in the inky blackness of night, heedless of hawthorn branches slapping her cheek or frigid creek water splashing against her calves as she raced to see the very same man. Frosty Highland winds burned her skin and whipped through her uncovered hair, the damp breeze penetrating a threadbare cloak. The leather of her worn boots provided little protection from the brooks overflowing with newly melted snow, the water seeping through cracks too numerous to patch any longer.

And although her heart pounded at a furious rate, the relentless thump had naught to do with the Lord of Blackburn, whose keep rested just beyond the next hill. Nay, her blood raced with hot fury through her veins for another reason entirely.

Fear.

Swallowing back the cold wave of dread that threatened, Brenna used the surge of emotion to nudge her horse harder, faster, over that last barrier between her and the only man she could turn to for help. Tears stung her eyes as she rode, but she told herself the damp streams coursing down her cheeks and streaking back into her hairline were caused by the bite of bitter mountain winds against her tender skin and not an outpouring of soft emotions she could ill afford. She intended to wall off her fears and feelings for now, a technique she'd perfected in the past three godforsaken years of her twenty-three summers.

Although she would give Lord Gavin Blackburn anything he required in order to secure his assistance just this once, she would not hand over the last scraps of her pride along with it.

She might not be the spoiled daughter of the noble house of Douglas anymore, but she still retained her noble bearing despite the yoke of an unwanted marriage, the realization that her dead husband was a traitor and the hardship of English imprisonment these past three years. No matter what life had doled out for her she had clung to her pride—in herself, in her father's clan and in her country. For no matter what her traitorous husband said to the contrary, Countess Brenna Douglas Kirkpatrick had always been a loyal Scot to the bone.

Brenna had traded her soul to hold her head up and make such a claim and, by God, no man would take it from her now.

There would be no indulging of weak emotions until she'd retained Gavin's help to recover the only precious thing left in a world that had forsaken her.

Gavin Blackburn sat upright in his bed, awakened by a sound. A movement. He could not be sure.

Fingers flexing against the crisp linens his servants had dried in the cold mountain winds the day before, Gavin held himself perfectly still. Listening. Waiting.

His hound, Rowan, tensed on the floor beside him. Even in the dark shadows of his bedchamber, lit only by scant moonlight that told him the hour was well past midnight, he sensed something amiss in his keep. Rising from his bed, he didn't have long to wait to discover the source of his unease.

A feminine voice raised in anger lifted through the gallery to echo off stone walls.

For the first time in a year, a woman had entered Blackburn Keep.

An interesting turn of events since his gatekeeper, young Alister the miller's son, had strict orders to admit no one. And Gavin didn't believe for a moment any of the village women would be foolish enough to enter the keep these days. They knew of his peculiarities. Respected his wishes. Left him alone.

Nay, the woman in his hall could only be an outsider. And heaven help young Alister if her purpose was treachery. The English had been known to use the lowest means to gain entry to Scots fortresses, and considering the way they had treated Scots noblewomen taken captive during Robert the Bruce's bid to free Scotland, Gavin would not be surprised if they resorted to using women as a way to distract young gatekeepers.

Pulling on his braies and shrugging into a tunic, Gavin did not bother with a hauberk as he leaned down to pat Rowan's head. He didn't even take time to tie his garments about him, assuming any woman who entered his keep past midnight without an invitation could damn well suffer his lack of attire. Gripping his sword grown ice-cold in the drafty chamber, he stepped out onto the gallery just in time to collide with Kean, his bailiff.

"I told Alister ye would kill him dead, my lord." Kean followed Gavin down the corridor leading to the stairs while Gavin craned his neck for a glimpse of this woman who—by the low fury of her tone—seemed to be raising bloody hell.

He could see naught but a few long shadows below, since he had never found a need to burn tapers all night.

"Did she give her name?" Gavin hit the steps at a brisk pace despite the fact that the stairs disappeared into blackness. "Lay a fire in the hall and make sure Alister knows the gate willna open again this night or I will personally toss him into a deep patch of poison ivy until next winter. Ye ken?"

"Aye." Kean nodded vigorously beside him, already moving toward the fireplace as they reached the bottom of the stairs. "And her name is—"

"Brenna." The woman herself stepped in his path, her face materializing from the shadows in the dim light cast from two narrow candles that provided the only illumination in his great hall after midnight. "Brenna Douglas Kirkpatrick, my lord, and I would have never come at this hour if I did not seek your aid in the most dire of quests."

Brenna.

Dear God, she hadn't needed to say any more than that. As if he had ever forgotten this woman who had become Scotland's most lauded patriot during the recent years of tumult with the English. She bore little resemblance to the fanciful girl he remembered from his youth. Her father had married her off to the English-sympathizing Kirkpatricks and by all accounts, Brenna had not gone to the altar quietly. Gavin would have stepped in to speak to her father himself if he hadn't been fighting at Robert the Bruce's side during those years.

"By all that is holy, how came ye here?" Gavin moved to put his arm about her and usher her toward a seat near the grate where Kean was busy laying a fire, but something about her rigid posture stayed his hand before he touched her. There was a wariness in her eyes now that had never been there in their youth. "Come, warm yerself by the hearth and Kean will fetch some wine. The last I heard tell of Brenna Kirkpatrick, she was locked in an English keep as Edward's own prisoner."

She moved toward the bench nearest the fire that now crackled and hissed as the wood slowly caught flame. Gavin could see her better in the reflected glow of the growing blaze, her dark brown hair glinting damply against her gray woolen cape. Her thin cloak molded to her body, the garment as lean and sparse as the rest of her. The soft curves of her youth had been replaced by willowy strength. Even her cheeks that had once dimpled in perpetual smiles now possessed a taut angle, bringing her green eyes into startling focus.

"Let me take yer cloak before ye catch yer death." He moved to help her with the wet garment and noticed her stiffen as if unaccustomed to another's touch. Or, mayhap, she simply feared the contact with a man. There was no telling what kind of atrocities she had faced while held captive, no matter that she slept in a remote keep instead of a public prison. Throwing the cloak over a table to dry, Gavin settled in beside her, taking wine from Kean before dismissing him along with two other servants who lurked about the echoing hall. Only his hound remained to keep them company.

Brenna accepted a stout wooden cup from the tray and drank deeply while Gavin tried to remember everything he knew about her daring in those early years of Robert the Bruce's campaign to unite Scotland. She'd wed as her father willed, he recalled. And although Gavin had had no plans to ask for her hand himself back then, he distinctly remembered being disappointed to learn another man had married the willful young countess who had grown up on neighboring lands.

He'd always thought of her as too young for him, too full of fire when he had sought simple things in life. Peace. Security. Good crops. But he'd long admired her spirit and he'd thought it a crime her father would shackle her to a craven English supporter simply because Fergus Kirkpatrick offered richly for her.

Gavin had put her out of his thoughts after that, consumed with his own role in securing Scotland's freedom. He'd heard no more about fiery Countess Brenna until he heard from the Bruce himself that the bold Scots noblewoman had personally chased him down to warn him of Kirkpatrick treachery and a bold new plan of attack by the English. 'Twas only hours after the king had sent the brave beauty back home that she was beset by the English on the shores of Dornoch Firth. Nearby, English knights had already captured a handful of other Scots noblewomen seeking refuge in a hallowed sanctuary, but the Scots hadn't learned until later that Brenna had been seized, as well.

Now, Gavin waited quietly while she finished her wine, his gaze soaking in the angular cut of her hollowed cheeks, the dark circles beneath her eyes. Two raw scratches across her temple told him she had made the trip across the dark moors in haste. Blasted hell, between her dripping boots and mud-soaked hem, she looked as if she had been riding for days.

"I was only released from my English prison last week." She did not look at him, but kept her emerald eyes trained on the flames in the grate. Her voice rasped slightly, as if she had not spoken in a long time. "I rode straight for my late husband's holding, but arrived to find his brother's standard flying above the keep. I was not given admittance because it seems I have been dismissed from the family."

"But 'tis no secret ye didna ever care for his kin. Have ye no dower lands to seek retreat? Or perhaps yer father will welcome ye home?"

"I would sooner take up residence in the nearest den of thieves than live under my father's roof, but I do have dower lands. I care not about the loss of my dead husband's holding so much as I care about something else his family has stolen from me." Her voice lowered to a harsh whisper, and at first Gavin thought she nursed a deep anger. A need for revenge.

But as she wrenched her attention from the leaping flames crackling merrily in the hearth, he could see that her vivid green eyes were filled with tears.

Gavin's heart clenched at the sight of this stiff, unbending woman who wore her muddy, threadbare clothes with pride yet could not hold back tears at the thought of some injury by the Kirkpatricks. Hell, she could have told him she wanted to retrieve a family ring, an heirloom brooch or a damn scrap of ribbon from her husband's conniving clan and he would have gladly picked up his sword to see it done.

His heart had been rent in two by another woman's tears, another woman's pain. He could not abide to see such tangible proof of feminine hurts.

"Dinna cry, lass. I'm sure we can make it right."

To his surprise, Brenna blinked before her tears were shed, her glimmering eyes turning cold and hard in the firelight. "Nay. I will not cry because I will not let them take the best of me, but I need your help to succeed in my quest. You have only to name your price." Her words were soft but sensible, as matter-of-fact as any man conducting his trade.

Gavin wondered if she realized how much the Highlands had faded from her speech in the years she'd been imprisoned, how much she almost sounded like one of *them*. He found himself struggling to recall her melodious lilt as a girl when they might have sat close to this fire with his siblings and hers, their clans friendly if not overly close. They had shared a bond long ago, and one stolen kiss that Gavin would never forget.

"Before I name any price, lass, I'd best know what it is ye'd like me to fetch for ye."

She hugged her arms about herself as if no amount of heat from the grate could warm her. Gavin did not miss the hitch of her breath as she drew in a long draft of air fragrant with the scent of burning cedar.

"'Tis my children the Kirkpatricks have stolen from me, my lord."

Gavin stilled, his heart slugging painfully in his chest as it had anytime he'd thought of children this past year. He had not forgiven himself for the loss of his fragile young wife who had been so determined to bear his babes despite the limits of her delicate body. After losing two bairns early in their terms, she'd managed to carry a third for nine moons only to lose the little girl during a delivery that had stolen his wife's life along with Gavin's heart.

Brenna peered at him with a desperation in her eyes that resonated clear to his toes. He knew well the sacrifices a woman was prepared to make for her children, and he would not let Brenna fight this battle alone.

She leaned closer, her visage glowing with fierce maternal love. "Not for anything else in the world would I confront the Kirkpatricks again, but I will not have my boys stolen out from under me. I have been denied three years of their young lives, my lord, and I will not be denied another day." Her voice cracked with a soft swell of emotion before she recovered herself, her hands clenching into frustrated fists in her lap. "I am prepared to pay you any price to secure your sword for the task. Will you help me?"

His heart eased somewhat as he separated his past from his present. He could never save Aileen's babes for her, no matter how much he had prayed and wept before God. But Brenna's sons could be freed by his sword, a weapon he needed no divine intervention to wield.

"How old are yer sons?" He had not even been aware she'd

borne any children with Fergus Kirkpatrick before the English had captured her. Her imprisonment, and the risk she'd taken to insure a free Scotland, had leveraged a high price indeed.

"Callum is six and Donovan is four. Fergus was killed in battle shortly after Donovan was born, and when I rode to give King Robert the news of Kirkpatrick treachery, I left my sons in the care of my sister at Montrose Keep. The gatekeeper will no longer admit me into the Kirkpatrick family holding, but I suspect the boys are still there, although I am not sure about my sister. Wherever they are, I am certain they have been usurped by my husband's kin and I cannot sit idly by while the Kirkpatricks steal away my children to be raised among their own traitorous kind. I saw firsthand the weak shadow of a man my husband became after a lifetime of his father's influence."

Gavin nodded as a more complete vision of Brenna's life formed in his mind. She was utterly alone in the world, divided from her family by old grievances and a marriage she never wanted, widowed by her husband and forsaken by her husband's kin. And although she had suggested earlier she could be content without the support of her family, she had children to think about, noble sons who needed a secure home and political connections to keep them safe.

All of which could be easily provided to them if only the proud countess could be convinced to accept his protection.

"I will undertake this quest, but I regret to say my sword will come at no small price."

"If it is within my power to give you, Gavin of Blackburn, I swear you shall have it."

Clearly Brenna placed too much trust in him and the youthful friendship they had once shared or she would not have made so rash a promise.

Gavin would never accept so much as a farthing for a cause so noble, but he had every intention of using her wide-open invitation as a way to protect this strong woman who had risked—and lost—so much. And it just so happened his proposed solution would mend a problem of his own he had feared he would never reconcile.

"I assure ye, lady, ye are well capable of paying, for I seek only this." Reaching for her, he drew her hand forward, untwining it from its resting place along her arm. "Handfast with me, Brenna, and I shall ride out for your children at first light."

Brenna wondered if the wine had distorted her senses.

She had not eaten in three days, and even then, she'd scarcely touched her last meal within the confines of the keep where she'd been imprisoned because she had been too anxious about her impending freedom. Perhaps the lack of food and sleep had conspired with the wine to muddle her thoughts.

Yet, as she looked into Gavin's inviting blue eyes in the firelight, she realized there could be no mistaking the warmth of his hand curled about her own. His callused palm spoke of his strength and sword prowess, the very reasons she'd sought him out today. But the tender way his thumb brushed the back of her fingers conveyed a more intimate message altogether.

For one heated moment, she took in the strong angles of his face, which remained unmarked except for the lines about his eyes that had squinted back too much sun and indulged in plenty of laughter. Dark hair so brown it was almost black fell in silken disarray above his brow. Many a maiden had surely dreamed about brushing her fingers through those locks. Indeed, one woman surely had touched him thus….

"But what of your wife?" Brenna yanked back her hand as she straightened her shoulders, reminding herself she could not trust any man, even one who had occupied more than his share of her thoughts in her youth. She had been disillusioned about men ever since her father had seen fit to wed her to a spineless knight who cared more about pleasing his greedy family than fighting for what was right.

And perhaps Gavin was lacking in honor, too. She knew very well that he was a married man, since her own sister had attended his wedding four years ago.

"My wife died in childbirth last spring." He spoke the news softly—slowly—each word drawn from him painfully as if they emanated from the most raw places inside him. Broad shoulders and thick muscles had been little defense against deeper hurts. "Our babe died with her."

Ah, she had been too quick to judge him. Sympathy tightened in her chest at the thought of his loss. Her memory of Gavin Blackburn had been that he was a good man. Even in his youth he had been noble and considerate, full of charm and ideals that set her girlish heart to fluttering. She might not ever be so easily taken in by a man again, but she had not been wrong in her vision of Gavin as a man of honor.

"I'm sorry." Her words of sympathy were quiet in the cedar-scented hall, too inadequate to comfort a man who had clearly loved his wife. "I should have known you would never propose such a thing. I fear I am overtired from a long journey and I am not thinking clearly."

Some of the pain diminished in Gavin's eyes as he shook his head. "Ye dinna misunderstand me, Brenna. I proposed a union between us before I go after yer boys. A handfast will bind us together for at least a year and that will strengthen my claim for the children when I ride into Montrose."

"You want to handfast…with me?" Brenna could see his point about having a strong claim to her sons, but wasn't it enough that she was their rightful mother? It had to be enough because Brenna had no intention of tying herself to any man again. Fear flickered through her for a moment until she realized how to discourage this man's misplaced interest in her—a task of vital necessity to a woman who would risk everything for her freedom.

"I appreciate your gesture, my lord, but perhaps you do not

recognize the full import of what you are suggesting. Allow me to spare us both further embarrassment by simply saying that I am unfit to be any nobleman's wife now."

Chapter Two

Silence hung over the hall until even the occasional pop and hiss of wood in the grate seemed a loud, resonating sound. Brenna's breath echoed in her ears, each intake of warm air rasping gently within her chest, reminding her that she could not push herself for many more days without rest. She needed her children back soon, and she needed Gavin's help to obtain them.

If only he could be dissuaded from this madness he'd suggested.

"Ye look quite fit for marriage to me." Gavin's eyes slid over her with slow precision, stirring unexpected warmth inside her. "I am sorry for any hurts ye incurred at the hands of yer captors, Brenna, but I will swear on my own mother's grave to protect ye and yer sons for the rest of yer days if ye'll only agree to a handfast. 'Tis more than passing reasonable."

The warmth in her chest increased the longer he stared at her with the liquid blue gaze she recalled so well from her wistful youth. She had daydreamed about those eyes, imagined such passionate declarations in her romantic thoughts many summers ago before she learned the cold, hard truth of noble marriage. She would not be swayed by idle promises anymore, even from a man who might strive to honor them in a way Fergus Kirkpatrick and her own father never had.

Still, his words touched her. He would consider taking her to wife even after all she'd been through, even when he knew there could be a chance she'd been violated by her captors? Few men would make such an offer. Although she could not help but wonder what he hoped to gain in return.

"I was not ill-used by my captors." She had not meant to mislead him. "In that instance alone, my connection to the Kirkpatricks proved valuable since the English owe much to the clan."

Before he could speak, she pressed ahead, determined that he would hear her out. "But I would not dream of saddling you with an unwanted wife and family because of my request. You are generous to make such a suggestion, but you must believe me when I say I could never accept such an arrangement." She stared down at her hands, which glowed red and chapped in the firelight, refusing to get lost in the lure of those blue eyes. She would not pretend the last three years had never happened. Nay, the last seven years, since in truth her captivity had started long before she ever rode to warn Robert the Bruce. "I am prepared to pay you in gold or land or even sheep if I find my dower properties have been profitable these last few years, Lord Blackburn. You have only to name a price."

"Gavin." His hands settled on her shoulders before he turned her to face him. "I was Gavin to ye long before I became laird of my lands, and I will remain Gavin to ye now. I willna accept anything save yer promise to live with me for one year, a handfast promise ye can walk away from if the marriage doesna suit ye. 'Tis more than fair for risking my neck by crossing swords with yer unholy Kirkpatrick kin."

Brenna's skin tingled beneath her surcoat where he touched her. The man's hands were dangerous and she would do well to remember as much.

"Why?" She shifted slightly, as if she could dislodge his grip, but he held her with gentle insistence. "How will you profit from a handfast that I could never promise will lead to a true marriage?"

His hands slid away from her arms then, and for one brief moment, Brenna mourned the loss of his warmth. His strength. She watched him as his eyes shifted from sky-blue to stormy gray, his dark brows knitting in consternation.

"I am a man without heirs, lass." He could not have boiled down the matter any more simply than that.

From a logical standpoint, Brenna could appreciate his position. But along with the thought of heirs came the thought of…coupling.

Her cheeks warmed, but she refused to play the shrinking maid when she was a mother two times over. No need to blush like a spring virgin. And yet…she had not thought of such things in a very long time. Clearing her throat, she banished all thoughts of coupling from her mind and attempted to regain control of their conversation.

"But you are a powerful laird. Surely you need to make a more advantageous match than a widow with a notorious past." She scrubbed her hands over her arms in an effort to ward off the chill that had crept through her ever since the loss of Gavin's touch.

"Ye've been away from the Highlands so long ye are not aware of my reputation." His jaw flexed in consternation, his whole expression stern and forbidding. "I was so stricken with grief after my wife died that I would allow no woman within the keep. And while I admit, my request for solitude might appear extreme, I didna realize that it would perpetuate rumors far and wide about my eccentricities. Apparently there are nae too many marriageable women willing to tie themselves to a harsh Highland laird determined to have heirs but canna stand the sight of a female within his walls, ye ken?"

Her heart softened as she realized his stern expression simply covered a deeper wound. A grief that had never fully healed.

"Aye. Gossip is as prized among these mountains as good ale and sturdy horseflesh, but I am certain you can find a struggling lord who will gladly give over his daughter anyhow. 'Twas how my own marriage was made."

"Aye, and look at the misfortune that ensued." He leaned forward, bracing his elbows on splayed knees as he looked her in the eye. "I willna have a bride who fears me. There is an accord between us, Brenna, one that was forged long ago in a stolen kiss before either of us was old enough to understand what it meant, and I mean to call upon that mutual understanding now that we both find ourselves in need."

Something stirred deep inside her, something warm and soft that scared her more than his words.

"Nay." She shot to her feet, unsettled that he would remember her long-ago foolishness. "You cannot assume anything from a mere accident of childhood. I was naught but a girl when—"

She could not finish the thought, unwilling to remember her only other encounter with Gavin alone. Her cheeks flamed hot at the memory of her boldness that day, her impish need to let the young Blackburn heir know she was not just a silly girl anymore. She'd happened upon him on the moors one afternoon when her father had come to sell the elder lord Blackburn a ram.

"I seem to remember ye were a bit more than just a girl." Gavin's eyes danced merrily as if he recalled the event in vivid detail.

Brenna's cheeks heated even more.

"Then your memory proves rather faulty, my lord. Let us dispense with the past and stick to our present agreement, shall we? I need your sword and your help and I am willing to trade anything to retain them as soon as you name a sum that is within my power to give."

"Ye keep speaking of yer willingness to pay this price, Brenna, but I've yet to see any proof of yer being amenable." He leaned back in his chair with the indolent arrogance worn by powerful men. "I can be every bit as stubborn as ye, lass. And I willna offer my help until ye swear—here and now— to live with me for a year as my handfast bride."

Regretting the need to make a decision so quickly, Brenna saw little choice but to agree to his price, curse the man. She needed her sons back now and she had no one else to turn to for help. Her father had made it clear that he considered himself free of obligation to her once she wed Fergus. And the Kirkpatrick clan considered her the enemy ever since she sold them out to the king.

She paced before the hearth, her feet treading the well-worn stones that had hosted countless Blackburns and their guests over the years, wishing she could go back to simpler days when she and Gavin had been friends.

"When you speak of handfasting, you mean that either of us has the right to walk away a year from now?" An idea began to form in her mind.

"Aye, but the traditional rules apply. I expect ye to live at Blackburn Keep with me for the year, but if we decide to act as man and wife within that time—" he paused, his gaze lingering on her until there could be no mistaking that he referred to consummating the union "—then we will find a priest and make an official marriage."

Brenna could scarcely remember their one shared kiss without flushing hotly. How could she think on lying with him? Flustered, she shook her head. "That will never happen, but I will agree to your terms if you can think of nothing else you would like better. I must have my sons back, no matter what the cost."

Gavin rose, his warrior's frame unfolding from the bench before the fire, his massive body flexing with muscles beneath a thin tunic he'd left open and untied. Brenna's gaze drifted to the open V at his throat where she absorbed the sight of lightly bronzed skin glowing even more warmly in the fiery light of the hearth blaze.

Her mouth dried at the sight of him so tall, so near. The young warrior she remembered had not been as broad of shoulder or as tall. He was now a man in his prime, a feared knight of the realm. That made him the perfect candidate to win back her sons, but a rather unsettling choice to share her bed.

Nay, her *home*.

There would be no sharing of chambers in this handfast arrangement. She would make certain of that. Later, she would find another way to repay Gavin for retrieving her children.

For now she simply needed to remember that staying out of Gavin Blackburn's bed would be the only way she could walk away from him at the end of their year together.

Gavin reached for Brenna, determined to hold on to this woman who had proved herself as fierce a warrior as any sword-wielding knight. That she could embody such strength in so slender a form amazed him even while it made him certain she was the right wife for him.

He could not bear to lose another woman he loved, could not endure the heartache that came with Aileen's death again. But Brenna was resilient where Aileen had been soft and giving. Brenna had looked death in the eye and defied it as she defied her captors, refusing to give in to her tender sensibilities when she'd been marched through Scotland with her hands tied.

Brenna Douglas Kirkpatrick—soon to be Blackburn— would bear him strong sons and make a formidable lady for his people. He had married for love the first time, a mistake he would not repeat with Brenna. He admired the proud Highland lass, true. And despite the dirt on her gown or the gaunt look of her once dimpled cheeks, the woman stirred his blood.

That connection was all the reassurance he needed that he did the right thing in handfasting with Brenna.

No need to wait to seek a priest to perform a marriage ceremony when a handfast would serve him just as well. They could speak their vows to one another here and now—and be done with it.

"Give me yer hand then, Brenna, and we shall see the deed accomplished." He took her palm in his, surprised at the cool smoothness of her skin there. He suppressed the urge to apply her hand to his chest and warm those cool fingers with the heat of his body, but he could not suppress his wayward thoughts.

"You do not wish to wait until morning?" Her low voice hummed along his senses, the words whispered as softly as a lover's confidences across a pillow.

"I ride at first light if I am to arrive at Montrose Keep the next day. If we speak our vows now, we can still steal a few hours of sleep before I must leave."

She tensed so sharply he was forced to squeeze her palm to keep it within his grasp.

"You wish to retire this night?" Her green gaze turned accusing, and as she glared at him he spied the slashes of yellow within the green orbs that reminded him of a cat's eyes.

"Retire to rest," he clarified, wondering how they would ever consummate a marriage if she found the thought of lying with him so distasteful. Or perhaps frightening? He could not imagine what horrors she'd been subjected to during her captivity and a surge of protectiveness made him all the more determined to keep her safe. "There is a guest chamber prepared where you may sleep in peace."

Her fingers seemed to cease their trembling enough that he loosened his grip on her. Pink color suffused her cheeks as she nodded.

"That would be fine." She bit her lip, hesitating as if she debated asking more of him. But she only shifted on her feet, her damp leather boots squeaking softly in response. "I appreciate your thoughtfulness, as I've had a long journey."

Empathy for her clogged his throat as he tried to imagine her fears for her children. Now more than ever he was certain his decision to handfast with her had been fated. She needed his protection. He needed her strength.

Squeezing her palm lightly, he spoke the words that would bind them together in the eyes of God and man for at least a year.

"I, Gavin Blackburn, take you, Brenna Douglas Kirkpatrick, to wife and to you I pledge my troth." He stared into those deep green eyes of hers and found himself wondering how long it would take to convince her to share his bed. His life.

She licked her lips, a small flick of pink tongue against her rosy mouth.

"And I, Brenna Douglas Kirkpatrick, take you, Gavin Blackburn, to be my husband." She met his gaze but did not hold it, her eyes glancing down to their joined hands. "To you I pledge my troth."

Gavin could scarcely believe the deed was done. After a year of banishing every female person from his keep, he had handfasted with the first one who walked into his great hall.

And although she was too exhausted and frightened of him now to consummate their arrangement into a true marriage, he had no doubt but that the deed would be done long before their promised year together was finished. Indeed, he would sleep little tonight knowing that his new bride lay but a few doors away, her cool skin awaiting the fire of his touch.

All the more reason for him to obtain her children for her as quickly as possible. Her mother's heart would rest easy once her sons were safely under his roof, and then there would be no reason to hold back.

For now, he would content himself with a taste of her lips before they retired.

"Thank ye, Brenna." He bowed swiftly over their clasped

hands, sensing she would retreat from him as fast as she could. "You would do well to rest now, but for my part I will never sleep until you answer one last question for me."

"Aye?" She blinked up at him, her dark hair beginning to dry in the warmth of the fire's blaze.

But his gaze flicked to her mouth and the enticement of her soft lips.

"I would know if you taste as sweet as I remember." Relinquishing her hand, he cupped the back of her neck, titling her face to just the right angle. He lowered his mouth over hers to savor her, his fingers sifting through her hair as he inhaled the damp fragrance of the moors that clung to her skin.

She tasted like heather and moonlight, a combination of natural and exotic, a heady blend of the outdoors and something more darkly sensual. Her lips parted on contact, and for all he knew she had been about to say him nay or protest in some other way. But whatever words she'd been about to speak, they were lost in the onslaught of heat that seemed to roar through them both at the contact. Gavin couldn't deny the hungry flames that licked over him just because of one simple kiss, and he could feel the temperature rise in Brenna's skin where he touched her, her throat warming beneath his fingers.

Desire surged for the first time since his wife had died, except this desire lacked the tenderness that had marked his couplings with Aileen. The molten ache that gripped him now was no gentle swell of affection but rather a need sharper than hunger or thirst, an elemental urge.

His hands slid down Brenna's shoulders, his fingers sinking into her worn gown to savor the feel of her subtle feminine curves beneath. He followed the line of her slender waist to the slight flare of her hips and told himself he could touch her no more. He needed to pull away. Had to assert some control over himself, over this moment, before he hauled Brenna to his chamber in spite of his earlier promise that she would have her own quarters.

But just then, she sighed against him, her whole body easing ever so slightly. The gentle exhale whispered over his senses, a soft feminine acquiescence that seemed so at odds with this fierce woman ready to take on her dead husband's bloodthirsty clan no matter what the cost.

Which reminded him she wouldn't even be here now, would never allow him such a liberty, if she hadn't been desperate to save her children.

"Hellfire." He backed up a step, knowing he could not keep from touching her without the benefit of some space between them. "I am—" too cursed bold "—sorry. I have nae excuse other than I have been too long alone. I promise I willna—" *devour you whole. Ravish every last delicious inch of you.* "—make so bold with yer person again unless ye wish it."

She nodded curtly, her straight posture bearing no sign of his kiss although her lips remained enticingly full. Red. Swollen.

His hunger for her had not abated, but he would not make the mistake of touching her again tonight.

"I am grateful for your assistance, Gavin of Blackburn, and for your restraint." She dipped her head in a display of courtesy that did little to diminish the proud nobility she wore like a regal cloak. "If you will show me to my chamber, I will bid you good night."

Visions of escorting Brenna—his wife—to any chamber containing a bed teased his senses for a long moment before he shook off the unwanted desire. He had not expected his self-imposed year without a woman to have wrought such a sharp appetite.

"My bailiff will show you to your room." He shouted for Kean to bring some balm for the scratches on her cheek even as he backed out of the hall, desperate to draw a breath that did not contain a hint of her scent. "I swear I will win back yer sons, Brenna, and ye willna be sorry we tied our fortunes to one another."

And although he meant every word, he half wondered if he had made a mistake following his first instinct to wed her. They had been handfast for less than an hour and already things were not proceeding as he had planned.

Brenna followed Kean toward the stairs to the gallery, her thin gown outlining her every graceful movement as the fabric molded to her body. "That is one promise I intend to hold you to, my lord. I bid you good night, Gavin, and may you sleep well until the morning."

Gavin followed her progress with his eyes, knowing that he would not sleep so much as a minute with the memory of their kiss still burning through him. And although thoughts of his new wife would plague him like the devil until he had the pleasure of her in his bed, Gavin consoled himself with the certainty that he wouldn't have long to wait to make their handfast into a true marriage. With the promise of shared kisses like that, the heat between he and Brenna would spill over into a conflagration all too soon.

Chapter Three

The pale rays of early spring sunlight had scarcely crept into the sky the next morning when Brenna made her way to the stables.

Her muscles protesting every step after days spent on horseback, she welcomed the cold rush of brisk air against her cheeks to keep her alert. Hugging her thin cloak about her shoulders, Brenna savored the last bit of warmth the garment retained. She'd slept deeply in Gavin's guest chamber after they'd parted, her tired body welcoming the soft kiss of crisp, clean linens against her. The scratches on her temple had been soothed by the balm Gavin had ordered for her, the angry cuts cooling almost instantly.

Too bad her dreams had been filled with images that were anything but cooling. A good mother would have thought of Callum and Donovan, the precious babes she missed so much. But no matter how much she wanted to conjure their dear faces, her wicked thoughts had strayed to visions of Gavin Blackburn. The man's kisses had awakened a sleeping heat she had not realized resided within her anymore.

Now, she peered into the stables, her gaze lingering on the horse she'd ridden hard all the way from her English prison.

The poor mount she'd been given upon release was a tired old field mare that should be enjoying a sunny pasture somewhere, not picking her way through frost-covered Highland mountains. Still, her only other option was to saddle one of Blackburn's horses.

As she debated what to do, a male voice startled her from behind.

"I didna expect to see ye awake this morn, Lady Brenna." Gavin's deep, masculine voice rumbled right through her, rattling her confidence when she needed to be strong. Invincible.

"I would not miss this first chance to see my sons." She pretended not to hear his growl of protest as she plowed ahead. "But I must admit I hate the idea of asking my tired mare to make another journey so soon after her last. Might I impose upon your stable just this once, my lord husband?"

She'd hoped reminding him of their handfasted status would buy her some leniency in an inevitable argument this morning, but the word merely reminded her that she'd willingly entered into wifely servitude once again, if only for one year's time. Even if Gavin honored his promise not to pursue an intimacy she did not seek, she was still subject to his rule. She'd left her father's household to be governed by a husband she had reviled, then moved from her Kirkpatrick confinement to English captivity. She'd thought to gain her freedom when her captors had finally released her, but she'd quickly traded one imprisonment for another by becoming another man's wife.

"Take yer pick of horseflesh, wife, but dinna think to ride with me this morn." He moved to saddle his own horse, the thick muscles of his arms managing the heavy leather with ease. "I ride into the stronghold of one of Scotland's most formidable families to steal away their heirs. Even if they were an honorable clan, the task would be risky, but we both know the Kirkpatricks are as wily and treacherous as they come. Ye willna put yourself in such danger."

Anger welled up inside her, a hot tide of resentment she could do little to suppress. Yanking another saddle from the wall, Brenna wrestled the leather toward a black Arabian whose back she could almost reach, unlike the huge warhorses that filled most of the stalls.

"I asked for help regaining my sons, Gavin. I didn't ask for you to take over the task completely."

Easing the saddle from her hands, Gavin settled it gently atop the horse. "Nevertheless, ye need to consider yer limitations." He eyed her meaningfully as he adjusted the stirrups for her. "Ye may be an uncommonly brave lass, but ye canna do everything yerself."

"I can do this." She reached for the saddle to pull herself up onto her mount, the earthy scent of horses and fresh hay wafting on the morning breeze.

Gavin imprisoned her wrist, holding her steady. "Ye recall where yer recklessness landed ye three years ago? 'Tis an admirable thing ye did to warn our king of yer husband's treason, but was the cost worth what ye gained?"

"I kept our king's head attached to his shoulders." She blinked up at him, hardly believing he would dare to suggest she'd made a mistake in riding to Robert that day. "As one of his most trusted knights, I would think you of all people would have appreciated the warning of an ambush. Has it occurred to you that I may have saved your ungrateful neck as well as his?"

A wry smile curled his lips as he relinquished her hand. "Mayhap ye did. But I would urge ye to recall that in a time of war, ambush is an everyday risk. Sometimes ye would do well to trust others to fulfill their responsibilities instead of needlessly risking yer own lovely neck."

Her skin still tingling from where he had touched her, Brenna relaxed just a little as she realized he thought she didn't trust him. Having been endowed with her own share of pride, she could appreciate his. From the tales she'd heard of combat with the English and Gavin's prowess with his sword, this man had earned the right to her respect.

"I have every confidence that you will free my sons or else I would never have ridden here to seek your help." In truth, she'd thought of him the moment she arrived at Montrose Keep to find a new standard flying above the parapets. In her mind, Gavin represented Scots strength at its most fearsome. "But because I have not seen my boys in three long years, I find I cannot wait quietly for you to return in a few days hence. I need to go with you so I can see their faces and hold them in my arms. The memory of them—" her voice caught on a trembling note before she cleared her throat "—it is all that carried me through the last three years."

Gavin swore softly under his breath. His gaze wandered from her face to the steady spread of sunlight across the sky just outside the stable doors.

"Very well, then." He strapped his gear to his mount with brusque movements, his frustration evident in every clipped word he uttered. "Ye may ride with my men to Montrose, but ye will wait outside the gates. Do I make myself clear?"

Surprised to have won her battle so easily, Brenna bit back the next round of arguments she had formulated to convince him.

"Yes. Absolutely." She hugged her cloak tighter about her and wondered if this would be the last time he would grant her any compromise during their year of handfast. "Thank you, Gavin."

"Dinna thank me." His tone scraped harshly over her nerves as he bent to lift her atop the horse. "My wife would have given anything to see her own child just once before she died. 'Tis against my better judgment to let you go, but I will allow it out of deference to her."

Brenna found herself roughly deposited on her mount before Gavin spun on his heel and led both animals from the stable into the weak yellow sunlight bathing the keep. A small force of men awaited him there, mounted and ready to ride.

As she watched Gavin secure extra blankets to his deep chestnut-colored horse, she understood for the first time that their handfast was as unwelcome for him as it was for her. He'd married her to give his keep a lady, but it remained clear no woman would ever take his first wife's place.

Knowing that should have made it easier for her to go through with her plan to walk away from Gavin after their year together elapsed, but instead, the knowledge pinched her heart with unexpected regret.

As they closed the distance to Montrose Keep, Gavin regretted the need to spend the night on the road. He'd sent his men ahead to scout the Montrose holding, leaving he and Brenna alone for the night.

After everything Brenna had been through the last few years and especially the last few days, she deserved to rest and recover her strength. A cold, damp bed in the woods was no place for a woman in her weakened condition, because whether she wanted to admit it or not, her health surely suffered when she pushed herself the way she did today. Old fears stirred from his first wife's death.

"Ye shouldna be here," he reminded her as his eyes searched the landscape for a suitable place to camp until sunrise. Montrose lay only a few more hours ride but it would serve no purpose to arrive at the keep in the middle of the night.

"I believe you've already expounded upon that point several times," she shot back at him, her shoulders achingly erect even after a long day on horseback. Her long brown hair had been woven into loose plaits that bounced on her shoulder in time with the horse's canter.

"Yer reunion with your sons will be a short one if you catch yer death of cold." His breath huffed white clouds into the crisp air as he spoke, the sun slowly setting in a purple blaze behind distant hills.

"I have survived worse than a Highland spring, I assure you." She slowed her horse to a trot as they neared a lightly beaten path into the woods. "Besides, I know something you don't know about the road to Montrose."

She turned a surprise smile upon him as he reined in his mount and Gavin's breath caught in his chest at the unexpected reminder of the carefree young woman she'd once been. She had flirted boldly with him long ago, full of confidence in her girlish wiles and brimming with curiosity where he was concerned. He'd known her father would seek a man with a larger fortune than Gavin possessed back then for his eldest daughter, but that hadn't stopped him from entertaining thoughts of Brenna for his own. But then Robert the Bruce had put out the call for warriors and Gavin had devoted himself to freeing Scotland.

"Is that right?" He studied her pink cheeks, still hollow from her long captivity, but infused with more color than the night before. "Do ye know of a warmer place to sleep tonight than the cold, hard ground?"

"I explored the terrain all around Montrose Keep during my marriage to Fergus and I am quite certain I know every crofter's shack and hunter's cottage within twenty leagues."

He peered around the silent forest bordering an open meadow, seeing no sign of outbuildings of any kind. "Ye have but to lead the way. Yer bones may nae protest a Highland spring, but mine do. I am more than ready to sit before a warm blaze."

"This way." She nudged her horse forward down a side path that led up a low hill. "It is not really a cottage or a shack, but a peculiar old ruin that may have belonged to a hermit or a holy person who sought seclusion. There is a tiny walled garden attached to a crumbling stone edifice that seems to have been built for a dwarf. It is honestly the most strange little ruin I've ever seen and I'm rather curious if it is still there."

They wound up the hill as the sun set, casting long shadows and a last glow of purple light across the land. The bare trees all around them looked more ominous in the half light, the pattern of their stark branches almost menacing in the dull gloom.

"I see it." Gavin spotted the slate roof among the trees, the clean angle of the man-made structure the only feature that gave away its presence. The eroded dark stone facade blended in with the trees and dark earth, making the small dwelling as much a part of the landscape as the fallen logs and moss carpet.

An hour later, Gavin had tied their horses and started a fire within the walled garden Brenna had remembered. He had laid out their blankets inside the small structure, although the crumbling dwelling would provide little protection if it rained. But Brenna lingered by the blaze he'd built, picking at the bread and wine he had packed for their journey.

"Did you come here often while you lived at Montrose?" Gavin wished he could have found time to hunt before the sun had set. Brenna's slender frame would benefit from weeks of hearty meals and he vowed to find a woman to run the kitchens at Blackburn Keep again once they returned home. The meals Kean struggled to prepare over the past year barely tempted his hound, let alone a noblewoman.

"Only when Fergus was plotting against our king," she scoffed at the memory. "But that put me here at least once a sennight, I suppose. I did not like being anywhere near his treacherous friends so I would bring Callum here for a few hours at a time, and later Donovan, too."

Night birds called overhead as the wind picked up, whistling through the cracks and hollows in the stone ruins.

"Donovan would have been naught but a babe when last ye saw him." He tried to envision what her sons would look like and hoped for her sake they'd taken after their mother. Fergus Kirkpatrick—like all his clan—bore a striking resemblance to a boar hog.

"He was a year old and growing bigger by the day, it

seemed." She smiled, the soft glow of maternal love lighting her face. "I have dreamed of him often, wondering how his features would have changed and shifted as he ages."

A sharp ache filled him as he thought of his daughter who had never taken her first breath. She'd been perfect, delicately made like her mother, with a head full of dark hair.

"I'm sorry." Brenna's quiet words called him from painful memories, comforted him with simple understanding. "I have often regretted the time lost with my children, but I have always known they were healthy and well cared for by my sister until the Kirkpatricks took over Montrose Keep. I can't imagine how hard it has been for you to lose your wife and your babe at the same time."

Heat seared Gavin's eyes for the first time in many moons. He had avoided all discussion of Aileen to prevent the dark pain that came with it.

"It canna be helped." He'd told himself as much a thousand times and still failed to be comforted by the thought. "Now that we have handfasted, we can think about our children. The Douglases are strong stock, after all. I'm sure any babes you bear will be equally healthy."

The soft sympathy in Brenna's green eyes faded, replaced by an inscrutable expression. She nodded stiffly before standing.

"I am sure you are right." With clipped movements she wrapped the rest of her bread and downed her wine. "If you will excuse me, Gavin, I am more tired from our journey than I thought."

"Of course." Gavin stood, reluctant to see her go but grateful she would be able to sleep long and uninterrupted tonight. "We'll ride for Montrose at first light so we can complete the journey back to Blackburn Keep by late tomorrow night."

Backing quickly away, Brenna ducked inside the small dwelling as if she could not escape his company fast enough.

Did she think he meant to foist himself on her this very night to beget his heirs?

Damnation. He possessed better manners than a Kirkpatrick, he just wasn't always delicate in his speech. He meant to have his children, but he was willing to wait until Brenna was fully healed from her long imprisonment.

But then their true marriage would begin. Gavin would fulfill his promise to Brenna on the morrow and then he would be ready for her to fulfill her promise in return. Sooner or later they would live as man and wife in every sense of the word.

After Brenna departed Gavin, she lay cocooned in blankets on the floor of the small dwelling, listening to wind whistle through the trees. Smoke from the fire in the walled garden curled through the chamber where she reclined, the wisps of gray mist floating over her like the memory of her conversation with Gavin.

She told herself her eyes did not sting simply because he had married her for her ability to bear healthy heirs. After all, she had not cried when the English had captured her three long years ago. Not even when one particularly brutish knave yanked her by the hair halfway to the border did she give up so much as a tear. Pride and anger wouldn't allow it.

Why then did a few simple words from Gavin have the power to sear her more painfully than any wound? The thought troubled her long into the night. Right up until Gavin finally lay down on the other side of the chamber from her.

She squinted through the darkness, able to see him only because his blankets lay close to the open archway leading into the walled garden where the fire still burned. He had arranged her pallet deep within the room, far from the door and any dangers that might come their way during the night.

He was thoughtful and brave, ready to put himself at risk

to protect her and her sons. She could not ask for a more worthy guardian for her children.

She studied him in the firelight as he readied himself for bed. She told herself she should close her eyes, yet found herself fixed greedily upon the sight of his strong arms bared to the cold night air as he removed his tunic.

Brenna shifted beneath the covers as she watched, fascinated by the play of shadow and light over taut muscle and bronze skin. He slid his sword just beneath the edge of his bedroll, hiding the silver glint of the blade from any night marauders yet keeping the weapon easily within reach should the need for it arise.

Careful and thorough, the laird of Blackburn Keep left nothing to chance. Not even the begetting of heirs. And although Brenna still stung at the reminder he had wed her solely for her proven ability to bear healthy children, she could not help a twinge of curiosity about what it would be like to lie with such a man. Foolish, dangerous imaginings. Yet the fanciful part of herself she'd thought long buried now teased her mind with heated questions.

What would it be like to share her bed with a man who was careful and thorough and left nothing to chance? Ah, yes, she was surely a wanton woman that such foolish wanderings of her thoughts caused her pulse to kick up most inappropriately.

Squeezing her eyes shut tightly, she ignored the blatant longing of her body to concentrate on the intelligent course of action she'd already mapped out in her mind.

Once she'd secured her sons, she would bide her time before consummating her handfast. She needed time to heal, time to think. She'd been rushed into their vows, a victim of her desperate need to hold her children in her arms again. Part of her still longed for freedom from any man's rule, yearned for a way to leave her handfast after their year together.

As for Gavin, whose mere presence fired her blood like no man she'd ever known, she would simply remind herself that his goals in their union had been as mercenary as hers. She needed protection. He needed heirs.

Still, he was risking his life to retrieve her children and she would be honor bound to repay him for his aid. If heirs were so important to him, perhaps she could help him find a more suitable wife, a woman more like his first bride who had so thoroughly stolen his heart. Maybe then Gavin's heart would heal, and he would forgive Brenna for walking away from their handfast promise.

Although the notion of finding Gavin a bride bothered her unexpectedly, Brenna recognized it as the only acceptable recourse with a man so intent on carrying on his clan. Satisfied she had seized upon a solution to her dilemma, now she only needed to be sure her handfast was not consummated. An easy task since Gavin had promised he would not make overtures of intimacy again unless she wished it.

She only needed to believe in his sense of honor to escape her handfast and secure her sons' futures. Unless, of course, Gavin became aware of her unwanted feminine interest in him. She had the feeling she would not be able to say nay should he ever come to her bed with the intent to seduce.

All the more reason to stay on guard. After everything she'd been through, she would not risk her heart for something so fleeting as passion.

After spending the night a few arms' lengths away from Brenna, Gavin could not deny the undercurrent of desire that connected him to his new bride. A current that flowed fast and hot even while he raced her through the last mountain pass to Montrose Keep, where they would join his small force of men.

Her eyes followed him today, shadowing his movements as they closed the distance between her and her sons. That quiet awareness had not been there when she'd first come to his keep two nights ago, but it was very much present now as she slowed her horse to a trot.

He did not want this desire. Not really. He'd hoped that binding himself to Brenna would force his mind out of the past and drag him back into the present. For even if his heart had died along with Aileen and the daughter he'd never been able to hold, he had enough pride in his heritage to want the Blackburn clan to thrive and prosper. That meant he'd need a son to take his place before he grew too old to protect his people.

Of course, the heat he felt for Brenna would naturally lead to children, but he hadn't expected such anticipation for the marriage bed. Somehow it seemed disloyal to Aileen to experience such keen hunger for another woman.

Over the next rise they met his man to journey the rest of the way together. He kept Brenna apart from the others, sensing her unease around other men. Still, the extra protection would keep her safe.

"There." Brenna pointed to the Montrose holding half-hewn out of a mountainside, its high walls melding seamlessly into the jagged gray cliffs at its base. "The gates are open today and will probably remain so even when they see us coming since we are naught but two riders. Think you we should just ride straight past the gatekeeper and into the courtyard?"

"And risk an arrow in the back?" He had to smile at her boldness, though her plan was sheer folly. "To what purpose?"

"To catch them off guard." She held his regard, steady and unblinking. Her green eyes narrowed after a long moment. "I would not have them forewarned so they can hide the boys. Perhaps this way we shall see them at play and your men can simply take them."

"No." He was surprised at her cunning, although maybe he shouldn't be since she'd lived in the Kirkpatrick stronghold for years before she was taken captive by the English. "We willna risk drawing the wrath of the clan lest the king decide to allow them to keep the children. The boys are Kirkpatricks after all. 'Twould be better to use a bit of charm to obtain the boys without a fight, ye ken?"

From her disgruntled scoff, he guessed that she was more than ready for a fight. "Ye've a bloodthirsty streak in ye, lass."

"Only where my children are concerned." She tilted her chin up at him, as arrogant a girl as ever he'd met.

She could not have been more different from Aileen, but Gavin found himself grinning in spite of himself.

"'Tis an admirable quality in a mother, especially one who must raise her sons in such an unforgiving land. But for today, ye'll wait patiently outside with my men while I retrieve yer kin and we'll be on our way home in no time."

Thinking the matter settled, Gavin nudged his horse forward toward the Kirkpatrick holding. It wasn't until much later in the day that he recalled his new wife had never agreed.

Chapter Four

Squinting up into the battlements of Montrose Keep later that afternoon, Brenna decided that waiting for things to happen must be a subtle form of torture. Could there be a more painful fate for a woman who had been locked away, unable to do anything of her own choosing for three long years? Every moment she waited for Gavin to bring her boys out of this den of Kirkpatrick vipers felt like a long, drawn-out eternity, the hours stretching into one endless torment.

They had reached the keep long before noon that day and by now the sun had passed its highest peak. At this rate they would not be back at Blackburn Keep until the next morn.

Lingering just inside the gates, Brenna had made conversation with a few of the villagers who had been her responsibility when she'd been their lady. They were a tight-lipped, suspicious lot thanks to Shamus's cruel ways, however, and she hadn't been greeted with anything more than passing curiosity. None of them had said anything to her about her sons, although she'd been tempted to question everyone she met. *Have you seen my boys?*

Had *anyone* seen her sons? The questions blared through her mind as she wondered what had happened to Gavin and why he had not brought them out already. Twice she had tried to urge one of his men to enter the keep and look for their laird, but twice she had been denied. Surely Gavin could not blame her for entering the keep after all this time to see what became of him? For all she knew, he could be engaged in combat with the Kirkpatrick laird, Fergus's stingy sire who would sooner sacrifice his knights in frivolous battles than give up so much as a farthing of his precious possessions. What if the old miser had decided her sons were valuable possessions, as well?

Gavin's men would have to cut down every knight in Montrose to free them.

Her mind made up, Brenna vowed she would wait no longer. As soon as she could elude Gavin's men-at-arms, she would enter the keep herself. Shamus Kirkpatrick was a wicked, dangerous laird surrounded by equally wicked and dangerous minions, after all. She could not allow his treachery to inflict harm on a man so noble as Gavin Blackburn.

Her promised husband.

Shaking off the peculiar clenching inside her chest at the mere thought of her intimate connection with the bold Scot, Brenna strode deeper into the courtyard under the pretense of talking with the local wise-woman, confident no man-at-arms would venture into the crone's domain. Once out of sight of Gavin's men, she ventured near one of the lesser-known kitchen entrances to the keep.

If there was treachery afoot, Brenna meant to root it out before any Kirkpatrick lifted a finger against Gavin or her sons. She had learned a thing or two about guile in her time as Fergus's wife and she would not hesitate to use it now when she needed it most.

Gavin liked to think he possessed more patience than many of his hot-blooded countrymen. But by now, he would gladly wring the neck of the next Kirkpatrick to enter the great hall and give him yet another excuse for why they could not produce Brenna's boys.

Curse the clan. The whole lot of false-talking turncoats could rot in hell at this point for all he cared. Brenna would be worried, and for all Gavin knew, the lying churls that lived in Montrose could be trying to spirit the boys away out a back entrance while they smiled in Gavin's face.

Shoving aside the second cup of wine he'd been given even though he hadn't so much as sipped the first, Gavin refused to dance attendance on the Kirkpatricks any longer. He'd hunt down the children himself and be done with it. He had found out Brenna's sister, Alexandra, had been sent home a few months ago, so at least he'd gleaned that much from his conversation with the old laird's wife. The boys were now on their own at Montrose Keep, with only a keep full of greedy relatives to watch over them.

Ignoring the protests from a couple of clay-brained louts in charge of watching over him, Gavin stalked through the keep with one hand on his sword. His Kirkpatrick guardians could object all they wanted, he refused to wait for Shamus to return to the hall with the boys any longer. With one battle cry, he could bring the wrath of his own men down upon the keep.

He peered from one chamber to the next while one of the knaves followed him and the other ran off—ostensibly to bring help. Gavin pondered that Shamus was an even bigger fool than he'd originally thought for the laird to send his wife in his stead. His son had been a spineless twit, so it shouldn't come as a surprise that his sire would be as craven as they came.

Gavin had entered the kitchens when he heard a strange noise from deep within that cavernous chamber. The sound was like a fierce yelp. A growl of warning.

Or a feminine war cry.

Feet kicking into motion, he sprinted across the smooth stone floor, followed by one of Shamus's men-at-arms. He skirted around a row of small cauldrons in front of the hearth, and then he spied the source of the sound half-hidden behind the wall of ovens.

Brenna held the old Kirkpatrick laird at knifepoint, while two dark-haired boys clutching large sacks stood frozen in the corner behind her. The boys looked ready for a journey, their packs bulging with new loaves of bread.

"He meant to sneak the children out a back gate," Brenna hissed, her words punctuated with a small jab of her knife against the old man's tunic. Her green eyes narrowed dangerously. "The lying, cheating, treacherous, no-good bastard meant to hide my children from me, but he will not succeed."

Her words sounded angry. Venomous. Yet Gavin noted the way her arm trembled just a bit, the way her rigid body shook with raw emotions that could not sustain her much longer. She'd been overcome with exhaustion and heartsickness before she ever began this journey and by now she quivered with weakness despite her sure hold on her narrow blade.

Curse her need to do everything herself. Did she think he could not handle one wily old laird? And how in Hades had she eluded his men to stand here unguarded and alone? Lifting his sword to Shamus Kirkpatrick's breast, Gavin stared down the patriarch of Scotland's most notorious clan.

"'Tis glad I am to be seeing yer face at the end of my sword, Shamus." Gavin nodded to Brenna, hoping she knew enough to get the children safely away. "I will join you outside the front gates." Thankfully, she lowered her knife, replacing it on the kitchen counter from whence it must have come before she hustled the children out a side entrance.

No doubt the same entrance Shamus had been heading for while Gavin cooled his heels in the great hall.

"I have nae quarrel with ye, Gavin of Blackburn." Shamus straightened his skewed tunic, although he moved slowly beneath the nearby threat of Gavin's blade. "The boys are my grandsons and there isna a Scotsman alive will contest it."

"Aye, but Brenna is their mother and, with our handfast, I am their new sire." He pushed his blade against Shamus's chest, halting the older man's attempts to smooth his garments. "The boys are therefore mine, and no Scotsmen will contest it or he will have the wrath of Blackburn to answer, ye ken?"

Calling on the last strains of patience, Gavin refused to give an inch until Shamus nodded his understanding.

"Good." Gavin tightened his grip on his sword and moved to follow Brenna from the keep. "Then I bid ye good day and expect never to see yer face again, old man. The enmity that was born here today will die here today so long as I ne'er lay eyes on a Kirkpatrick again."

Backing away from the laird, Gavin left the kitchens, still seething with anger at the Kirkpatricks and frustration with Brenna. How could she put herself at risk that way?

Prepared to take her to task for interfering, Gavin called to his men as he mounted his horse and tore through the gates. Yet he stopped cold in his tracks when he spotted her in a small clearing with her children. She knelt before her sons in the shade of a tall pine tree, all signs of rigid posture vanished while she hugged each child in turn, her arms wrapped tight about them as her head inclined to each small shoulder.

The boys' wide eyes suggested they were a bit bewildered by the outpouring of emotion from a woman they might not remember, but the eldest patted her hair awkwardly when she kissed him, as if he knew his mother had come for him at last.

Gavin's throat closed up tight at the tender scene, his eyes burning for a moment until he blinked away the ghosts of his buried dreams. He signaled to his men to ride ahead, knowing they would shadow him the rest of the way to Blackburn Keep.

For a year he had shut himself off from the world to prevent this ache inside him, but as he watched Brenna run her fingers over each boy's face, Gavin realized the old hurts did not have as much power over him anymore.

Instead, seeing Brenna with her sons gave him hope, a warm sense of possibility that maybe he could find a measure of contentment.

Gavin slid from his horse as she stood. "We'd best put Montrose far behind us, lass. Yer sister was turned out by the old laird three moons ago and one of the maids said she thinks Alexandra was headed for yer dower lands to take refuge."

As she turned to look at him, the gentleness in her eyes lingered, catching him off guard with the hint of vulnerability he had never seen.

"Thank you, Gavin." She called to her horse before peering around the pine-scented clearing where no one seemed to be following them. "These are my sons." She laid a protective hand on the shoulder of the taller boy whose light brown hair looked as though it hadn't seen a comb in a long while. A dirt smudge across one cheek balanced a dimple on the other although he did not smile. Tall and lean at six years of age, he would be a warrior of intimidating height one day. "This is Callum, the elder."

The dark-eyed imp nodded solemnly as he seemed to size up Gavin, his eyes lingering appreciatively on Gavin's sword.

"'Tis a pleasure to meet ye, young Callum." Gavin bent closer to speak quietly to the child. "I hope ye'll ride with me back to yer mother's new home because I dinna think yer little brother will manage the bigger horse."

Callum nodded, standing up straighter as if rising to the occasion of his new task.

Brenna squeezed the shoulder of the other boy whose mischief-filled eyes and round cheeks looked as if he had stolen more than his share of cakes from the kitchens, but his young body was already growing tall and strong, even at four years. "And this is Donovan."

Gavin shook the child's hand. "Ye'll like yer new home,

lad. I've got a hound named Rowan who is ready to give birth to a whole new slew of pups. If we hurry, we'll be there in time to see them."

Donovan grinned and held up his sackful of belongings that his Kirkpatrick grandsire had given him. "We can go now. I've got bread."

"Well, that settles it then." Gavin couldn't help but smile at Brenna, who was already situating herself on her horse. He handed Donovan up to her before lifting Callum on his mount and riding far away from Montrose Keep.

There would be time enough to confront Brenna about the risk she'd taken by facing down old Shamus Kirkpatrick with a knife. Gavin had the feeling that the treacherous laird would not let such an affront pass without retribution, but Gavin would allow Brenna to enjoy her reunion with her sons.

Besides, she needed to recover before he gave her anything else to worry about. She had survived hardships before, but she was not invincible. She needed to rest and regain her appetite to grow strong again, and until then, Gavin would stay out of her way.

Once she recovered her health, they would devise a way to protect themselves and the boys from Kirkpatrick retribution. Only then—when they were all safe and she had regained her strength—would they consummate the handfast promise that was never far from Gavin's thoughts.

The month of April passed in a blur for Brenna. For the first time in years, she felt safe enough to let her guard down, safe enough to sleep deeply at night without any fear of rogue English knights descending on her prison to make free with her person.

That had never happened in all her years as a captive, but she had been threatened with the scenario during her hellish march from Dornoch Firth to the English border. After that, she had lain awake in fear many a windy night in her isolated keep, startling at every creak of the old edifice while she mindlessly felt for the blade that always rested under her pillow. Only much later did she learn from a quarrelsome old serving maid that her virtue had been spared because she was a Kirkpatrick. The English king owed many a debt to treacherous Shamus and his kin, and for this reason alone, Brenna was safe from a more humiliating captivity.

Now, she fastened a silver circlet about her head and ran her fingers through her loose hair before turning to the looking glass in her chamber at Blackburn Keep. Blinking at her reflection, she realized that Gavin had been right. She'd scoffed at him the night before over supper when he remarked that her newly recovered health made her look younger. After weeks of being subject to his undeniable charm, she had learned to deflect his lavish compliments wherever she could so she wouldn't lose any more of her heart to the strong Scot who had saved her boys.

But this time, he had been correct. She did indeed appear younger than she had a mere moon ago, her cheeks filled out with gentle curves instead of strong angles, her hair sailing over her shoulders in smooth, shiny waves. Even her green eyes seemed brighter.

Not that it mattered, she reminded herself, turning away from the reflected image. Beauty was a fickle beast that had drawn the wrong kind of attention from Fergus Kirkpatrick. She'd rather live anonymously and alone than as the chattel of some ignoble man who would only shame her and teach her sons the ways of treachery.

Not that Gavin was such a man. Still, if she followed her plan, she would not wed Gavin after their year of handfast. She had thought of a much more suitable woman for him in the weeks she'd spent healing, although she had not yet told him as much. Nor had she spoken to the woman she had in mind—her sister.

Brenna stepped into her slippers to protect her feet from

the cold stones of her chamber floor on this sunny spring morning. In an effort to introduce the topic to her sibling, she had sent an invitation to her sister, who had taken up residence on Brenna's dower lands after being turned out of Montrose Keep by Shamus Kirkpatrick. But after four weeks, Brenna had heard no reply from her. If Alexandra would consent to come to Blackburn Keep, she could at least meet Gavin again before deciding anything with regard to Brenna's plan.

She could not be sure Alexandra would be amenable to Gavin as a husband, but her sister had sacrificed three marriageable years of her own life raising Brenna's children during her English imprisonment. Besides, Alexandra was more gentle natured than Brenna had ever been, more like how Brenna envisioned Gavin's first wife.

Tamping down a flash of jealousy over the thought of Gavin with another woman, she reminded herself that he deserved to be happy. He was a noble, admirable man to whom she would forever be indebted after the way he'd helped her.

Brenna had felt a stirring of guilt at sending the missive without mentioning it to Gavin, but what if her sister declined Brenna's suggestion? She would not have Gavin subjected to any more slights.

A small knock at her chamber door called her from her worries and Brenna moved through her small solar to admit her guest.

Callum, Donovan and Gavin all stood framed in the doorway, each carrying a bouquet full of spring wildflowers. Their knees grass-stained and their hair coated with bits of leaves and sticks, they looked as though they had rolled in the meadows to obtain their colorful offerings.

"Happy May Day!" Donovan shouted the greeting with youthful enthusiasm while Callum, her quieter, thoughtful son, bent over her hand to give it a gallant kiss.

And as if that show of affection didn't fill her heart to overflowing enough, Gavin winked at her over their heads like an eager coconspirator.

"We thought ye might like to welcome spring with us today. 'Tis a fine morn for fishing." Gavin helped the boys deposit the flowers into a water urn near the hearth, the old iron vessel looking newly festive with the crown of cheerful blooms.

Callum watched her with worried dark eyes while she considered the offer. "Are you feeling better now? Do you think you can come?"

She longed to smooth away the worry in her son's wrinkled brow, but she had learned that he was no longer a babe and it embarrassed him when she fussed over him. She'd gotten to know her children again slowly over the past few weeks, spending time with them in the evenings while Gavin kept them busy during the days.

Restraining herself to a dignified nod and a warm smile, she reached for a light cloak.

"I am much better, Callum. Certainly well enough to join you for a day of fishing. I can't think of a better way to spend May Day."

No sooner had she finished speaking than the boys ran off toward the hall, their garments shedding bits of grass and leaves as they began boasting how many fish they would catch.

"Yer sons are an ambitious lot." Gavin pulled her chamber door shut behind them before offering her his arm. "I had forgotten how many things a boy can accomplish in a day."

"I fear they have kept you too busy while I've been convalescing." Brenna hadn't seen the children as much as she would have liked, but it pleased her that Gavin made time for them, taking them hawking and hunting, or playing endless games of blindman's buff. She had seen the children in the practice yard sometimes, watching Gavin's men engaged in swordplay or trying out their own moves with wooden swords Gavin had crafted for them.

But Gavin's crowning achievement in the eyes of her sons had been his encounter with a wild boar a fortnight ago. With one thrust of his sword, he had dispatched the beast bearing down on Donovan in the forest nearby. Although the boys had been well and truly impressed with their new sire's sword prowess, Brenna had not slept for two nights, thinking about what might have happened if Gavin had not been with them.

"Not at all." He shoved open the main doors leading into the courtyard where the boys were already loading fishing poles and assorted sacks onto the back of a patient field donkey. "I find I am invigorated by all the hours outdoors. Spending these days with Callum and Donovan has made me realize how dreary my life had grown."

Brenna watched Gavin secure the sacks to the donkey's back before leading him out of the courtyard toward the wide stream that wound through the holding. The boys were already running ahead of them, pushing and shoving each other good-naturedly until they reached the top of a long incline and began rolling down the hill to the brook.

"You are kind to say they have not been an imposition, but now that I am well again, I'm sure I can manage them."

Gavin's raised eyebrows seemed to disagree. "Manage? Somehow I doubt there will be any managing going on. Ye might have forgotten how difficult it can be to keep up with two hellions determined to stay busy at all hours of the day."

He looked so disheveled, Brenna had to laugh. "The twigs on your tunic seem a testament to your words, my lord."

"No risk is too great to obtain spring's bounty for my wife, although I canna discern why the best flowers seem to grow in the most unreachable places. I'll have ye know I scaled a cliff side for the hollyhocks."

Her heart melted in soft appreciation for his gesture. He deserved so much more in a wife than her. The knowledge soothed her conscience whenever guilt gnawed at her about walking away from their handfast. He should marry a woman with a more sheltered past, a woman who would not be gossiped about for the rest of her days.

Still, she wondered how she would maintain her distance from Gavin today when all of nature had put on its best finery for their outing? Peonies and lilies bloomed side by side with roses and gooseberry bushes. The sun shone with so much vigor that even the new grass beneath her slippers radiated a gentle warmth.

"Your efforts were not wasted, for hollyhocks are my favorite." She'd always loved the simple flower that was so easy to grow and had planted dozens of them around Montrose Keep many summers ago.

"Aye, so says Callum. He doesna have much to say to me yet, but whenever the boy speaks it is always worth listening to. I think he has missed ye sorely."

Hurt for Callum stung her to the core. "I have spent many hours wondering if it was wrong of me to leave the keep that day. I will never be able to give back to my boys those years that were stolen from them."

Her eyes fixed on her sons in the distance as they raced to the fishing spot. It was obvious Gavin had taken them along this route before, as they seemed at ease with their path.

"But ye have shown them the importance of honor." He held aside a branch for her as they passed through a hedgerow. "One day they will take pride in singing their mother's praises because she helped our king free Scotland. 'Tis a noble heritage for any knight."

Her heart warmed at his words and for a moment, Brenna wondered what it would be like to allow herself the security of marriage with such a man. But even though such a union would serve her, it would never heal Gavin's heart or provide him with the happiness he deserved.

No matter that Brenna had not been abused during her English captivity, people would always wonder about it, and the incident would make her tainted in their eyes somehow. Especially since she had ridden to warn Robert the Bruce of her own free will. In the eyes of her Highland neighbors, such brazenness was not a woman's place. She did not care, for herself, but she resented the fact for her sons' sakes. And she would not wish such a notorious wife upon a good man like Gavin Blackburn.

"Your words comfort me," she told him finally, keeping her tone light so she wouldn't be tempted to fling her arms around his strong neck and kiss him with gratitude. "I hope that Callum and Donovan will come to look at my captivity with so much forgiveness."

They walked on in silence for a little longer, picking their way through bramble bushes, marshes and weeds until at last they reached a small clearing by the stream. The boys were already there, skipping stones across the water, their excited words drowned out by the gurgle of water over rocks.

Sunlight sparkled on the water while the bank remained shaded by a gracious old oak. Brenna found herself wondering if Gavin had often visited the spot with his wife.

But as she watched him unload the haphazard supplies from the donkey's back—the children had brought their wooden swords, plenty of sweet cakes and cream—Brenna didn't see any signs of old ghosts between them.

Later, after he had helped the boys catch a small bucket of fish, Gavin settled himself on a blanket beside her while Callum and Donovan jousted with the trees.

She passed him a jug of wine that the cook had thought to pack along with the boys' sweets. "Is it difficult for you to visit places you used to go with your wife?"

He leaned up against the oak beside her, his long legs

sprawled out before him, his thigh resting a mere hand's span from hers.

"I dinna spend much time with Aileen outside the keep because she was in more fragile health and her expectant condition kept her close to her bed. It doesna seem right she missed out on such a view, does it?"

Brenna couldn't be sure if he spoke of the picturesque brook or the sight of her two strapping sons whose sword skills were being well tested by a tenacious young vine. Gavin's attention, it seemed, lingered on the children.

"It is very unfair." She could not help but reach for his broad hand that rested in the sparse grass between them. Squeezing his palm, she offered what comfort she could for a hurt she knew might never heal completely. "I cannot imagine losing someone I cared about so deeply. 'Twas different for me with Fergus, for I never loved him. And in a way, I think that is sad, too, for he was not so wicked a person that he did not deserve to be loved. But I could never respect the way he always acted as his clan bid without ever thinking over the matter for himself."

Gavin soaked up Brenna's tender touch, amazed at how deftly she'd interpreted his mood today. He had been thinking of Aileen ever since they'd stepped into his favored fishing haunt this morn, but he had not experienced the biting waves of grief. Instead he had begun thinking how much Aileen would have enjoyed the antics of Brenna's children, and oddly, the notion had brought a new sense of peace along with it.

Maybe the best way Gavin could honor his first wife's memory would be to simply enjoy the sons he had been given. While he couldn't be sure Brenna would allow Callum and Donovan to take his name, he would certainly offer it. Now that Brenna was his wife, he had every intention of raising her sons as his own.

"I hope that ye can find more happiness in yer second marriage, Brenna." He reached over her to turn her chin toward him, to stare into eyes as green as any Highland hillside. "I canna promise we will find love, but I swear I will value yer thoughts, and I promise to give ye reason to respect me in turn."

She bit her lip as if caught in a moment of indecision. Teeth sinking gently into the soft fullness, Gavin found himself longing to taste her again. The boys were engaged in their own games farther down the stream, after all. And Brenna had definitely recovered her strength.

Why should he hold back from his new bride any longer?

"You deserve a chance at love and happiness again, Gavin." She looked up at him so earnestly that he felt, for the first time since Aileen had died, maybe he could discover healing. Peace.

"Then perhaps ye can help me find those things, Brenna." Wasting no more time with words, Gavin covered her mouth with his.

He was not sure he could ever find love again, but he knew that tonight he would find happiness in Brenna's arms.

Chapter Five

Brenna had never imagined that drowning could be such a pleasant sensation. Yet right now, with Gavin's kiss dragging her under the waters of reason, she wanted nothing more than to succumb to the warm tide of pleasure rippling through her.

His mouth took absolute possession of hers, his kiss sure and knowing as he drew her close, his fingers pressing into her surcoat to urge her near the heat of his body. Her hands reached for him reflexively, settling on the wide expanse of his strong shoulders, savoring the contrast of his soft linen tunic with hard muscle beneath.

She tipped her head back, losing herself in the heady sensation of his tongue stroking over hers. Never had she been kissed this way before. Her first husband had seen no need for kissing, and in light of their awkward couplings, Brenna had certainly never been enticed to offer him her lips, either.

But *this*... She could not begin to appreciate all the ways Gavin's mouth made her senses sing. The heat of his body next to hers, pressing against hers, made her aware of womanly needs she thought had faded along with her girlish youth. This was the sort of kissing a young woman dreamed of late at night in her most secret imaginings. Indeed, in her fanciful youth, she had sometimes envisioned kissing Gavin in precisely this manner. But those innocent yearnings could not compare with the reality of his broad chest pressed against her breasts, or his large hands smoothing down her sides to cup her waist. Her hips.

A twitchy hunger awakened deep inside her at his touch, causing a small cry of need to manifest in her throat. The sound was only the barest of noises, but Gavin answered it with a dark, masculine growl, his hand cradling her scalp as he deepened his kiss.

The scent of warm man and fragrant pine needles filled her nostrils, while the sound of the gurgling stream drifted to her ears. Along with the shouts and laughter of her sons.

Children.

The reminder that her boys played nearby couldn't have come at a better time. She couldn't allow herself to become so carried away with them so close. And more importantly, she would never be able to help Gavin find the wife he needed if *she* became legally bound to him—a fate that would be accomplished the moment she allowed his honeyed kisses to overrun her common sense.

She pushed at his shoulders even while her blood rushed through her veins in heated waves. "I can't."

Gavin broke the kiss that held so much power over her, but he did not release her. "Ye surely can, lass. The weeks of convalescing have well agreed with ye."

As if to prove the point, his hand smoothed over her hip which had filled out again in the past few weeks of renewed appetite and rest. Warmth radiated from his palm to tease and tempt her body, which already wanted more from this man.

Fortunately, her mind knew better. She just hoped she possessed enough strength of will to follow where her common sense led.

"But I thought we agreed to wait before we—I mean, I am

just not certain that this is the right time." She needed to hear back from Alexandra first, since she would be doing Gavin a grave disservice to allow his deft touches to sway her from a noble cause. He needed a woman who would be a credit to his clan and the pride of his household.

Brenna's name was known far and wide in the Highlands for her rash deeds, and with the way gossip spread like spring heather, she was wise enough to realize many would consider her a fallen woman. Damaged. Soiled. And completely un-worthy of a good man like Gavin, no matter what anyone said of his overwhelming grief for his first wife. Surely he could be forgiven for such deep devotion?

"Ye're right. I should have asked ye first before I in-dulged in a kiss, Brenna, but truly there is no better time to celebrate our handfast." The fire in his blue eyes turned them to bright quicksilver. "Yer health is regained, yer chil-dren are happy and it is May Day when the old rites of spring are still practiced by even the most God-fearing of Christians. Lie with me tonight, lass, and I think ye shall be well rewarded."

His lazy, arrogant smile made her heart skip a beat at the same time it called a red-hot blush to her cheeks.

"I am a widow, my lord." She trotted out her best stern voice, but it failed her utterly by turning low and breathy in the middle of her rebuke. "I am certain you cannot provide any rewards I have not already experienced."

His gentle laughter sounded as though he was not con-vinced. "We will soon see about that. Come back to the keep with me before the sun is set, Brenna. 'Tis almost time to sup and I willna allow you to miss yer meal because I am hungry for naught but ye."

Standing, he offered her his hand while he called to Cal-lum and Donovan. Flustered at his easy manner in the wake of so much hot emotion and rampant confusion on her part,

Brenna hoped that the walk back to the keep would allow her thoughts to clear.

Perhaps she could speak with Gavin over supper about Alexandra. Her sister's gentle spirit would soothe Gavin while her pristine reputation would be well respected.

Although, truth be told, the idea of seeing her sister with Gavin already sparked a fierce pang of envy. Brenna's sacrifice would not be easy to make, especially after this afternoon's vivid reminder of how good things could be between Gavin and her.

Her lips remained swollen from his kisses, her cheeks burning from the light abrasion of his masculine jaw against her tender feminine flesh. But although the sensual enticement of his touch would be difficult enough to walk away from, Brenna feared she would miss his tender concern for her even more. Memories of the protective way he had guarded her while they were on the road to Montrose Keep floated through her mind's eye. He had given her a whole month to recover her health since then, demonstrating a thoughtful regard for her person and her feelings that no other man had ever given her.

He would be a difficult man to leave, but Brenna would do so because Gavin was a good man. A deserving man.

A man she could easily fall in love with if she wasn't more careful.

Gavin wondered at Brenna's silence on the short walk back to the keep, finally deciding she might be nervous about their first night together as man and wife. A reasonable fear, perhaps, considering she had probably known very little kindness at the hands of Fergus Kirkpatrick.

Promising himself to take things as slow as possible that eve, Gavin struggled to keep his mind off the sweet taste of her lips and the hot response his touch had ignited earlier when they sat upon the banks of the stream. A big part of the reason he had handfasted with her had been to protect her after all. He would not compromise that task by inflicting any harm upon her himself.

Although she did seem brimming with good health, thank the saints. He stole a sideways glance at her as they neared the courtyard, her cheeks full of rosy pink color and her bright green eyes alight with her own deep thoughts.

She was still as beautiful a woman as Gavin had ever seen, and if not for his certainty that he could never love a woman of such feisty spirit and independence, the brazen lass might have captured his heart.

Hauling the donkey along the path behind him, Gavin shouted to Callum, "Take yer mule to the stables and see she is fed some hay for her troubles, lad. Ye can unload the beast before ye come in to sup."

Callum and Donovan had just grasped the lead rope when Gavin noted strange horses in the courtyard.

"Were you expecting visitors, Gavin?" Brenna shaded her eyes to get a better view of the newcomers.

"They bear no standard. A messenger from the king, perhaps?" Gavin thought of his king and hoped that Robert did not need him in battle again. Gavin had no wish to depart Blackburn Keep with Brenna and her sons still settling in, but he would go if summoned. Leaving would be made somewhat easier by the fact that Brenna believed in the king's cause as much as Gavin. Perhaps there would be benefits to having a wife with warrior instincts.

"I do not think the messenger comes from the king," Brenna said slowly, as if the matter were of grave concern. "Gavin, perhaps we should talk first."

Taking in her furrowed brow, he wondered if he had misjudged her. Would she be worried if he needed to leave to join the king's forces?

"There will be time enough to talk." As his feet reached the smooth stones of the courtyard, he realized Brenna had paused a few steps behind him. He reached back to draw her forward. "I willna head off without making sure ye have everything ye need first."

She looked as though she wished to say more on the subject, but then he spotted their visitor as a young man approached them with a thin white scroll in hand.

"Greetings my lord and lady." The gangly messenger swept a low bow before them, his light riding cloak covered with spatters of mud as if he had ridden hard through many an overflowing brook. "I bring word of yer sister from yer lands at Balfour."

"And how fares Alexandra?" Brenna asked, although her face had lost some of its pink glow.

Gavin reached for the scroll, but the young man pressed the parchment into Brenna's hand.

"'Tis news for Countess Brenna." He bowed again over Brenna's hand, which trembled lightly as she accepted the missive from her sibling. "And may I take the liberty of extending my heartfelt thanks for yer noble sacrifice for yer king, my lady? All of Scotland sings yer praises."

Gavin might have taken more offense at the young whelp's obvious adoration of his future wife, but he was curious to hear news of the younger Douglas sister.

"I wonder how Alexandra knows of yer freedom? For that matter, I wonder how she learned ye've taken up residence at Blackburn Keep." Gavin excused the messenger, offering the man a coin along with whatever day-old bread he might find in the kitchen.

When he finished, he turned back to see Brenna's eyes traveling quickly back and forth over the page.

"What news?" He wondered if Alexandra wrote simply to inquire after her sister's health, although he still could not fathom how Robert would know she was here.

Unless…

"She is already taking a husband." Brenna frowned, her gaze traveling rapidly back and forth down the page, unaware of Gavin's dawning realization.

"Ye wrote to her." A decision that did not strictly concern him, perhaps, but he was surprised she had not told him. Not even when they puzzled together over the arrival of the messenger. "Yet ye didna think to mention it?"

"I had wished to discuss with her a matter of some privacy." Her fingers curved protectively about the scroll.

"I trust ye realize how much weight ye give this matter since ye didna mention it to me?" He would not have been surprised that Brenna wished to write to her sister. Why the need for secrecy?

Licking her lips, she searched the courtyard as if to seek out the nearest way around him. "Actually, I have been meaning to speak with you about it, but I had hoped to put the matter of our handfast to rest first and then—"

"Put it to rest?" His voice boomed throughout the courtyard, but Brenna's sons—his sons too, by God—were still off on their errand of securing the donkey. His suspicions mounted, fueled all the more by her guilty manner. "Hellfire, woman, what is there to put to rest?"

Did she think to change her mind about their vows? Would she call in her family for aid in leaving Gavin now that she had secured her sons?

"You must admit we rushed into our handfast promise rather hastily, Gavin, and I had thought maybe—"

Her halting words doing little to allay his fears, he yanked the missive from her fingers to read the news for himself.

Scanning the page, he noted that Alexandra assured her sister the dower lands were doing well. She went on to say she looked forward to her own marriage to a blacksmith well beneath her in social standing, but she had cut herself off from their father in order to marry where she wished.

It was the last lines on the page that ripped through him with more force than any battle wound. He read the words aloud to be sure he had not misunderstood.

"'…and although I appreciate your kind suggestion that I consider marriage to Gavin of Blackburn, I assure you, I have already found more happiness than I can say.'"

For a long moment, words escaped him as the reality of her cunning radiated through his limbs. He had not imagined such careful deception from Brenna, who had proved herself a loyal Scot by undergoing great personal risk. How could she plot and scheme this way behind his back?

"I had every intention of fulfilling my vow to you, Gavin—"

"By having me wed yer sister after our handfast year was up? Or would ye have even waited for the year to end?" Anger pounded in his head and gnawed at his gut with sharp, unrelenting teeth. "I see that ye learned a thing or two about treachery from yer time spent among the Kirkpatricks."

"I would never have walked away from the handfast without talking to you first. I thought you deserved a better woman than me."

Gavin scarcely heard her words with the blood whooshing through his veins. "All this time I've been avoiding yer bed thinking to give ye time to recover. Yet all along ye've been plotting how to remain chaste so ye could walk away from our bargain."

"Alexandra would have made you a better wife." She stared him in the eye, as if she spoke the truth.

But Gavin could not weigh her words now, not when the realization of her scheming to leave him sent a frigid blast across the warm feelings he'd had for her.

"Just how did ye come to decide who should be my bride? Ye know me so well that ye can choose a wife for me even though ye canna commit to fulfill the role yerself?"

"It was probably an ill-conceived plan, but my sister is more even tempered and sweet, just the sort of woman you would want."

For a moment, guilt nipped at his conscience since he had often thought that was exactly the sort of woman he wanted.

But hellfire, why should he feel guilty when Brenna had sought to deceive him all this time? Anger rumbled through him anew.

"So ye found a woman ye thought I should wed." He narrowed his eyes. "That's assuming ye could have escaped the lure of the marriage bed for the rest of the year, yet ye didna appear so intent upon protecting yer virtue down by the stream just now."

He recalled the way her body had warmed against his, could still hear the way she'd sighed softly into him when he kissed her. Had she forgotten how her breathing had gone shallow while her fingers clenched helplessly in his tunic? "Perhaps the time has come to consummate our handfast once and for all."

Crushing the blasted missive from her sister in his fist, Gavin tossed it aside and tugged Brenna toward the keep, renewed determination to make her his wife firing his steps. At the very least, they would conduct this discussion in a private place away from any servant who might overhear.

He shouted for Kean to watch over the children as he hauled her through the front doors and toward the steps to the gallery. Gavin had been ten kinds of fool to ever suspect the woman nursed a hint of vulnerability since she had deftly used her feminine weakness to keep him at bay for weeks while she searched for another wife to take her place.

"I did not make excuses." Brenna's voice was no longer soft as she denied his words with a passionate avowal of her own. She halted at the foot of the stairs to point an accusing finger at him. "You promised me that you would not kiss me again or initiate intimacy unless I asked you to, remember?"

"A promise I made to give ye time to heal yer heart and

body after all ye had been through." It galled him to remember how careful he had been to protect her tender sensibilities when she had meant to deceive him all along. "I dinna think ye can force me to honor my promise when ye've had no intention of honoring yers."

Gavin spied a new young maid scurry from the shadows of the hall back into the kitchens and cursed himself for his lack of discretion. He drew Brenna up the stairs and into his chamber, barring the door securely behind them.

Brenna glared at him from the center of the master chamber. "Keep in mind I did not ask you for such a promise." She folded her arms about herself, her slender frame appearing deceptively delicate. "And although I feared that I would never be the kind of woman you deserved, I had hoped I could help you find a woman you would be able to love. I said right from that first night you agreed to help me retrieve the boys that you did not deserve to encumber yourself with an unwanted wife simply because you were willing to help me."

"And just what made ye think I dinna want ye, Brenna?" He stepped closer, fresh anger blending with the simmering hunger he'd never fully quenched during their fishing excursion earlier.

"You had banished every woman from your keep for a year's time. It took no great wisdom on my part to realize you were not ready for another wife since you still grieved so deeply for your first."

Her words made sense, and yet he could not get around the fact that she had made a vow to him, curse her eyes. "A promise is a promise, Brenna Douglas Kirkpatrick *Blackburn,* and I'll thank ye to remember it. I deserve more loyalty from ye than Fergus Kirkpatrick did."

"Aye. And I had hoped that if I was ever to marry again, I would deserve to be loved as much as your first wife." Her green eyes, which reminded him of the Highland hills, also reminded him of her stubborn strength, her courage and resolve in the face of his anger. She truly possessed the same fortitude as her mountainous homeland. "You are fortunate that you have known love, Gavin, and I am sorry you lost it. But I have never known such tender sentiment from any man and I did not think it fair to either of us to enter into a union where we would have no hope of discovering that kind of accord."

Her words finally succeeded in reaching through his anger. Was he being selfish to wed her? Maybe. But his intentions were noble, damn it. He would protect her and her sons, who had already been through too much.

Yes, he could understand her desire for love, but how could he forgive her deception?

"Then ye should have said nay when I asked ye to wed." Although, at the same time, Gavin thanked his stars that she had not. He'd only begun to realize how much he needed her.

"I wanted to think of my sons' futures before I considered my own hopes."

He knew her staunch practicality and fierce maternal love should come as no surprise. Yet he resented the fact that she would not have chosen him as a husband because she preferred some romantic notion of love. Still, a part of him could not help but admire the way she'd protected the boys from their sire's wily clan and put their happiness first.

"Well, now their future resides with me at Blackburn Keep." He reached for her in the falling darkness of the chamber, the sinking sun imbuing the scant tapestries and furnishings with a red-orange glow. "As does yers."

His hands settled on her narrow shoulders, soaking up the feel of her soft silk surcoat and fine linen kirtle beneath it.

Brenna's eyes widened as she looked up at him, her body quivering ever so slightly as he touched her.

"For what it is worth, I am sorry for plotting to find you another bride. I should have discussed my reservations about the marriage with you as soon as we returned from Montrose. My only excuse is that I have spent many years living in fear—first of my husband's kin, and later my captors. It has been difficult for me to trust anyone."

Surprised by her confession and the raw honesty he sensed behind it, Gavin suspected that her admission had not come easily to a woman so unbending and proud.

He did not know that he would be able to trust Brenna again, but this was a start.

"Since ye've clearly wronged me this day, Brenna, might I hope ye'll make amends by inviting me to kiss ye?"

Chapter Six

Brenna held herself steady in the soft hush that had descended over Gavin's bedchamber, willing herself to call upon cool reason instead of her churning emotions to make a decision.

Gavin would allow her to choose whether or not to lie with him? Even after she had plotted his future without him? That made him an uncommonly generous man.

And uncommonly wise.

If she went to him now, the way her aroused body urged her to do, she would have no one to blame but herself for her fate. She could never point a finger at Gavin to accuse him of constraining her with a marriage she had not wanted. And hadn't she always longed to be the mistress of her own destiny?

She had chosen Gavin to help her retrieve her sons because she'd remembered him to be an invincible warrior and a man of honor. At the time, she had trusted him as much as she could ever trust any man. And although that had not been an overwhelming amount of trust, she had come to have all the more faith in him as she spent more time with him.

And stubborn Gavin himself seemed intent upon having her for a wife. As long as her sons would have a father to protect them, she had told herself she could sacrifice her selfish wish for love.

Besides, all her life she'd longed for the freedom to choose her own way, and Gavin had delivered the power into her hands with a few simple words. By God, even if she made a mistake, she would always be grateful for that power.

Licking lips gone suddenly dry, she peered up into his eyes and made her decision.

"I seek much more than a kiss from you, Gavin of Blackburn." In truth, her body had burned for him when he touched her earlier by the stream, and all it had taken was the brush of his hands over her shoulders to reignite the desire now. "I would know the feel of your hands on my skin and the press of your body against mine."

It seemed an endless moment that he gazed back at her, his eyes turned so darkly blue they loomed as fathomless as the night sky. But it was probably only a scant instant that she stood there, pinned in his gaze and caught in a web of want.

She might never find love with this hardened knight who'd lost so much, but she knew as surely as she breathed that she would find scorching heat. Right now, that seemed like enough.

She needed that heat to burn away old fears and unwanted memories.

At last, Gavin's hands moved slowly down her arms in a heavy, languid caress.

"Ye willna regret it, Brenna, I swear." His whispered words warmed her ear before he leaned in to kiss the tingling skin of her neck, his lips soft and hot.

Ribbons of pleasure unfurled from that sizzling point of contact. His tongue darted along her throat, painting a damp path lower to the neckline of her gown.

Wrapping her arms around his neck, Brenna drew herself closer to the source of all that male heat. Her fingers wound into his silky dark hair, her breasts grazing the solid strength of his chest.

It amazed her that he did not toss her onto the bed with all haste. She could have never ventured this close to her last husband without landing underneath him for an unremarkable—although mercifully fast—joining.

But Gavin seemed intent on taking his time, mouth seizing possession of hers while his hands moved over her waist and down her hips. Her lips parted beneath his kiss, welcoming him inside as her tongue dueled with his in a slick, heated dance.

He tasted like the wine they'd shared by the stream earlier, his kiss a new intoxication she had never experienced before. Her head swirled with the effect of so much heady sensation, her breasts tightening to painful peaks beneath her kirtle from the friction of his chest.

A low growl rumbled through him before he pulled away. "I need to see you."

Only then did she realize that the chamber had grown dark. The sun had set outside, allowing no light to penetrate the two large windows with leaded panes of colored glass. With no fire in the grate and no tapers lit, they were swallowed in shadow.

"Let us retire and I shall light a candle." She was more than ready to lie with him, her pulse pounding with her body's demand for more of this man.

"Nay, I need to see all of you." He moved away from her long enough to pull a soft fur from the seat of a chaise. "Lie here before the hearth and I will build a fire."

At her nod, he hefted her into his arms and settled her on the soft expanse of fur. She stretched on her side to watch him work, his body illuminated once he struck a few sparks with his flint. Normally Kean would have started the evening blaze in the bedchambers with a hot coal from the kitchen fire, but since Brenna and Gavin had been closeted alone in the room since dusk, he must have simply been giving them privacy.

A very good thing. Brenna could think of many ways she would like to be intimate with the man who'd promised to be her husband. She took in every ripple of masculine muscle as he bent over his task. When he had finished, the blaze bestowed a golden light over them both. Gavin stripped off his tunic before returning to her, his chest a mouthwatering enticement of bronzed muscle and intriguing shadow.

"That's better." Gavin surveyed her body before he knelt over her where she lay. His fingers unfastened her girdle and untied the laces of her tunic beneath her surcoat. The soft linen fabric slid decadently over her skin, heightening her awareness until the barest swipe over her flesh seemed a sensual touch.

She'd never burned for a man's hands before, but now she thought sure she would flare up into a blaze hotter than the one in the hearth if Gavin did not remove her clothes soon.

"I can't wait," she whispered, her fingers exploring the bare expanse of his chest. His skin possessed a velvet quality made all the more intriguing by the rock-solid muscle that rippled beneath.

She could feel his smile against the crook of her neck where he kissed her. "Are ye always this impatient, Countess?"

"I cannot say since I have never been in such a hurry before." Determined to have her own way, Brenna reached for the hem of her gown and tugged it up and off her body.

When next she sought Gavin's expression, she noticed he was no longer smiling. He was now fixed on the thin tunic quickly sliding off her shoulders, his hand already reaching for the swell of her breasts.

Arching forward into that touch, she could not help the cry of pleasure sobbing forth from her throat as he cupped each breast in turn. Her thighs twitched with pleasure as he bent his head to each taut pink crest, his tongue swirling around the tight peaks until liquid warmth coursed through her.

"Ye're so beautiful." He paused his kisses to lean away enough to study her in the firelight.

She knew she no longer possessed that first blush of womanhood that gave every female a bit of a glow. For that matter, she'd nursed two babes and had seen more fear and sorrow these past seven years than she cared to remember. Brenna did not deceive herself that she possessed any great beauty, yet she knew by Gavin's eyes that he had somehow found her pleasing indeed.

The notion warmed her heart as thoroughly as his touch heated her body.

"You are more than passing fair yourself, my lord," she whispered back, fingers skimming the broad expanse of his chest before she allowed herself to trail them slowly down the center of his hard, flat belly to the barrier of his braies. "But I would like to see the rest before I make my final decision."

Where did she find this boldness? Perhaps it had been there all along, next to her fierce will to protect her children and her king. She had just never found cause to use it in her marriage to a man she could not respect.

"I'm finding a lot to admire about a brazen lass. Maybe 'tis nae such a bad quality in a woman." He restrained her grip as she ventured her touch lower still. "But the impatience—we may have to work on that."

She let him keep his grip on her wrist, but she took her revenge by arching her lower body to rub over his. "Or maybe I should just work on making you as impatient as me."

The raw groan in his throat sent a thrill through her, but her movements only served to make her more hungry, more wild for him. It had been so long since she had been touched with intimacy. And even during her marriage she had never been touched with so much reverence for her person, let alone so much care for her pleasure.

She wanted Gavin's hands all over her. Now.

By this time, Gavin seemed to be thinking the same thing.

He stripped off her tunic and then stepped out of his braies before lying down beside her again.

Her daydreams hadn't done him justice. She had sometimes entertained visions of him at night before she fell asleep. In truth, she had been dreaming of the man since she was little more than a girl. But not in all her fanciful imaginings had he been so solidly impressive.

"I have made my decision now," she whispered with hungry admiration as her fingers fell to trace a delicate path over his thigh. "And I've come to the conclusion you are a sight to behold."

He rolled her onto her back, nudging his thigh between hers. "And I've come to the conclusion ye have succeeded in making me impatient."

Heat simmered through her veins, making her more than ready for him. For this.

He palmed the small curve of her belly then edged his way lower to sift through the dark curls between her thighs. She gripped his shoulders as he found the hot center of her, tracing his finger around and around that sensitive flesh until her thighs fell open even wider.

Already she could see the coming conflagration, sensed that there would be more to this joining than Gavin finding fulfillment. His deft touches across her slick heat gave her a hint of the sensual rewards she might find if she just allowed herself the freedom to feel and not think.

Concentrating on feeling, she seemed to float on a wave of pleasure while at the same time, a jolt of lightning struck at her insides. Seized by the sudden searing heat of the sensation, Brenna clung to Gavin. Stars appeared behind her closed eyes, her whole world narrowed to this man and the keen satisfaction he wrought with naught but his hands.

Her body tightened and clenched, seizing in spasms of delicious pleasure that rocked her hips and left her thighs trembling in their wake. She cried out with the force of that fierce heat, her eyelids fluttering back open just in time to see Gavin position himself over her. Blinking up into his eyes, her gaze locked with his as he edged his way inside her. The pressure built, thick and hot, until he was sheathed completely. She pulsed around him, her body succumbing to tiny aftershocks of pleasure even as an all-new wave of tension built inside her.

She skimmed her hands up his arms as he braced himself above her, her warrior husband taking time to gentle his strength for her sake. Her heart swelled with tender feelings for him that she should not allow. It would be dangerous to let any man hold such sway over her, and yet it was impossible to deny the wealth of emotion she'd always harbored where Gavin was concerned. What if she allowed herself to care about him? She could not imagine a man more honorable. More noble.

Amazed that he was in her arms at last after dreaming of him for so many years, Brenna curled her palm around his neck to tug him closer. To taste him.

"Ye're mine forever now, lass." He breathed the words over her lips between kisses. "There will be no more talk of leaving."

"But remember, my lord, you belong to me just as much as I belong to you." She traced her fingers over his temple down to the angular line of his jaw. "Perhaps one day, you will find I am as worthy of your heart as ever my sweet-natured sister."

She noticed that he made her no promises on that count, but soon she was too swept away by the delicious sensations soaring through her to care. She clung to him as heat pooled in her womb and tiny spasms undid her. Gavin's hoarse shout mingled with her cry as he found his own release.

Contentment warmed her as she curled into his arms, the night air blowing lightly over them through the open casements. She did not know if she could win this man's heart, but at least she had been honest about her reservations before they consummated their marriage.

Now, they were well and truly wed, an arrangement that brought her peace and security, both for herself and her sons. Why then did a cold cloud of fear hang over her in the aftermath of Gavin's heated lovemaking?

Perhaps because, deep inside, she knew she had already made herself vulnerable to more pain than she had ever experienced. Against all her better judgment, she had fallen in love with Gavin Blackburn.

Dawn approached and still Gavin had not fallen asleep.

He tugged the blankets up and over Brenna's shoulder as she slept. If only he could protect her from the rest of life as easily as he warded off the night chill for her.

He'd consummated their handfast vows in a moment of heated lust, his desire for her overwhelming his better judgment. But now that she slept peacefully at his side, her newly healed body so slender and delicate, he could not believe he might have put her health at risk so soon.

She might have already delivered two strong sons into the world, but that had been before she had been subjected to harsh captivity. She claimed no man had ill-used her, but he knew that the English were notoriously rough with their Scots captives—even noblewomen. What if her body was no longer fit to bear children? And, far worse, what if a birth took a dangerous toll on her?

Angry with himself, he vowed to be a better husband to Brenna than he had been to Aileen. He was a stronger man now, old enough to harness his lust for the sake of his wife. Perhaps he could name Brenna's sons his heirs and then he would not have to worry about childbirth claiming her the way it had taken Aileen.

Watching his wife weaken and waste away had been a brutal punishment, a humbling reminder of how little power he wielded no matter how fearsome his sword. He would have given all he possessed to trade places with her, to grant her one wish of becoming a mother, but in the end he could do no more than hold her hand. He prayed that those last few moments he'd held her, whispered to her, had provided her with more comfort than they had given him. That night still haunted him, the memories all the more vivid now as he thought of losing brave, beautiful Brenna.

How had she become so frighteningly important to him when he had purposely wed a woman so unlike his first wife?

"What troubles you, Gavin?" Brenna's sleep-husky voice called him from black thoughts.

He peered over at her by the first rays of dawn streaming in through the open window, her green eyes bright with new feminine moods he had not seen in her. Was she happy this morn, or did she regret their new bond as husband and wife?

"I was contemplating our sleeping arrangements."

She slid closer in the bed, her bare skin brushing his in a tantalizing touch. "They are much more interesting this way, don't you agree?"

Gently he rearranged her pillow and inserted a hand's space between them once again. "It occurs to me that ye could become pregnant again."

"I trust that news would be more welcome to you, Gavin, but I had rather hoped it would not be the sole pleasure we took in our marriage bed." She frowned, her soft pink lips curving into a pout.

This would be far more difficult than he had imagined. Steeling himself against the undeniable allure of his bride, he tried again.

"I would not ask too much of your body after everything ye've been through. And while I am grateful that we are now bound as man and wife, I am not without care for yer health." He hoped she would understand his meaning, but she continued to look upon him with hazy confusion in her eyes. "Perhaps it would help matters if we were to maintain our own chambers."

"You do not wish to sleep with me?"

Regret pounded through him as he remembered all the ways she had touched him so sweetly—and, by turns, so brazenly—the night before.

"It is nae a matter of what I *wish* for, believe me—"

"I thought you married me because you have seen with your own eyes that I can deliver heirs? You said it yourself that night on the road to Montrose Keep." She propped her elbow beneath her head, her dark hair spilling softly over her arm to pool on the bed linens.

"I hoped you would one day bear a babe with me, Brenna, but that doesna mean it has to be next year. Ye must give yerself time to heal after all ye've been through."

Swiping a hand through her silky dark hair, she propped herself on her elbow to lean over him, the linens slipping low on the swell of her breasts.

"I understand your fears, Gavin, but I am certain in my heart that we would bear strong, healthy children together." She smoothed a feathery touch down his cheek. "You must trust in me."

"Ah, lass, ye ask for my trust when I have seen childbirth steal my own wife. And recall that when I asked for yer trust at Montrose Keep, ye didna give it."

"Of course I gave it." She sat up in the bed, covering herself with her pillow, although her bare arms and legs remained a tantalizing view. "I would never have vowed to handfast with you in the first place if I hadn't been certain you were the man who could retrieve my boys. I had every faith in the world that you would free them that day."

"Yet when I asked for ye to wait for me while I saw the deed done, ye repaid me by pulling a knife on old Shamus Kirkpatrick. 'Tis nae very trusting at all." He sighed his frustration, knowing he was straying too far from the topic at hand. "I only mean to say that ye canna simply ask for trust when ye give none in return."

Her spine stiffened to that painfully straight posture he recalled from the first night she had arrived at Blackburn Keep.

"Begging your pardon, my lord, but it seems to me you are saying far more. Not only are you unwilling to trust me, but you also will not be sleeping with me." She slid from the bed with quiet dignity, her gloriously naked body a mocking reminder of all the pleasure he would be forsaking. Slipping her tunic over her head, she glared at him with cool fire in her eyes. "Then I pray you will excuse me, Gavin, while I seek my own chambers. After having fallen in love with you, I had hoped that you would begin to care for me if we spent more time together as man and wife. I see now that was a foolish notion indeed."

She had already donned her surcoat over her tunic and was reaching for the door when her words finally sank fully into his brain.

"Ye speak of love for me?" He could not comprehend that she would harbor such depth of feeling for him. Just yesterday she had been ready to forsake her handfast vows to maintain her precious freedom.

"A foolish fancy, perhaps, but I find I cannot command my heart in this matter."

Gavin shook his head in wonder, not sure whether or not to believe her. Worse, he feared the damage it would do to *his* heart if he allowed himself to trust her in this. "Ye're the only woman in all the Highlands who could make a declaration of love sound as encouraging as a death knell."

She smoothed elegant fingers over the creases in her rumpled surcoat. "It seems I have little to celebrate when you are relegating me to my own chamber."

"I had forgotten how unreasonable fears could be when yer

heart is at stake, Brenna." And if he allowed himself to love her…the thought of losing her would be all the more devastating.

"I am stronger than you know." Her eyes glittered with tears he knew she would not shed over him.

"Aye. So strong that ye're willing to put yerself at risk far too often." He thought of her reckless ride to Robert the Bruce, her bold wielding of a knife when her children were about to be spirited away by the Kirkpatrick laird. "When will ye see that there is strength in holding back on occasion?"

Frustration churned in her eyes and he knew she did not understand him or what he wanted. Would she ever?

She drew herself up, her proud bearing dignified despite her wrinkled garments. "If you will excuse me—"

Whatever she might have said was lost in the sudden pealing of a deep, resonant chime.

"What is it?" Brenna turned toward the window while Gavin grabbed up his tunic.

"The watchtower bell." He knotted his braies and reached for his sword. "Alister signals to me that an enemy approaches."

Chapter Seven

Brenna heard the chamber door slam behind Gavin before the last echo of the ringing bell faded. Fear scuttled up her spine as she wondered what dangers awaited outside Gavin's gate. English troops come to seize a Scots keep? Or could the Kirkpatricks have mustered an army to take back the six-year-old heir to their clan?

Scrambling to finish dressing, she donned her hose and slid into her slippers before following her warrior husband down the steps of the gallery and out of the keep. Lifting her skirts enough to allow her to run, she caught up with his long strides as he crossed the quiet courtyard.

"Ye need to secure the boys." He didn't spare her a glance as he surveyed the outer walls, pausing on Alister's watchtower.

"I saw their door is still shut." Brenna stubbed her toe on a wooden peddler's cart and tried not to wince. "I thought I should know what sort of enemy we face before I make preparations in the keep."

"Aye, but once ye've spied yer enemy are ye sure ye'll be able to walk away?" His blue eyes pinned her for a scant moment as they met Kean and Alister near the watchtower. "Now is the time to make yer choice. Do ye trust me to protect yer sons today, come what may?"

Alister, the same young man-at-arms Brenna had wheedled her way past that first night she'd set foot in Blackburn Keep, stepped forward. "Two riders, my laird. They say they come on behalf of Shamus Kirkpatrick and they only wish to talk."

A chill chased over Brenna's skin despite the warmth of the late-spring morning. Gulping back her fear, she kept her eyes on Gavin, knowing he expected her to make a decision.

Follow his will and remain safely within the keep? Or fix her person on her old enemy to prevent the wily Shamus from spiriting away her sons?

Both actions frightened her. But only one would provide her with a chance to earn Gavin's love.

"Brenna?" He remained utterly still while his men moved along the outer walls, taking up their positions should Gavin call for their arrows.

"I will stay inside the keep to make sure my sons are safe." The words stuck in her throat a bit, but she spoke them nevertheless, determined to demonstrate her trust. "I know you will protect them out here as well."

The relief in his eyes was fleeting, but it had been there. Gavin gave her a short nod before he turned to Kean and climbed the watchtower, leaving Brenna to handle any Kirkpatrick treachery on his own.

"Gavin will get them!" Donovan shouted his prediction so loudly Brenna feared his little voice would carry down from the stable loft into the courtyard.

"Shh." She thrust another piece of bread toward her youngest as they watched Gavin face off with two of Shamus Kirkpatrick's men from their perch in the small hayloft above the stables.

She had meant to secure the boys in the keep. Truly she had. But by the time she returned to their chamber, their door was wide-open and they were no longer in their beds. After a bout of heart-stopping panic, one of the kitchen maids told her she'd seen the boys head for the stables after snatching a bit of bread.

By the time she found them, there hadn't been enough time to take them back to the keep. Alister was already opening the gate to admit the enemy. Now, Gavin spoke in tones low enough that Brenna could not hear their exchange, much to her frustration. She was curious how Gavin thought to settle the matter of Shamus Kirkpatrick's stolen heir.

He did not seem inclined to make war over the matter, and for that, Brenna could not blame him. But all the Highlands knew of the legendary Kirkpatrick greed. Gavin must realize old Shamus would never rest until his legacy was secure. He would not wish to name another heir, only to have Callum claim the family seat—and the family wealth—when he was old enough to lead his own men.

Her hand went to rest instinctively on Callum's shoulder while he lay on his belly beside her in the hay.

"I pray he ends this today," she murmured, grateful Shamus had not made an appearance himself. No matter how much she loathed the old man's clan, she did not want her sons to see their grandfather battle with Gavin.

"He will do this…" Donovan lifted his wooden sword and drew it across his neck with a childish flourish that included much gagging and his eyes rolling back in his head.

"No, he won't," Callum said simply, his dark eyes trained on the conversation between Gavin and the two men who Brenna recognized as Shamus's sons by marriage.

"He won't?" Brenna wondered where Callum found his quiet confidence in Gavin. She studied her eldest in the bright rays of the morning sunshine, the contours of his face endlessly fascinating to her after three long years away from him.

"He says 'Never engage yer enemy unless ye hafta.'" He

tore his attention away from Gavin and the other men long enough to peer up at Brenna. "And I don't think he'll hafta today."

She sincerely hoped Callum wouldn't mind a kiss on the forehead, because Brenna could not resist embracing this young man who already made her so proud.

He squeezed her back while Donovan cried out, "Hafta! Hafta!" raising his wooden sword in the air.

"Hush!" Brenna murmured, her wary gaze darting back to the courtyard as she drew Donovan the fearless warrior into her arms too. How many lands would he conquer one day? Assuming he did not draw the wrath of his Kirkpatrick clan down upon their heads first.

"Gavin says waiting to engage your enemy gives you time to think and plan," Callum continued, rattling off his practice yard lessons like a seasoned commander as he pulled away from Brenna's arms and returned to his post at the window. "He's probably thinking of something right now."

Brenna watched Gavin where he stood in the courtyard, her thoughts traveling back in time to those years when she had admired him as a girl. He had made himself invaluable to Robert the Bruce at a very young age. Wouldn't it make sense that he possessed more complex battle skills than a lethal sword arm? Perhaps she had underestimated his skills as a tactician.

Had she underestimated him as a husband, as well?

A twinge of regret pierced her as she recalled his anger over Alexandra's note. He had done so much to help Brenna and she had repaid him by scheming to free herself from their handfast. Now that they were married, she would concentrate on making him happy and freeing him from the ghosts of his past.

"The Kirkpatricks are leaving." Callum's excited announcement caused Donovan to stop jousting with a broken oxen yoke while Brenna blinked herself free of wishful dreams.

And, lo and behold, outside in the courtyard, the Kirkpatrick riders leaned over their mounts and kicked the animals into a bold run. Winding between a few crofters' cottages and then bolting past the watchtower, the men disappeared as quickly as they had arrived, and Brenna's sons still remained by her side.

Gavin had done it.

Giddy with gratitude, she muffled a happy sob as she squeezed them both to her again, the brief moment of joy too sweet to be overshadowed by the thunderous way Gavin called out her name over the whole courtyard.

Gavin had felt Brenna's presence the whole time he'd been negotiating with the beef-witted louts sent by Shamus to retrieve his grandsons. Not that Gavin would ever allow it to happen.

Silence greeted his ears in the wake of his call. He did not know precisely where she had positioned herself during his negotiations with the ruthless Kirkpatricks, but she had been there. Watching.

He was about to call to her again when the door to the stables burst wide-open, Donovan leading the charge with his wooden sword twirling. Even the more cautious Callum ran toward Gavin, his skinny knees pumping. At a glance, he could see he'd won the boys over to his side, but he could not tell about his most staunch judge, who came his way more slowly, bits of hay still clinging to her purple gown.

Would she be pleased with the bargain he'd made with her sons' clan? Or would she only resent not being there to negotiate her own terms?

Her expression remained inscrutable, her features, which used to be so animated when she was a girl, were now tempered by age and wisdom. He would gladly spend a lifetime coaxing smiles from her lips, but would she be content with him after the way he'd forced her to choose between meeting her enemies head-on and protecting her children in the background?

Perhaps he had been unwise to give her such an ultimatum, but after his first wife's death, he found he could not suffer to see Brenna put herself in danger.

Donovan reached him first, the rambunctious four-year-old launching himself into Gavin's arms for a hug before he cavorted about the yard, tilting his sword at sacks of grain from the mill while he played hide-and-seek with one of Rowan's new pups.

Callum slowed his steps as he neared Gavin, but the serious boy bestowed upon him something Gavin had rarely seen from him before—an undiluted, childish grin.

"They won't be back this time, will they?" Callum held his hand out to Brenna, drawing her close and squeezing her hand tight.

He might have done it to draw some comfort for himself, but Gavin had the sneaking suspicion Callum wanted his mother to hear the answer.

"Nay, they won't be back." Gavin knew Shamus was smart enough to take the solution he'd waved in front of him. "Ye've seen the last of yer grandfather, I'm afraid, but ye can see the rest of yer clan when ye are old enough to rule Montrose Keep for yerself."

Callum glanced up at his mother. "It is for the best. Grandfather yelled at Donovan a lot."

While Gavin hoped Callum's indictment would not have his mother saddling the nearest horse to do battle with the old laird, he was surprised to feel Callum's arms slide around his waist for a hug. He squeezed the boy back, allowing himself a moment to ruffle Callum's baby-fine dark hair.

The unexpected show of affection left Gavin's throat raw with emotion while the youth scampered off to play with the puppies and his brother. Leaving Gavin to face his wife alone.

Tears welled in her eyes as he turned to her, and for the first time, she did not seem concerned with swallowing back the telltale emotions. Two neat streams coursed down her cheeks.

"You have put their hearts at ease," she remarked, watching Callum pile as many pups as he could find in his brother's lap. "For that, I can never repay you."

"Let there be no more talk of repayment." He drew her close, heedless of who might see them in the middle of the courtyard. Gently, he swiped away her tears. "And I promise I will not ask ye to choose where to fight yer battles in the future. We are both on the same side—now and always."

"I have no need to fight all my own battles," she admitted, blinking up at him in the warm spring sunshine. "I found myself very at ease in the hayloft today, content to hold the boys close while you chased away the enemies from the gate."

"Did ye now?" He plucked pieces of straw from her hair. "Yet I noticed ye didna stay put in the keep where ye belonged."

"It seems you have imparted the warrior spirit to the boys. They were already in position to ward off the enemy with their swords by the time I found them."

Some of the tension in his shoulders slid away as he realized she had not been in the stables to watch over his actions with the Kirkpatricks. She had merely been protecting Callum and Donovan.

"What makes ye think they got their warrior spirit from me?" He cupped her chin, his thumb grazing the lips he had spent all night tasting. "Their mother is as strong a warrior as ever I've seen."

She grinned up at him in the warmth of the May sunshine and his heart paused a beat at the glimpse of her old self, the cheeky Highland lass who had caught him off guard with a kiss one long-ago spring.

"Then let me be a warrior in the childbed, Gavin Blackburn, so that I may bear you all the sons you will need to carry on the legacy of your clan." Her grin faded as she traced her fingers over his tunic, slowing around the region of his heart. "I am touched that you would fear for my pain, but I know in the very fiber of my being that I was meant to be the mother to Blackburn babes."

Stifling his old fears, Gavin knew he could not ask her to have faith in him if he gave her none in return. Silently vowing to do everything in the world to keep her safe and healthy, he nodded.

"Aye. Ye were destined to be the mother to our babes. Why else would ye have sought me out on a windy moor all those years ago to have yer brazen way with me?"

She poked him in the ribs and he gave an exaggerated wince before pulling her against him for a long, thorough kiss. He did not set her free until they were both breathing hard, their thoughts already leaping to the night ahead.

"You are an arrogant man to kiss me in full view of any of your clan who might happen to be looking, Gavin Blackburn," she whispered, her lips full and damp from his mouth. A gentle breeze played with her hair, blowing the silky strands temptingly about her shoulders as she stared up at him in the middle of the quiet courtyard.

"Ye are an incredible woman, Brenna Blackburn, and I love ye to distraction and beyond. I dinna care who knows it."

"Does that mean you will sleep in my bed tonight, my lord?"

"Nay. That means ye will sleep in mine."

He would have kissed her again, but her green eyes narrowed with curiosity. "Tell me something, Gavin. How did you make the Kirkpatricks leave, and what makes you so sure they won't be back?"

Gavin couldn't help a moment of pride in his scheme. "I told them they had best depart Scotland for good lest ye make public all the incriminating letters Fergus Kirkpatrick wrote."

"I don't have any of Fergus's letters." She frowned, a small shadow of worry in her eyes.

"But they don't know that." He squeezed her to him, enjoying his unusual craftiness. "I told them ye kept the letters to protect yerself in case Robert the Bruce ever came after ye or yer sons to avenge Kirkpatrick treachery."

"And they would leave Scotland on the mere threat of exposure?" Her whole body tensed against him.

"Aye. Along with a bit of gold to ease their way in a new homeland. If Shamus isna swayed by the threat of hanging, I've no doubt that he'll be wooed by the pleasing weight of gold in his hand. And before ye ask, I swear to ye, what I offered him is a small price to pay to insure he never returns."

It was an even smaller price to pay for the reward of Brenna's grateful kisses and the look of relief in her eyes. When she finally released him, her eyes turned serious once more.

"There has been no marriage contract between us, Gavin, but I want you to know that I trust you to watch over my dower property and take whatever rents are necessary to send Shamus and his legion of whey-faced foot-lickers to the outer ends of the earth."

Smiling, he reminded himself never to cross swords with his ruthless wife. "Thank ye, Brenna, but I will keep yer dower lands profitable so that they may one day pass to Donovan as ye've planned. My guess is, he will conquer many holdings far and wide to add to his own coffers, but it is only just that he receive the holding. Callum shall one day inherit Montrose, which my men will keep safe for him until he is ready to rule. And as for our babe…"

His hand trailed to her belly where he could almost think about a little Blackburn heir without his gut knotting.

"Your son will have Blackburn Keep." She made a sweeping gesture to encompass the courtyard and expansive lands. "But what if I prove as fruitful a mother as Rowan?"

They looked down at Gavin's gentle hound. She watched over Callum and Donovan, who were now covered in happy, barking puppies.

"Perhaps we should wait and see how yer health fares before we borrow trouble." He would take no chances with this woman who had healed the hurt inside him.

"That's right. I'd forgotten Blackburn wisdom says never engage your enemy unless you have to. Does that mean you are hoping for a household full of girls so you won't have to worry about dividing up your lands?"

The image brought a smile to his face. "Heaven deliver us from a brood of willful young Brennas. Can ye imagine a little she-devil with Donovan's sword arm and her mother's sense of justice?"

"You are right." She nodded solemnly before she drew him toward the keep. "Let us not worry about the future and concentrate on the first Blackburn heir. In fact, I think it would be remiss of me not to get to work on the task of motherhood right now when I feel so healthy and full of love for you, my lord."

And just as it had been that first night when she had appeared in his hall, dripping wet and desperate for his help, Gavin found he could not say nay.

Epilogue

Sun streaming down on her favorite haven, Brenna reclined on a blanket near the shallow stream that coursed past Blackburn Keep, promising herself she would close her eyes for only a moment. Her youngest, Elizabeth Aileen, had fallen asleep at her breast after an afternoon picnic, and mother and babe now lay together in the shade of a tall hawthorn tree while the other children played nearby.

At six months Elizabeth was already the very image of her mother, her cries more fierce than any of her siblings had been at that tender age.

When she was born, Gavin had delighted in their newest babe the same way he had celebrated each child she had delivered him—first Ian James who had just turned four, then Gwendolyn Mae who was almost three, and finally, Elizabeth. Each birth had been as easy as her first two—relatively speaking. Of course each one hurt like Hades, but they had all been blessedly quick and uncomplicated, much to Gavin's relief. Seeing his face strained with worry each time her birthing pains started let her know in no uncertain terms that she meant everything to her husband.

Thus, it had pained Gavin to leave his family to answer Robert the Bruce's call four months ago, but he had sensed an end to the long struggle for the throne. And from everything Brenna had gathered from traveling knights over the past two months of his absence, a battle at Bannockburn had indeed ended the Bruce's long struggle.

Scotland was free at last.

Which was very well and good, but the happy news had not yet brought her husband home. Blinking sleepily at ten-year-old Callum, where he helped his younger brothers bait their lines to fish, Brenna smiled contentedly. Gwendolyn slept on her nurse's lap on her own blanket a few feet away, a tattered rag doll clutched in the little girl's fist even in sleep.

Brenna might have succumbed to the urge for a nap, especially with Gwendolyn's young and able-bodied nurse assuring her she could watch over the children. But a twig snapped a little way up the path, making Brenna bolt upright. Even Rowan seemed to sense something, the dark hound coming to her feet a moment before she sprinted up the path with as much enthusiasm as one of the pups from her most recent litter.

"'Tis a fine life of leisure ye've made for yerself, Brenna Blackburn." A sorely missed masculine voice boomed over the creek-side haven just as her long-lost warrior husband came into view, a grin on his face and a heavy traveling bag slung over his back.

Cheers went up from the boys as they ran to greet him, and even little Gwendolyn pried her eyes open and toddled over. She held her arms out to him, doll in hand.

Smiling in spite of herself, Brenna covered the baby with a bit of the blanket before she rose to her feet.

"I'll warrant my life of leisure has required more effort these last few months than your trudging around Scotland to help your king, Gavin Blackburn." She knew full well he only teased her, but she gladly chastised him to uphold her half of their game. They both agreed raising children could exhaust the strongest warrior, but that seeing a babe grow strong and happy was a greater reward than any gold in the household's coffers.

"Aye, but at least I managed to help him free Scotland in the meantime. And I'll warrant ye've had more fun than me." He smiled at her over Ian's head as he hugged his son. Callum and Donovan held up two of Rowan's new pups for him to see.

"I do not doubt it." She could scarcely imagine being away from the family for any length of time ever again. Missing those three years of Callum's and Donovan's lives had made her all the more grateful for every moment she spent with their children now.

Thanks to Gavin, Shamus Kirkpatrick had stayed far away from her sons these past four years. The old man had set up residence in England after departing Montrose Keep, but she'd heard he passed quietly after a bout of chest pains last winter. One day, Brenna knew Callum would bring peace to the disjointed remains of his father's clan, but for now, she simply cherished each day of watching him grow strong and smart, his quiet assurance a calming influence on all their children.

After doling out hugs all around and kissing his sleeping baby, Gavin lifted Brenna into his embrace. Her feet dangled just above the ground as he kissed her, his sun-warmed scent surrounding her as surely as his strong arms.

"I've missed ye." He kissed her deeply, his mouth molding to hers for a long moment before he leaned back enough to peer down at her through half-closed eyelids. "Are ye taking care of yerself? Eating enough?"

His hands spanned her waist and smoothed over her hips as if to decide for himself.

"Aye. But perhaps we are a bit inappropriate in front of the children." She made a halfhearted effort to wriggle away, though she didn't really mind when he continued to hold her close. The children were already occupied arguing about how many opponents Gavin had taken down with his sword in the summer's battles anyway.

"I'll tell ye the whole of the story over supper tonight, and not a moment sooner," he promised them before winking down at her.

She could not think about Gavin in the midst of a battle-field without a flutter of nerves and was glad when the children found something else to discuss. "Congratulations on the Bannockburn victory, my lord, but more than anything, I am just grateful you are home at last."

"Aye." His word was hoarse with emotions she recognized well. Together they had built something strong and wonderful out of the ashes of old pains and fears and not a day passed that they were not thankful for second chances. "And I want to hear every bit of news, but first I think it's very important that ye retire for a little while to rest."

Brenna smiled. Of all the games they played in their marriage, she liked this one the best. "Do you mean to suggest I look tired, my lord?"

"I mean to suggest ye deserve to rest and I'm just the man to make sure ye get everything ye deserve." The heat in his eyes never failed to send an answering flicker of warmth through her.

"I will be eager to see how much rest this plan of yours involves, but I do not think your children will allow you to escape so quickly."

He nudged the dark traveling sack at his feet with the toe of his boot. "Then ye underestimate the power of presents."

The warmth in Brenna's womb kicked into a full-blown fire as she imagined spending a few hours in her husband's arms before the meal.

"Have I told you lately that I think you are vastly clever?" Her heart pounded in anticipation.

"It is my aim to please ye, lass."

Brenna threaded her arms around his neck and thought how truly blessed she'd been to handfast with such a man.

"Believe me, Gavin, you do."

* * * * *

*Be sure to watch for Joanne Rock's next medieval tale,
MY LADY'S FAVOR, coming in June 2005,
from Harlequin Historicals.*

A MARRIAGE
IN THREE ACTS

Miranda Jarrett

For Brides Everywhere:
Love and Be Happy!

Chapter One

Staffordshire, England
May, 1805

In spite of his rank, Lord Ross Howland, Earl of Mayne, was commonly regarded as having one of the greatest minds of his generation. His mathematical calculations were a marvel, his scientific conclusions profound and inspiring. Yet as brilliant as his intellect was reputed to be, there remained certain questions so complex and eternal that not even Lord Howland could fathom an answer.

"Perhaps you can tell me, Dawkins." With a great sigh of frustration, Ross pushed his empty tankard across the counter for the barkeep of the Tawny Buck to fill again. "What do ladies want?"

"Ah, now that's a true puzzle, my lord, isn't it?" Dawkins puffed out his lips and shook his head as he poured the ale. "Do you be referring to a particular lady, my lord, or the species as a whole?"

"A particular one." Ross watched the bubbly foam subside, automatically calculating the precise rate at which the tiny bubbles must pop and vanish or spill over the side of the tankard. "My sister Emma."

"Lady Emma?" Dawkins's disappointment was palpable. "Not any of those darling pagan lasses, the ones what wear no clothing beyond flowers and grass? Them that chased your boat on your journeys to Tahiti and other such places? Not the ladies the papers made such a fuss about?"

"Oh, no," Ross said, unwilling to be distracted. The women of Tahiti *had* been beautiful and startlingly unconcerned with their nakedness, but they were also so inconstant in their attentions and such born thieves in the bargain that their appeal had soon waned for Ross, as it should for any proper-thinking Englishman. "Those ladies were easy enough to please. A new iron cook pot and a pair of green glass ear-bobs, and they're happy as can be. My sister's a different challenge altogether. You have heard she is to wed?"

Dawkins's grin spread from one broad cheek to the other. "'Course I have, my lord! The entire county's rejoicing with the news. Could there be a prettier couple than Lady Emma and Sir Weldon Dodd?"

"No, there could not." Ross nodded with satisfaction. In the decade since their parents had died of the same fever, he'd been Emma's sole family, and he was delighted that she'd managed to settle herself this way with so much joy and so little fuss. "My sister has wanted Sir Weldon since she was in the nursery, and to her good fortune, he felt the same admiration for her."

"They say the best matches are the ones made in the cradle, my lord."

"Dawkins, that's precisely where I still picture her," Ross said. "I can scarce believe she's old enough to marry, but somehow since I've been away, she's turned seventeen. Seventeen, for all the world! When I sailed, she was still climbing in the lofts to look for kittens, with bits of straw in her hair and pinner."

"Time does fly, my lord. And you have been gone from England for a good long time."

"Nearly three years." Ross glanced out the window to see

how the repair was progressing on his coach's wheel. His appointment as an astronomer on board a navy-sponsored voyage of discovery had taken him clear around the world without serious mishap—until, that is, he'd come within the last ten miles of Howland Hall, and the rutted ditch that had broken a wheel spoke. That irony had tempered Ross's impatience, and the two tankards of good country ale—ah, what he and the rest of the *Perseverance*'s crew would have given for such a taste in Buenos Aires, say, or Honolulu!—were making the wait easier still to bear.

And if he were honest, he'd admit that this homecoming would be different from any of the others. For one thing, he had never before been away from Howland Hall for so long. In the middle of the Pacific Ocean, time hadn't mattered, and each day and night had blended into the next, and the next after that.

Yet when he'd been reunited with Emma in London a fortnight ago, he'd been shocked by the change in her. Since he'd been away, she'd finished her schooling and become a grown woman, a beauty. She was ready to marry and have children and God knows what else while, at thirty, Ross himself remained a wanderer and a dreamer more occupied with the stars in the sky than the mortals on this earth.

Each morning his looking glass showed he even appeared the same—amiable, agreeable, a bit disheveled and a bit distracted, enough to prove he was a gentleman but no fop. He had seen and learned more of the world, certainly, but he hadn't evolved or grown or changed, or whatever else it was a man was supposed to be doing, and despite Dawkins's ale, the idea was sobering.

He sighed again, running his fingers through his hair. "So you see my problem, Dawkins. What can I give to my sister to mark her wedding? What do I offer to a young lady who has never wanted for anything?"

"What to offer, what to offer." The barkeep wiped his

cloth over the bar in slow circle. "That iron cook pot won't do for Lady Emma. What of a new jewel? Don't ladies like those?"

"She already has more baubles than she could ever wear," Ross said. "And I intend to give her the pick of our mother's jewels from the strongbox before the wedding."

"You're a most generous gentleman, my lord." Dawkins frowned, thinking. "A new gown, then, or bonnet with rare feathers?"

"I've already granted her free rein with her mantua-maker for her wedding clothes." Ross recalled the bills forwarded by his sputtering accountant. "I told her to indulge herself, and she obeyed. If Weldon holds firm, Emma won't need so much as a new pair of stockings for a good five years."

"Maybe a smart little gig, my lord, with ponies to match?"

"That's Weldon's gift to her." Ross's smile was becoming more of a desperate grimace. "She wrote an entire letter to me about it."

"Then there must be something rare you've brought back from your voyaging, my lord. A seashell, or a unicorn's horn, or some other such marvel of nature?"

"Unicorns are creatures of the fancy, Dawkins, with no basis in science or truth." Ross took another long drink of ale, finding comfort in the warmth and well-being spreading through his limbs. "With Captain Williams's approval, I did name an uncharted island after her—Emmalasia—but she did not seem impressed."

"Ahh, well, you know how females be, my lord. If they can't show a thing off and preen before their friends, then what's the use for it?"

"Exactly." Ross nodded, grateful for Dawkins's enormous wisdom in these matters. "But Emma is my only sister, the dear, sweet lamb, and I must give her a gift that is rare and special and worthy of her."

Beside Ross, another man cleared his throat, a great, portentous rumble.

"Forgive me for catching your words, my lord," the man said, "but I could not help but overhear the nature of your sad, sorry dilemma. And I can offer you hope, my lord. I can offer you a miracle. In short, my lord, I can offer you a wedding gift among wedding gifts."

Ross turned, taking care not to spill his ale. It was good that he did, for the man was not at all what he'd expected.

Instead of the farmer's smock or ostler's leather waistcoat that was the usual dress here at the Tawny Buck, this man wore a long purple cloak like a druid wizard's, trimmed in tarnished gold braid, and oversize rings on his fingers. His curling white hair flowed to his shoulders with leonine luxuriance, and his face was craggy with nobility: a nose fit for Caesar, a brow broad yet solemn, and blue eyes, the startling color of deepest midnight, that had seen much suffering and joy yet had flinched from none of it.

Ross frowned and gave his head a little shake to clear it. Was it the ale, or the old man himself that was making him think in such...such a poetical fashion?

Waiting for Ross to reply, the man folded his arms over his chest with an exaggerated sweep, the purple cloak furling like a plush wave around him.

Still Ross remained silent, not quite sure what to say, and the old man raised his chin, and his voice.

"Yea, my lord, I have the answer you seek," he boomed. "The one sure way to make your lady sister rejoice with delight, with gratitude, with—"

"That's enough now, you old rascal." Dawkins had come around from the bar, and with one hand twisted in the shoulder of the old man's cloak and the other grasping his arm, he began ushering him toward the door. "His Lordship don't need the likes of you bothering him about his private affairs."

"No, no, Dawkins, let the old fellow stay." Ross smiled. One thing he'd learned from sailing in a navy ship was that the best information often came from the most unlikely of men. "I'd like to hear this wondrous suggestion of his. God knows I don't have any of my own."

With a contemptuous look for Dawkins, the old man pulled free of the barkeep's grasp, then bowed low to Ross.

"I am Alfred Lyon, my lord, your most humble servant." He curled his hand through the air with an extra flourish. "Exclusive proprietor, director and leading player of the esteemed and venerable Lyon Company of Traveling Thespians, and now entirely—*entirely!*—at my lord's service and whim."

"An actor." Dawkins shook his head with disgust. "Which is the same as saying rubbish and trash. Have you heard enough, my lord? Shall I put him out on the dung heap now, before he picks your pocket and steals your drink?"

The old man drew himself up with full-blown indignation. "Sir, I am neither a thief nor a gypsy, but a practitioner of the most noble of the dramatic arts."

"I'll vouch for anything Mr. Lyon steals, Dawkins," Ross said. Of course the old rogue was a dissembler and a deceiver—what else was acting, anyway?—but Ross had drunk the precise amount of ale to find Mr. Lyon vastly entertaining. "Especially if he can tell me what to give my sister."

"I can, my lord, and I shall, and fully recognize the privilege it is to share your noble company. But—but—" Lyon coughed and stretched his neck up like a chicken in distress. Popping his eyes, he fluttered his fingers over his throat. "Forgive me, my lord, but—but—my speech is inhibited by the dryness, quite as parched as the great Sahara."

"He wants you to buy him a drink, my lord," Dawkins said. "I told you he'll take your coin one way or another."

Ross motioned towards the tap. "Then give Mr. Lyon a tankard of his own to dampen the great Sahara."

"Forgive me, my lord, but my throat is my instrument, a gift from the gods." Lyon made a strangled cough. "Brandy, my lord, only gentleman's brandy, by my surgeon's decree."

"Then your surgeon's a horse's ass," Dawkins began, but Ross nodded.

"Give Mr. Lyon his brandy," he said, "and in return he will tell me his idea."

"Not an idea, my lord, but a proposal." Lyon took the tiny tumbler of brandy and held it up to window's light, frowning at the liquid like a jaded connoisseur before he downed it in a single gulp.

"To whit, my lord," he began. "My company of players finds itself, ah, between engagements, and able to address and accommodate your dilemma. Because my company includes the most inspired of playwrights, we can create a play in honor of the bride and her groom, a performance so exquisitely tailored to honor their especial love that they and your guests will marvel at your inspiration, your cleverness, your generosity!"

Dawkins snorted. "There now, my lord, I told you he'd nothing of use to offer you."

"I'm afraid that my sister wouldn't judge it as rubbish, but as the most exciting thing imaginable," Ross said, bemused. "To see herself prancing about the stage, the heroine of her own romance—why, there'd be no living with her afterward."

"Maybe not when she'd seen the actress meant to play her, my lord." Dawkins flicked his thumb toward the old man. "If she's the mate to this one, then Lady Emma would demand your head for supper, my lord, and who could blame the lady?"

"I assure you, my lord, that the fair lady bride would be played by my own daughter, a maid of twenty." Lyon bowed again. "Though a doting father might be faulted for bias, I can say with perfect honesty that Miss Lyon is a beauty of pure and unaffected grace, such as would only honor your lady sister."

Dawkins made a skeptical huff for Miss Lyon's beauty, but her father chose to ignore it.

"Your guests will only applaud the likeness, my lord, I am sure," he said. "I absolutely guarantee it."

"Indeed." Emma would be entertained, true, but when he thought of the wedding guests—Weldon's family, the oldest, dearest friends of his late parents, elderly aunts and uncles and godparents, officers and gentlemen that he knew from the admiralty—he could not imagine they'd share Emma's delight in this ragtag old actor and his company of gypsy players. They'd whisper that he must have lost his wits while the sailing round the Horn, to offer such an entertainment for such an occasion. Dawkins would simply call him daft.

And if he accepted Lyon's proposal, they'd all be right.

"Can you confide to me the date for Hymen's visit to your home, my lord?" Lyon asked, ruffling his fingers across the edge of the bar. "If we are to honor the lady bride as she deserves, then we must begin to make our arrangements as soon as—"

"Your coach be ready, Lord Howland." The stable boy raced up to Ross, his cap in his hand. "They say th' wheel now be better'n new."

"Thank you, lad." Ross finished the last of his ale and rose, fishing in his pocket for a few coins to settle his reckoning. "Here you go, Dawkins, for your ale and your ear."

"Thank'ee, my lord." Dawkins touched his forehead. "Much joy to Lady Emma and Sir Weldon, and a happy homecoming to you, my lord."

"The return of Ulysses from his many voyages, my lord!" Lyon flung his beringed hands up to the heavens to show his gratitude for such divine inspiration. "What more noble way to begin the piece! The tragedy of the fall of Troy, the shrill wrath of the Harpies, the awful majesty of Scylla and Charybdis! Ah, what potential for spectacle!"

For a brief moment, Ross contemplated the full horror of

himself at the center of such Homeric mayhem. "No piece, Mr. Lyon, and no spectacle," he said, settling his hat on his head. "I am sorry to disappoint you, but I fear my imagination isn't equal to yours."

His purple cloak fluttering, Lyon hurried after Ross as he headed for the door. "But my lord, if you please, if I can but explain further how we would—"

"Mr. Lyon, I have not seen my home in more than three years."

"All the more reason to celebrate!"

"Mr. Lyon." Ross stopped, and Lyon stopped beside him, blinking up into the bright afternoon sun. He took the old man's hand and pressed another coin into his palm. "Here, drink another brandy to my sister's happiness, and we shall be even."

Lyon's fingers curled over the coin, and before he could speak again, Ross had climbed into his coach, the door latch shutting behind him.

Scylla and Charybdis, indeed. Ross sighed, leaning back against the leather squabs to watch the familiar green fields and villages unwind by the coach's window. The excitement of the past three years was over, and his adventures were done for now. He might not have earned the hero's reputation that Ulysses had, but after traveling so far, he'd gladly exchange a hero's welcome for a bit of quiet and peace in his own bed.

He yawned, drowsy from the ale, and settled more comfortably against the cushions. Emma's wedding, then quiet and peace.

Quiet…and…peace….

Chapter Two

With a stride that was brisk and full of purpose, Cordelia Lyon walked up the long drive to Howland Hall, the white crushed shell crunching beneath her feet. She walked quickly because that was how she did everything—with speed, with haste, without a single second squandered—but also because the faster she walked, the less likely she was to be seen before she was ready. She was a Lyon; she knew the power of a good entrance.

She wanted to appear on the front step, composed and ready as if she'd just stepped from her barouche on a morning call, and not clambered from the wagon of the farmer who'd given her a ride from the inn to the gates. She did not want to be spotted here, on the driveway, flushed and damp and holding her skirts bunched to one side to keep them clear of the white shell dust. If she really were to salvage anything from her father's latest brandy-soaked misadventure, she'd have to be at her best.

She paused at the bottom of the wide marble steps and looked up, blotting her face with her handkerchief as she made her appraisal. Howland Hall wasn't a palace, but it was grand, very grand, and perfectly fit for the Earl of Mayne and his sister. Yellow limestone that gleamed golden in the early-morning sunlight, a double row of tall arched windows, a new slate roof with strange carved figures supporting the chimneys, and everything neat and tidy with the blandishment of wealth. How on earth had Father bumbled into so agreeable a situation in a country tavern?

Shaking out her skirts, she hurried up the steps. The blue traveling gown and redingote from the costume trunks were at least ten years past the fashion, but the silver lace and buttons still showed well enough, and once she'd blotted out the creases and folds with white vinegar, she doubted any mere earl would know the difference. With her fingertips she fluffed out her hair and tipped her broad-brimmed hat at a sharper angle. She squared her shoulders, imagined her spine to be a steel bar for perfect posture and took three deep breaths to steady her voice. She grasped the dolphin-shaped knocker, and rapped it twice.

The play had begun, and Cordelia was ready with her lines.

"Good day, miss." The footman at the door looked down his long nose at her, doing a measure of appraising himself as he glanced past her for her carriage.

"Good day." She lifted a single brow, just enough to indicate that she did not wish to be kept waiting now that the groom had already taken her horse back to the stables. "Pray tell His Lordship I am here to see him."

The footman hesitated, just long enough for Cordelia to glide through the half-open door as if she'd every right.

Which, of course, she believed she did.

"What name, miss?" The footman was watching her closely, still unsure whether she was to be trusted, and he'd kept the door open, too, in case he needed to usher her back outside. "Whom shall I tell His Lordship has come?"

"It is my business that His Lordship will recognize, not my name." She perched on the edge of one of the side chairs that lined the front hall, sweeping her skirts to one side to hide the toes of her dusty shoes. This footman was no more daunting than any other overbearing rascal she had faced for the company's sake, except that this one wore an earl's livery.

"You may tell Lord Howland that I am here to see him regarding Lady Emma's wedding," she said, "and I wish to do so as soon as possible. I know His Lordship's here, too, because it's far too early in the day for any gentleman to have gone out. Go on, now, tell him."

The footman frowned. "Lord Howland does not see any caller who refuses to give a name."

"I should venture that that is your rule, not his." Cordelia tipped her head to one side, remembering how impressed Father had been by the earl's generosity and kindness. "To my mind, His Lordship is less quick to judge others than you would make him seem."

The footman's frown deepened into a menacing glower. Oh, now she'd gone and been too forceful, too much Cordelia Lyon and too little the sort of fine young lady who would be admitted into Lord Howland's drawing room. What manner of actress was she, anyway, to forget her character like that?

She made her face soften, beseeching, and added a tremor of emotion to her voice. She smiled but managed to bring a glisten of unshed tears to her eyes. Weeping at will had always been a specialty of hers.

"I know it is your task to be stern, sir," she said, letting her shoulders slip into a forlorn droop. "I cannot fault you for that. If you go to His Lordship, and if he refuses to see me, then I shall leave, quiet and meek as you please. But I must try to see His Lordship. I promised my father. I cannot go until I do."

She watched the footman's expression shift as his sympathy for her grew and his suspicion wavered. At last he made up his mind.

"I'll tell His Lordship you're here, miss," he said, finally closing the front door. "But he is at breakfast, and may not choose to see you."

"Thank you," she said, folding her hands in her lap. "Thank you so much. I shall be perfectly happy to wait."

She watched the footman walk down the hall, his footsteps on the polished floor echoing with a slow, stately measure. The intense quiet of the large house seemed unnatural to Cordelia, whose own life was always surrounded by the crowded, noisy chaos of the company's members and second-rate inns and boardinghouses. What must it be to live in a world of such constant quiet? Beyond those footsteps, all she could hear now was the equally stately and measured ticking of a case clock somewhere upstairs, and, when the footman opened another door, the gentle clink of silver cutlery against porcelain and the voices of a gentleman and girlish lady: the earl and his sister.

With renewed interest, Cordelia leaned forward, striving to catch every morsel of their conversation. She was accomplished at eavesdropping—how else did an actor glean proper accents and mannerisms except by listening?—and she'd also hoped to learn more of the earl, in case she needed it in their own conversation.

She could hear the footman announce her and the earl reply, though she couldn't quite make out his words. He sounded far younger than the venerable figure she'd pictured from Father's description. A world traveler, that was what Father had said, a learned, scientific gentleman who sailed to exotic places for years and years at a time. Perhaps he found the quiet of his home unnerving, too.

But most important to recall was that the earl had been enjoying the ale for which the Tawny Buck was famous. Perhaps not as much as Father—precious few men could keep pace with Alfred Lyon—but enough that likely his memory of last night would be hazy.

"His Lordship will see you now, miss." The footman gave the slightest bow possible. "This way."

Cordelia gave her hair an extra pat as she followed, composing herself. This would be the important entrance, and she was determined to make the most of it.

"The, ah, the young lady, my lord." The footman held open the door, and Cordelia sailed inside, taking the tiny, quick steps like a dancer's that would make her skirts flow with grace around her legs. Sunlight splashed through the tall doors, open to the lawns and gardens, and across the white-clothed table spread with a breakfast lavish enough to feed the entire Lyon Company, instead of just this brother and sister.

Cordelia made her smile as winning as she could, and ignored how her stomach was rumbling at the scent of grilled bacon, shirred eggs with cream, and rolls fresh from the bake oven.

"Good day, my lord," she said, sweeping a spectacular curtsy with her arms extended and her wrists cocked. "How honored I am that you would agree to see me, my lord."

"Good day to you, too." The girl—the earl's sister—was as pink-and-white pretty as a spun-sugar shepherdess, albeit a very young shepherdess, heedless of the buttery toast crumbs peppering her lips and chin. With a silver spoon, she ladled marmalade onto another triangle of toast as she studied Cordelia with unabashed curiosity. "I say, you don't look at all like a menace."

"Because I am not, my lady," Cordelia said. "Because I am here only to bring you the greatest joy possible."

"The greatest joy, miss?" At the far end of the table, the earl rose from his chair, his napkin clutched in an oversize hand with faded ink stains on the forefingers. He was larger than she'd expected, his broad shoulders hunched as if he spent too much time over books or a desk.

He was more handsome, too, in a shaggy sort of way, his face browned from the sun and his dark wavy hair in need of cutting. Father really should have warned her. Oh, the earl wasn't handsome in the classical manner of the best-paid London actors, or even in the costly, groomed way of the fine gentlemen in the expensive boxes, but in an easy, unselfconscious way that was still quite manly. And his eyes were wonderful, so deep a brown as to be almost black, and—

"Miss?"

Oh, Hades, he'd caught her gaping and was too polite to tell her. What had she missed? What had he said that she hadn't heard? She deserved to have that footman return and toss her out as a witless ninny.

She gave a bright, rippling laugh, partly from embarrassment and partly as a distraction as she tried to recover. "Yes, my lord, the greatest joy."

He nodded, letting her inattention pass. "Offering my sister the greatest joy is a powerfully large promise to make."

So she hadn't missed anything at all. She allowed herself the tiniest sigh of relief and gave thanks for his kindness. "But Lady Emma is soon to be married. Every bride deserves such promises."

He smiled, and though Cordelia understood the smile was more for his sister than for her, it still gave her a little ripple of reflected pleasure.

"I'm sure my sister would agree with you. As you can see, she is abominably indulged."

"Of course I would agree," Emma said, reaching for the silver teapot. "And I am not indulged, at least not to an abominable degree. You should accept it. You've done the indulging."

"More's the pity," the earl said, but the expression in his eyes only showed he'd spoil her a hundred times again, he adored her that much.

Emma gave a quick nod of satisfaction. "And even if you don't know who this lady may be, Ross, you must admit that she is surpassing wise. Here, miss, please sit by me, and I'll pour you a dish of tea."

"Thank you, my lady, I shall." As if she were any other genteel guest, Cordelia sat with a graceful nod as she took the dish of tea from Lady Emma. She hadn't dreamed matters would proceed so well, and so fast. "You are too kind."

"Do I, ah, know you, miss?" Perplexed, the earl remained standing at the head of the table, his napkin still bunched in his hand. "From what Thomson had said, I felt sure you'd be some old acquaintance, come to welcome me back home, but for the life of me, I cannot put a name to your face."

"Of course you can't, Ross," Emma said, "because you've never met her. I told you before she couldn't possibly be one of your old acquaintances. They all grew weary of waiting for you to return and married other gentlemen."

"I'm afraid Lady Emma is right, my lord," Cordelia said. "I've yet to have the honor of a proper introduction to you, though you have met my father. I am Cordelia Lyon, my lord, the first lady player of the Lyon Company, and the only child of Alfred Lyon. I believe you met him last evening at the Tawny Buck."

"Indeed." The earl dropped heavily into his chair, and Cordelia now noticed that, unlike Lady Emma, his breakfast consisted only of pale tea, without cream: no ham, no bacon, no eggs, no sweet buns slathered with rich butter. If ever she'd needed proof that His Lordship had indulged in too much ale with her father to lead him astray, then proof there was aplenty in that spartan breakfast. The real question would be how much he remembered.

"Miss Cordelia Lyon, Alfred Lyon's daughter." His frown seemed to stretch across the table to her. He wasn't happy to have her appear this morning, that was clear enough. "That would explain why you bear no resemblance to those other ladies."

"Miss Lyon is vastly more pretty than any of those others ladies, Ross, that is why," Emma said. "Not that you would necessarily notice, not with your nose always in a book."

The earl took a deep breath, almost a groan. "Where is your father now, Miss Lyon? Has he come with you?"

"Oh, no." Cordelia smiled, trying to win him back. "Father prefers to devote the morning hours to wooing his muse."

That was what Father called it, anyway, though much of the world might regard his snoring away until noon in the garret with the rest of the company's members as something far less creative.

"Is your father an author, Miss Lyon?" Emma asked with interest, her small white teeth biting into the orange marmalade on her toast. "I've never met anyone who worshiped a muse."

"Mr. Lyon is an actor, Emma," the earl said, "and Miss Lyon is an actress. They both belong to a gypsy dramatic company that is passing through the county just now."

Cordelia's smile tightened. She'd hoped for better from him, and her disappointment had a bitter taste to it. So much for kindness and generosity and warm dark eyes. She'd recognized the earl's chilly disapproval at once. Like every player, she'd been the target of some version of it her entire life. Father should have warned her of this, too.

"My father is the proprietor, director, playwright and leading actor of the Lyon Company of Traveling Thespians," she said, "and I am one of its actresses. We have performed in London, Bath, Edinburgh, and many towns in between, and we have entertained royalty, nobility, and other audiences of the better sort."

Emma's blue eyes widened. "Ooh, fancy that! Did you know that, Ross? That Miss Lyon has entertained Their Royal Majesties? And here I've yet even to be presented at court!"

The earl didn't fancy it at all. "Miss Lyon's trade is playing with words, Emma. If you took more care to listen, you would realize that by saying 'royalty,' she could have meant His Royal Highness the King of All Apes and Asses."

"And I could also have meant His Royal Highness the Prince Regent, my lord," Cordelia said with a dismissive shrug of her shoulders. "Interpretation is everything in life, my lord."

The earl snorted. "I rather thought truth was more important."

"Indeed, my lord." She smiled with extra sweetness. "But then what else is interpretation but truth in moderation?"

"Indeed, Miss Lyon." He frowned as he sorted this out, and Cordelia turned back to Emma before he did. She hadn't planned to play her trump card unless she needed it, but the earl was forcing her hand. Nothing ventured, nothing gained, and no booking for the company, either, and no way to pay their bills for another four weeks.

Now she leaned toward the girl, the teacup still balanced in her fingers. "But as much as His Lordship may wish to deepen the mystery, my lady, I cannot keep the secret from you any longer. Your brother is a most generous gentleman, my lady, and he has arranged with my father for the Lyon Company to give a special command performance in honor of you and your upcoming wedding, with every line we speak tailored to celebrate the special love and respect between you and your bridegroom."

There, she'd done it now. Either the company would be beginning rehearsals tomorrow here at Howland Hall, or she'd be feeling that footman's hand on her back as he shoved her down the steps.

She didn't dare look at the earl.

Not that Lady Emma noticed. "For me, Ross?" The girl's voice rose to a squeak of delight as she clasped her hands together. "Oh, Ross, you would make such a wonderful gift to me? A play with me as the heroine and dear, darling Weldon as my hero, here at home for all our friends to watch?"

The earl held up his hands. "Now, now, Emma," he cautioned. "Don't become overwrought by something as foolish as this."

"But a play about *me!*" She hopped from her chair and bounded around the table to her brother, throwing her arms around his neck in a death-lock hug. "Oh, Ross, this is too, too perfect! How wicked of me never to credit you for conceiving such a gift!"

The earl tried to shift free of her embrace, his unruly hair now even more rumpled. "It's not settled, Emma. It's most likely not even feasible, given there's so little time before the wedding."

"We've two weeks, my lord," Cordelia said. "With hard work and rehearsing, that's more than enough to concoct an entertainment to delight Her Ladyship."

"Oh, Ross, did you hear that?" Emma was already reeling with delight, without a single word of rehearsal. "Miss Lyon and her people will concoct for me!"

"And such a delicious concoction it will be, my lady!" Cordelia rose to sweep her hands before her, as if shaping the concoction from the very air. "We will delight you, my lady, I promise. We will amaze you! The only trick will be finding lodging for the company on such short notice, and with—"

"But that is no problem at all," Emma said. "This house will be filled with wedding guests, to be sure, but there is no one at present living in the gatehouse, and Cook is clever enough to feed a few extra mouths at meals."

"You are too, too kind, my lady." Cordelia curtsied, trying to sound grateful instead of gleeful. She'd seen the gatehouse from her walk up the driveway, and she couldn't remember the last time the company had had such fine lodgings—so fine, in fact, that she'd let the question of their fee slide for now. "Our company is known for its talent, not its size. The gatehouse will do most admirably."

Emma nodded, all eagerness. "I fear the ballroom must pass for your theater, Miss Lyon. Will that do for rehearsing, too?"

"Now hold, Emma, hold right there!" At last the earl twisted free of his sister's fervent embrace. "I've been home not even a day, and here you are, turning our home into a playhouse full of rascally gypsy actors!"

Cordelia gasped with indignation, folding her arms over her chest. "Forgive me, my lord, but we are a company of professional thespians," she declared, her head high and the plume on her hat quivering. "We are not rascally gypsies, not at all, and if that is how you judge us, why, then I—"

"You cannot change your mind and leave, Miss Lyon," Emma cried, frantic with disappointment. "You *cannot!* Ross, this was going to be the most perfect present you've ever given to me, and now you're taking it away by insulting poor Miss Lyon!"

The earl sighed, drumming his fingers on the arm of his chair with the irritation of a man who knows he is losing.

"I am not insulting her, Emma," he said with wounded patience, "nor am I taking away anything I've given to you. I want you to be happy, Emma, that is all, and I want to do what is right and best for you."

But instead of looking at her brother, Emma frowned down at a greasy butter spot on the cuff of her sleeve, rubbing at it with her thumb.

"Then you will let me have my wedding play, Ross?" she said, wheedling. "You will make me happy with this best possible present from you?"

The earl grumbled without answering, his fingers still drumming away on the carved mahogany.

"We'll keep quite from your path, my lord," Cordelia said, lowering her voice. She was certain he'd agree now—Lady Emma had taken care of that—and she could afford to be conciliatory, even soothing. "And I swear by Shakespeare's own grave that not so much as a single teaspoon will go missing while we're with you."

He didn't smile, and neither did she. "How reassuring, Miss Lyon."

How arrogant, my lord, Cordelia thought. "It is meant to be reassuring, my lord. You'll scarce know we're here. Until, that is, on the night of the grand, glorious performance, when you may claim all the credit for your inspired gift."

"Then you *are* giving me my own wedding play, Ross," Emma said, bending down to kiss him on the forehead. "My own dear, dear brother! Can you ever know how happy this will make me?"

"I only hope you'll feel the same when the last curtain falls." He sighed as she kissed him again, and for a long, surprising moment his doleful gaze met Cordelia's over Emma's golden blond curls. She looked away quickly, but not before she felt her cheeks flush.

He really was quite handsome. What a pity he'd turned out to be such a pompous, self-righteous prig in the bargain.

"I know it will be perfect, Ross," Emma said fervently. "And I vow I'll never forget this."

His attention swung back to find Cordelia, the challenge in his eyes unmistakable.

"So help me," he said, "neither shall I."

Chapter Three

❧❧❧

With a wordless growl, Ross tore the page from his journal, crumpled the paper into a tight ball and hurled it across the room at the grate. It wasn't the first page to suffer this fate today. The parquet floor of his library was littered with his rejected efforts, a snowy bank of misguided thoughts and clumsy reasoning.

He shoved his chair back from his desk and stalked to the open door that led to the gardens, standing there with his hands clasped in frustration behind his back. The week after Emma's wedding, he must return to London to present the first paper of his findings on the relationships of wind and tide in the Southern Pacific trade currents. The Lords of the Admiralty were fierce, practical men, and they were expecting hard facts, irrefutable answers to justify Ross's place on board the *Perseverance.* Soon after that, he'd have to share his work with the Royal Society, and his friends among the scientific men who met at Slaughter's Coffee House in St. Martin's Lane were eager to hear his conclusions, too.

So here Ross sat now, surrounded by his books and journals and bushels of notes from the voyage, supported with letters from friends and academic admirers, in the comfortable study he'd designed for himself to be conducive to the deepest concentration and the brightest daylight. He'd even had a special long, lead-lined tub constructed to hold water, with a large bellows at one end to mimic the effect of the wind over waves. It was an absolute embarrassment of scientific inspiration, and yet he was as unable to write anything worthy as the sorriest dunce in a dame school.

He groaned and swore out loud, not caring who heard. Where was his much-vaunted concentration? He'd just spent three years at sea living and working in a cabin so small that he could touch each bulkhead with his hands outstretched. He had been surrounded by the unending din of shouting sailors and stomping marines, the roar of the waves and the creaking of the timbers of the ship. Yet as the seamen said, he had been happy as a clam.

How in blazes could he have been so productive then, and now produce nothing?

His frown darkened as he looked across the gardens to the north wing, which housed the hall's ballroom. There was his distraction, the reason why he could not think. How had he possibly allowed a pack of ne'er-do-well actors to invade his home? He hadn't seen them yet—he'd made sure to keep from their path, leaving their arrangement to his servants— but he still *sensed* their presence. How could he make meaningful calculations and conclusions based on purest facts when he must share his roof with people whose entire lives were crafted from deception and fiction?

He heard a woman's laugh ripple across to him through the open windows. Laughter that frivolous must belong to Cordelia Lyon, the most impetuous, conniving creature he'd ever met. No wonder she'd bewitched his sheltered little sister. Emma should never have crossed paths with a woman like that, and Ross thought again of how different they had looked standing side by side: his small, rosy, round-faced sister with her gold-blond hair—innocence itself!—contrasted to Cordelia Lyon, the sort of brazen Amazon accustomed to having every male eye on her.

Even he'd had difficulty looking away. Her skin was ivory pale, her hair deep mahogany, her eyes the same deep midnight as her father's, and full of flash and fire and trickery, too. The moment she'd swept into his breakfast room yesterday morning, he'd known she couldn't possibly be a lady, and it hadn't been just that tawdry silver-laced habit. Some sort of wild fairy queen, perhaps, but never, ever an English lady.

A lighter, more girlish laugh: Emma's. What was she doing there, anyway, in the middle of those people? It was bad enough that they were rehearsing in his ballroom, but his sister didn't need to be there, too, learning all manner of wickedness from them.

He threw open the door and marched through the garden, the shortest route to the ballroom. Cordelia Lyon might have caught him by surprise yesterday, quoting some sort of commitment that he'd supposedly given to her father at the Tawny Buck, but enough was enough. He wasn't fuddled now. His thoughts were clear as a crystal. He'd send them all packing in their gypsy wagon this afternoon, before they caused any more havoc in his household.

Muttering with outrage, he climbed up the steps to the ballroom and flung open the door. To his bewilderment, the enormous room was almost empty, the pier glasses and chandeliers still shrouded in dust cloths and the little white side chairs pushed into one corner.

And instead of the hooting, raucous pack of actors he'd expected, only his sister and Cordelia Lyon were there, sitting at the far end of the room in side-by-side armchairs. Each young woman was curled comfortably in her chair, her stocking feet tucked under her skirts and her slippers dropped on the floor before her.

"Ross!" Emma slid from her chair and scurried toward Ross in her stocking feet. "You will not believe how much progress Cordelia and I have made on my play this morning!"

"I'm glad to hear that at least one of us has accomplished something." He shifted his frown to her feet. "Why are you not wearing your shoes? We're not in Tahiti, you know."

Emma swatted at his arm. "Oh, Ross, don't be so stuffy. If you had enjoyed Tahiti, the way the sailors did, instead of merely studying it, then you wouldn't even be noticing my feet."

"Who has spoken to you of Tahiti, Emma?" He was going to miss his little sister once she wed, but he was also looking forward to handing his responsibility for her over to Sir Weldon. "That's hardly a fit topic for a young lady. What could you know of sailors' ways?"

"Oh, I have heard this and that." She shrugged, admitting nothing. "Everyone has. Young ladies are not by definition deaf, you know. But once you hear what Cordelia and I have been—"

"'Cordelia'?" He glanced back at the other woman, writing away like a governess in a book propped in her lap. "Don't become too familiar, Emma."

Emma rolled her eyes toward the ceiling. "I can call her the Queen of Sheba if I please, Ross, and no lasting harm will come from it. Now come, listen to what she has written so far."

"Why is she writing it?" He once again looked back at Cordelia Lyon. It was an observation, nothing more, a scientific study, as if she were a rare lizard or palm tree.

He noted that Miss Lyon wore a white muslin gown similar to Emma's, except that the hem of hers was bordered with a deep band of red, black and gold Grecian-style embroidery. Her dark chestnut hair was pulled loosely back from her face with a narrow red ribbon and drawn into a careless knot at her nape, with loose tendrils curling over her brow and around her cheeks. Today she struck him as less like a gypsy queen than some ancient Sybil or female scribe, and he envied her her concentration—even if what she was scribbling was most likely the worst kind of drivel.

He cleared his throat, hoping he hadn't been staring at Cordelia—that is, *observing* her—so long that Emma noticed. "I thought her father was the playwright."

"He is," Emma said, "and a most esteemed one, too."

"Then why isn't he here? That was our, ah, agreement." Neither Lyon had mentioned a fee as yet. God only knows how much this would finally cost him, but he should at least get the best value for his money. "Why is *she* doing the writing?"

"Because it is a wedding play," Emma explained with the kind of simplification usually reserved for the elderly. "*My* wedding play. Cordelia wants to incorporate as much of my courtship with Weldon into the play as she can. She thought I'd feel more at ease telling things about Weldon to her rather than to her father, which of course I would. Sharing our female sympathy, she calls it."

Ross could think of a few other, better words for it. Most likely the old man was still too inebriated this morning to write so much as his name, and his daughter was covering for him.

"Come with me, Ross, and listen to what she's written so far." Emma slipped her hand into the crook of his arm, looking up at him with the same wide-eyed beseeching that she'd used with him since she'd been little. "Please. You have gone around the world and back. You can go this little bit farther for me."

"For you." He grumbled. Here he'd been ready to take action against the players, and now they'd confounded him by not being where they were supposed to be, disobliging him so he couldn't have them tossed out and leaving him with this vague, uncharacteristic discontent swirling around inside his head. It was completely illogical, and illogic went cross to every fiber of his being. "Why else have I stumbled into this mare's nest than for your sake, Emma?"

"It is not a mare's nest, and you are far too surefooted to stumble into anything." Emma led him forward, refusing to let him drag his feet any longer. "And I hope you will manage to be agreeable to Cordelia, Ross. I know Miss Lyon is not half so fascinating as your musty old specimens, but it will not injure you to smile at a young woman. At least not fatally."

"Good day, my lord." Cordelia rose and swept Ross a curtsy grand enough for His Majesty himself. Everything she did seemed to be overdone like that, and gave Ross the uneasy suspicion she might be mocking him.

"Good day, Miss Lyon." His bow was as awkward and stiff as her curtsy had been graceful. "My sister tells me you are writing the play."

"Yes, my lord," she said. "Lady Emma is offering me every assistance in my composition. No one could inspire me more."

She smiled, but he couldn't quite bring himself to smile back. Sun slanted in from the window across her face, and he was surprised to realize she wore no paint, the way all actresses were supposed to. She was also younger than he'd first guessed, likely not much older than Emma, her skin as fresh and clear as if she, too, lived in the country and not in the dank, unhealthy disrepute of the theaters he'd seen in London.

He cleared his throat. "I, ah, I thought your father was writing the play. That is, I thought he was your company's playwright."

Her smile seemed to become more determined, less charming. "For a classical drama or high tragedy, yes, my father would write the play. But when a lighter touch is required for a play such as this, then I am the preferred author."

"Aren't you too young for such a responsibility?" he asked. "I am aware of only a few—a very few—female authoresses, and they are all ladies of, ah, of more years and experience than you."

"Talent knows neither age nor sex, my lord," she said, her words clipped with resolve. "And I am certain you will feel neither robbed nor cheated by the result."

"I didn't say that, Miss Lyon," Ross said, but in so many

words he had, and he knew it. "That is, I only wish the best for my sister."

"As do I, my lord." How in blazes did she manage to look serene and challenging at the same time?

"You see, Ross, everything will be fine." Emma's little fingers tightened like a vise into the crook of his arm. "Quite fine."

Cordelia glanced down at her notes. "Because I wish to protect your sister's sensibilities, the play will be cast as an allegory, with Lady Emma and Sir Weldon given different names. The title describes it to perfection: *The Triumph of Love*."

"Isn't that splendid, Ross?" Emma sighed with delight. "My very own *Triumph!*"

"First will come the prelude," Cordelia continued, "a conversation between Venus and Hymen to introduce the bridal couple. But the scenes from their love will be true to life, as you wished, my lord, so as to be recognized by friends and family."

Emma nodded eagerly. "The play should really begin when we were little children, but because there aren't any children in the Lyon Company, things must begin later, when Weldon and I are older."

"A Twelfth Night party here at Howland Hall," Cordelia prompted. "The first time Lady Emma was permitted to come down among the gentlemen and ladies for the music, and the first time Sir Weldon could ask her to dance."

"To begin with Christmas? When it is now spring, almost summer?" Ross shook his head, not understanding. "What is the sense in the play beginning so far from the actual time of the year in which my sister's wedding is taking place?"

"Because it is an amusement, my lord," Cordelia said with excruciating patience. "It must no more be set in the present month than Julius Caesar must be set in London instead of Rome."

"It's not the same at all. My sister and Julius Caesar? I see no similarity, Miss Lyon." He waved his hand through the air, dismissing the likeness and scene with it. "You must invent a different beginning."

Emma made a little squeak of protest. "Oh, Ross, do not be dense. This isn't one of your scholarly treatises where everything must be exactly correct. This is a play. For fun."

He patted her hand. "I am not being dense, Emma. I only want the best for you, and that includes having a play that makes sense."

"Very well, my lord." Cordelia slashed her pen across the page with a squeaking spray of ink, deleting the offending Twelfth Night party. "Does May Day make more sense, my lord?"

Ross considered for a moment. "The day does, yes," he said. "Though I am not at all certain that a pagan holiday celebrating fertility is suitable for a young lady's wedding."

"Perhaps it is your scientific inclinations that make you view May Day is such a way, my lord." The tension in Cordelia's voice had increased another fraction. "I believe the audience will see only the innocence of Sir Weldon crowning Lady Emma with a ring of flowers that he has picked himself."

"But she was not Queen of the May, Miss Lyon," he insisted. "The queen was one of the crofters' daughters. It's never a lady."

Without lifting her chin, Cordelia looked up at him. "I never said Lady Emma was the Queen of the May, my lord."

"No, no, Miss Lyon, but you did imply it," Ross insisted. "I do not wish my guests to think I am claiming a false distinction for my sister. For the sake of verity, it should be removed."

Cordelia's jaw tightened. She let her pen hover over the page for a moment before she deliberately dragged the quill along the paper, making sure Ross would understand how much was being sacrificed. "Very well, my lord. That scene, too, is gone. What a short entertainment this will be for your guests, my lord!"

He knew she was being sarcastic. Not wishing to encourage her, he decided to ignore it.

"The length of the play will not matter to my guests," he said, "as long as they are amused."

"Oh, Ross, you are being dense!" exclaimed Emma. "There is scarcely anything left to my *Triumph!*"

Ross cleared his throat. "Don't exaggerate, Emma. If Miss Lyon is indeed a playwright, then she is accustomed to revisions and edits of her work."

From the murderous expression on Cordelia's face, even Ross could sense that that might not quite be the case.

"At least my favorite scene is left." Emma gave a wounded sniff. "Do you recall how I dressed in a plain cap and apron like a serving girl, so I could go meet Weldon at the harvest dance?"

"Of course I remember, Emma," he said. He had been away from Howland Hall, attending a symposium in Cambridge on the nature of lightning bolts, but there had been plenty of people eager to tell him every detail of Emma's scandalous behavior when he'd returned. "That is not something I'm likely to forget."

She shrugged, smoothing her hand along his sleeve to calm him. "I know you were so angry with me then, Ross, and sent me off to that dull school because of it, but I didn't care, because that was the first time Weldon kissed me."

"He did?" Appalled, Ross made the calculation in an instant: his sister had let Weldon kiss her when she'd been only fourteen. "For God's sake, Emma, let's not put all your folly on public display."

"A first kiss from the beloved is not folly, my lord," Cordelia declared. "It is a mark of admiration and respect. Besides, the kiss gives great sentiment to the scene as I have written it."

"Well, then perhaps you should just unwrite it, Miss Lyon," Ross said sternly. "How can you call this a decent entertainment for my guests, making the bride a center of ridicule and shame?"

Again Cordelia paused, and held Ross's gaze for so long that he began observing the little flecks of gray and silver in her dark eyes, like tiny stars in a midnight sky. He ordered himself to look away and ended up only looking lower to see—no, to *observe*—her full, red mouth.

"If my lord prefers," that mouth was saying, "I can move the first kiss until later in the play. We can begin with a scene that is less…inflammatory to your tastes, my lord."

"Thank you, Miss Lyon." He nodded, making himself look slightly to the left of her face to avoid any more of those wretched observations about her person.

"You are welcome, my lord," she said, her voice tart. "I will find that other scene. That is, if such a scene exists."

"But I like the kiss coming first, Ross!" Emma cried. "It was such a perfect kiss that it would be the perfect way to start."

Ross closed his eyes for a moment, collecting himself. On board the *Perseverance,* his life had been tidy and well-ordered with the Navy's all-male precision, but here at home—here there were females, and no order at all.

"Emma," he began, striving to emulate Captain Williams's authority. "Emma, you are a lady, the daughter and the sister of an earl, a peer. You must understand how improper this would be."

"But it is not really her, my lord. It is a character," Cordelia said with clipped, maddening reason. "Surely you must see the distinction, my lord. Besides, who will be shocked by the sight of a young woman—even a lady—kissing the man she is to marry? Isn't that so, my lady?"

"Here now, I won't have you offering Lady Emma your advice, Miss Lyon," Ross said. "An impressionable young lady like my sister does not need to hear your dubious views on morality and virtue."

Cordelia gasped, her eyes round with outrage. "You do not have the slightest notion of my views on morality or virtue, my lord, though indeed I am forming an excellent view of yours!"

Ross's hands clasped and unclasped behind his back as he

worked to control his temper. He must remain calm, reasonable. He must recall who he was, and not sink to her level.

"You are an actress, Miss Lyon," he said, "and as such I suggest instead of advising my sister on—on *kissing,* you keep to your acting and playwriting and such."

"But it's not Cordelia's advice, Ross. It's fact." Emma's curls bounced around her cheeks. "Why, I've kissed Weldon so many times now I can't recall the number. I doubt there's a person in the county who hasn't seen us together."

"I haven't." Ross stared, aghast. "That isn't a fact, Emma, that is—that is—"

"The wicked influence of an actress." With swift jerks of her wrists, Cordelia rolled her papers into a tight sheaf. "You might as well say it aloud, my lord, and finish what you've begun."

"It's nothing that I must say, Miss Lyon," Ross said. How in blazes had she twisted his own words against him like this? "The whole world knows that actors and actresses live by their own version of, ah, of moral behavior."

"You know, my lord, even if the rest of the world does not." She clutched the sheaf of papers to her chest, her chin high and her voice ringing through the empty ballroom. "And since you are so vastly more knowledgeable and virtuous than I can ever be, my lord, I humbly suggest that you write your own play for Her Ladyship, and act every part, too."

She turned away without asking his leave, her back ramrod straight and her heels clicking across the floor as she marched toward the door.

"Now look what you've done, Ross!" Emma wailed. "You've insulted Cordelia and made her leave, and now I'll never, never have a wedding play, and you have spoiled everything!"

"Hush, Emma, she'll come back," Ross said, though he wasn't sure Cordelia would. "And I didn't insult her. I was only stating the truth, and she let her passions run away with her judgment."

"You did so insult her," Emma said with an indignant sob as she groped for her handkerchief. "You told her she had no morals or—or virtues!"

"I said that was commonly known of actresses. I didn't say it of her precisely." But Ross respected the truth enough to know when he was bending it, and right now he was bending it over backward. He sighed with exasperation as he looked after Cordelia's departing figure. Here he'd come to the ballroom intending to ask the Lyon Company to leave, and instead it seemed that now, for the peace of his home, he'd have to ask Miss Lyon to stay.

"Miss Lyon!" he called. "Miss Lyon, wait!"

She stopped, turned and swept him another of those grandiose curtsies.

"Forgive me, my lord," she said. "Good day, my lord."

And having had the last word, with a swirl of skirts, she left,

Chapter Four

"So we are to leave before we've fair begun, then, Cordelia?" Gwen twisted one of her bright yellow curls around and around her finger as she leaned against the doorway to Cordelia's room. "True, is it? Before I've a chance to play the Aphrodite that you say you'd written just for me?"

"Yes, Gwen, we are leaving, and as soon as possible, too." Cordelia raised the curved lid of her traveling trunk and began tossing her belongings inside. "Your Aphrodite is the least of it."

"So you say, Miss Lyon." Gwen sniffed and flipped her hair back over her shoulder. "Mayhap you've mucked up this booking, but I'm not inclined to leave such fine lodgings just yet for sleeping in a nasty field again."

"Then the sooner you pack your things, the less you'll have to regret." Cordelia glared at the older actress. "Go, Gwen, and leave me. Go."

Gwen sniffed again and pushed herself clear of the doorway. "Why should I want to stay, I ask you, with you in such a piss-poor mood?"

Cordelia didn't answer, and soon she heard Gwen's backless slippers clumping down the stairs. Although Cordelia would be just as sorry to leave this tiny bedchamber in the gatehouse, she refused to stay another night here under the protection of the Earl of Mayne. What choice did she have, truly? She might not have two coins in her pocket to rub together, but she did have her pride.

She heard someone else in the hallway outside. Doubtless Gwen was regaling the rest of the company with an exaggerated version of her disastrous morning, but Cordelia was in no humor to discuss it with anyone else.

Unless, of course, she had no choice.

"Sweet daughter," Alfred Lyon said behind her, his voice purposefully cheerful. "Such tales I've been hearing below!"

She glanced over her shoulder and made a face. "Gwen cannot resist."

"She never can," Alfred said, "so now you must tell me the truth. What did happen today at the hall? What manner of tempest have you swept down upon us, eh?"

"The foul wind that blows from a sanctimonious mouth." She rolled a pair of stockings into a tight ball and jammed it into a corner of the trunk. "It seems we will not be performing at Howland Hall after all."

"Ahh." Alfred came to sit on her bed, resting one elbow on the edge of the trunk. He had been out-of-doors, strolling through—and likely sleeping—in the hall's apple orchard, and while he was for once wearing conventional breeches and a shirt, he had braided his long white hair into a tight queue down his back and had tucked pink-and-white apple blossoms behind his ears like some ancient sailor gone giddy with shore leave. "His Lordship has had a change of mind?"

"It will not work, Father," Cordelia said, fists at her waist. "I'm sorry to disappoint Lady Emma—she's a lovely girl— but her sanctimonious fool of a brother has made our performance impossible."

"Has he now." Alfred drew one of the blossoms from his hair, twisting the stem in idle circles. "You know how happy

I've been with your management of the company, Cordelia, with those tedious bookings and billings and the rest that tax my poor old head. But this decision makes me wonder. If we are to leave here, have we another engagement waiting for us elsewhere? Have you made other arrangements that my ancient head has forgotten?"

Cordelia took a deep breath. The company had been booked for a fortnight at a theater not far from here, a theater that had inconveniently burned to the ground last week. That was why the wedding play had seemed like a magical plum falling from the very skies—until this morning, when that sweet plum had turned so sour.

"You know there's no other engagement, Father," she said. "Not until Bath at the end of the month."

"That is what I thought." Alfred nodded. "Then how do you propose our little family amuses itself until then, my dear? Have you a secret hoard of gold and silver that will pay our way?"

Cordelia ran her hand back through her hair. "I am sure something will present itself, Father," she said, though she wasn't sure at all. "It always does for us."

"It already did, Cordelia." He smiled over the flower. "The Earl of Mayne did not strike me as either sanctimonious or a fool. In fact, Cordelia, he rather reminded me of you."

Cordelia gasped. "Of me? Of *me?* Oh, Father, not at all!"

"Oh, yes." Alfred pointed the flower at her. "He's a handsome fellow, too, and just as unaware of it as you are of your own beauty."

"Stop it, Father." This was an old, old conversation between them, and one she didn't wish to have again now. "I'll grant you that he's handsome, yes, but that has nothing to—"

"One moment, pray, one moment, so that I might rejoice, and give thanks to the great goddess Venus herself!" With a gusty sigh, he clasped his hands over his heart and threw back his head, the long, white plait flopping down his back. "At last my daughter has taken notice of a handsome man! She is of mortal blood after all, a woman made of passion instead of a lovely creature carved of ice! Now if only he were an actor, a thespian, a true practitioner of the dramatic art!"

"Enough, Father. Enough." Cordelia turned away, folding a petticoat with brisk purpose to avoid letting him see the flush on her cheeks. It wasn't that she didn't admire handsome men, or wished to be a hard-hearted spinster all her days. She wanted the same things that other ordinary girls wanted, to fall in love and marry and have a husband and a home and children to fill it, and listening to Lady Emma's joy today had only made Cordelia long for such things even more.

But her life wasn't like other girls', and it certainly wasn't like Lady Emma's. There were no examples of happy wedded bliss within the company. How could there be, when they never lingered longer than a month in any one place? The romances of actors and actresses tended to be quick and intense and burdened with far more lust than love—and loud, unhappy partings.

Everywhere Cordelia looked were sorry examples of love gone wrong. The only women who risked everything for love and won lasting happiness were the heroines she played on the stage. The best any actress seemed able to expect was to find a rich gentleman who'd keep her as his mistress. Even Cordelia's own parents had not bothered to marry, and Cordelia had only the vaguest of memories of her mother from before she'd left Father for a French marquis who swept her off to the Continent. No wonder the earl's assumptions about the dubious morality of actresses had struck far too close to home.

Alfred cleared his throat. "I didn't intend to upset you, Cordelia," he said, contrite. "It was only a jest, that was all, and a poor one at that. What I want for you is happiness with a fellow of our own station. Ecstatic, mad-with-joy happiness, which for most of us lowly mortals means love."

"Love doesn't always mean happiness and joy," she countered. "From what I've seen, there's a monstrous amount of misery and heartache, too."

Alfred clicked his tongue, scolding. "Oh, my dear Cordelia, you are too young to be such a cynic. Someday you will find that man who will love you as you deserve, and then you'll know your old pater was right."

That was part of the old conversation, too, and Cordelia sighed, her hands quiet. "I am not really like the earl, am I?"

"Well, yes, you rather are," Alfred said. "I did believe you'd much in common, and might enjoy one another's company while we were here. That part was true. His Lordship struck me as intelligent and clever and more concerned about keeping his sister happy than being happy himself. Which is a great deal like you, daughter."

"He is also pompous and arrogant and enchanted with the weight of his own opinions," she declared, turning about to face him. "The amount of pleasure to be found in his company would not equal the little toe of a gnat."

"That much, indeed?" Alfred looked back down at the flower. "Then if there is no pleasure in his company, no troubling, dangerous attraction between you two, it shall likewise be no great trial for you to return to the hall and apologize to His Lordship."

"Apologize!" Cordelia stared, stunned. "Apologize to him, after what he said to me?"

"Yes," Alfred said. "Apologize, or beg, or weep, or grovel. Whatever method you deem necessary to regain his favor, and our employment here for the next two weeks. Better you do that then we play the local poorhouse, with the bailiff as our audience."

"But Father, I have never before done such a thing!"

"True enough, sweet," he said. "Before this, you have always put the company's welfare before your own. It's what has made you such a splendid manager."

"But this—this is different." She thought of how when

she'd first met the earl, she'd thought him merely handsome, in the visual way of peers. But then she'd discovered he was intelligent, too, which was quite unlike most peers—quite unlike most men of any station, really. Perhaps she'd liked him too much for it. Why else would she have been so angry when he'd scorned her for being an actress, branding her as immoral without bothering to learn the truth? Angry, yes, but she'd also been hurt, more hurt than she'd admit even to her father. "Very different."

"I expect it is, Cordelia," Alfred agreed. "But you have always done what is proper for the good of the company, and I expect you will do so again. You are the most honorable actress I've ever known, for all that you're somehow my daughter."

"Oh, a pox on honor." She looked down at the flower in her father's fingers. He was right, of course. The good of the company must come first. Without it, they were no more than a ragtag pack of wanderers—exactly the kind of gypsies that the earl had so blithely dismissed.

Alfred took her hand and gently pulled her down to sit on the bed beside him. "If it makes it easier, then I shall come with you to the hall this evening. We can begin by thanking His Lordship for his hospitality and the largesse of his kitchens, and proceed from there."

Wondering where the heat of her anger had gone, she shook her head and sighed. All she felt now was tired, and oddly sad. "It's better that I go alone, Father. I'm the one who made the mess. I should be the one who tidies it up, yes?"

"Didn't I say you were a most honorable creature?" He smiled, smoothed her hair behind her ear, and tucked the flower there, beside her temple. "Pride has a bitter taste when swallowed, but thankfully no lasting purgative effects."

She looked up at him sideways. "Who wrote that?"

"I don't know." He raised his thatch of white eyebrows with

pleasant surprise. "It's rather good, though, isn't it? Perhaps I shall claim it for myself."

"Only if I don't take it first." She rose, pushing the flower more firmly into her hair as she grinned. "I believe it would do most wonderfully as advice for my bride to deliver to her older brother."

"Take thy revenge as ye may, rascally child." Alfred winked, then laughed. "No wonder I've never doubted that you're my daughter, eh?"

The nightingales were singing in the orchard, the new moon had risen and stars hung high in the sky, and still Ross had not apologized to Cordelia Lyon.

He knew he had to do it. If he didn't, his sister was going to have a headache that would prohibit her from speaking to him for the rest of their lives, or so she'd sworn in the note brought by her grim-faced lady's maid. He didn't believe the dappled blotches on the paper that were supposed to be Emma's tears, but he did believe her resolve. Emma was stubborn enough to outlast Father Time, if she wanted to. Ross hadn't answered her note, because the only answer Emma would accept was that the Lyon Company was once again producing her *Triumph of Love*.

He shoved back the tray with the dinner he'd barely touched. He hated eating alone, and eating alone here, in his library at his desk among his papers and books, only seemed more bleak.

Her blasted wedding play. Three days ago, she'd never known such a thing existed, and now she was convinced she and Weldon couldn't be married without it.

He swore to himself, using one of the choicest sailor's oaths he'd learned on board the *Perseverance*. But it didn't sound right from his mouth, and it didn't help, either. He couldn't put this wretched apology off any longer. He had to find Cordelia Lyon now, and without bothering to pause for a coat or a hat, he left for the gatehouse.

The evening was clear, the air warm. He didn't doubt that Cordelia and the others would still be awake at this hour. Those people stayed up all night long, didn't they? No, the real question was what exactly he was going to say, and as he cut through the gardens, he tried to frame an apology that would admit enough for her to accept it without humiliating him. He'd make it brief, neat, so that there'd be no confusion, no possibility of—

"Oh, my lord!" She stood before him as if his thoughts had been brought to life, there with the pink-and-white petals from the apple trees drifting about her like lazy snow. The gown that had seemed so tawdry earlier now seemed elegant and ethereal enough for the moon goddess Diana herself. She'd draped some sort of gauzy, sparkly shawl over her shoulders that twinkled like tiny stars pulled from the night sky, like—

Like he'd become some third-rate poet, dreaming of goddesses in hackneyed prose. Ross shook his head in disgust. What in blazes was it about the Lyons that did this to him?

"You frown, my lord." She looked down, her fingers twisting in the hem of her shawl. "I know I displeased you this morning, but I—"

"No, no, not at all." He cleared his throat. Now was the time to apologize—now, *now*. "That is, Miss Lyon, I was in fact coming to find you. To talk about my sister's play, that is."

"You were?" She searched her face, worry replacing her first surprise. "Oh, my lord, then I *am* too late!"

"Too late?" Blast, he must sound like a wooden parrot. In all the learning he'd acquired in his life, why hadn't he ever studied what to say to beautiful young women under the stars? "To be sure, it must be nearly nine, but that is hardly too late for—"

"I was coming to apologize, my lord," she said in a rush, "to say that I was sorry for being prideful and rude to you, and for disrespecting your wishes, and disappointing Lady Emma, and I hope that you will forgive me and not send us away, so we can still perform for your sister's wedding. There, my lord, I've said it. There."

"Indeed," he murmured, marveling that she'd any breath left at all. He wouldn't have to apologize to her. She'd done it first, and now all he'd have to do was graciously accept her offer, and everything would be set to rights. But as easy as that would be, it also wouldn't be entirely honest, and honesty was a quality he held very dear, even with an actress.

Once again Ross cleared his throat. "This is, ah, a great coincidence, Miss Lyon, because I was, ah, on my way to apologize to you."

Her eyes widened. "You were, my lord? To *me*?"

"Yes." He nodded, observing how the stars reflected in her eyes as she looked up at him. "I made several ill-advised assumptions about your—your past, about which, as my sister reminded me, I know nothing. I was wrong to determine conclusions without facts, Miss Lyon, and so I must apologize to you."

She shook her head. "But you do not have to do that, my lord. You are an earl."

"I am foremost a man who prides himself on his reason," he said solemnly. "Until you prove yourself otherwise, Miss Lyon, I must ignore hearsay, and conclude instead that you are a lady of impeccable virtue and modesty."

"Ohh." She smiled, a wobbly, lopsided smile. "Oh, my lord! So you *are* as intelligent as first I thought!"

He paused, mystified. "Because I corrected my preconceptions and apologized for them?"

"Well, yes, you did that, but you did it with such—such eloquence!" She sighed with what seemed like inexplicable happiness. "I *relish* fine words, my lord, with the same delight as a glutton views at a feast. And so do you, my lord, don't you?"

His mystification remained, though he'd stopped worrying

about it. "There is a great art in choosing the proper word to express one's feelings."

"Did not I say you were intelligent?" She sighed again. "I must make a confession to you, my lord. No gentleman has ever, ever said such lovely, fulsome words to me before."

"Then I suppose no other gentleman has been as foolish as I, to need to say them."

She tipped her head to one side, appraising. "You are different in the moonlight, my lord."

So was she, but he suspected she would not find that complimentary. "A moon so new gives off precious little light, Miss Lyon."

"Then it must be the starlight, my lord." She swept the shawl in an arc through the air between them. "'The starlight has cast its magic spell upon you / And changed you for the better.'"

With her smiling up at him like this, he couldn't help grinning back. "You playwrights always know the proper words to say, don't you?"

The wobbly smile widened as she spread her hands on either side of her face, her palms open to the sky. "'True, I talk of dreams / Which are the children of an idle brain / Begot of nothing but vain fantasy.'"

"See, there you are," he said. "What right do I have to criticize your writing, when you can invent pretty things like that?"

Her laughter rippled around him, as light as the drifting petals. "Alas, alas, my lord, I didn't. I was reciting from *Romeo and Juliet,* a play by Mr. Shakespeare."

Even Ross had heard of *Romeo and Juliet,* though he wasn't overcertain of the plot. "That's the sort of play you're writing for Emma, isn't it?"

Rueful, she shook her head. "Only if the muses lavish an ocean of talent upon me. Though for your sister's sake, I mean to try." She smiled again, and swept him one of her grandest curtsies, the shawl twinkling around her shoulders. "I will not keep you longer, my lord, so I wish you—"

"Don't go," he said, and realized at once how lordly and presumptuous that must sound. "That is, Miss Lyon, I, ah—have you ever observed the stars?"

"The stars, my lord? The ones I see each night in the sky?"

"But have you ever *seen* them, Miss Lyon? Come, come, let me show you." In a rush of enthusiasm, he seized her hand, leading her in and out of the twisted trunks of the apple trees to the open field beside them. He stopped and leaned his head back, still holding her hand.

"Not until I went to sea did I truly understand the stars," he said. Here he was at home, and knew what to say. "The astronomers at Greenwich can explain this planet and that nebula, but it is the common English sailor who understands the stars with his heart. Now there, that brightest star—that is the North Star, the king of them all."

"There, my lord?" She curled her fingers more closely into his as she leaned back. "With the others clustered around it?"

Her hair brushed his shoulder, and from instinct he tucked her into the crook of his arm to keep her from tumbling backward. He decided certain instincts were very agreeable, as well as providing a way to preserve the species from harm.

"That is the constellation known as Ursa Minor, or the little bear." She smelled like roses, sweet and spicy and distracting. "The North Star is centered over the North Pole, and no matter where on earth a sailor may be, once he finds it, he can find himself."

"Imagine, my lord," she whispered, the soft curves of her body leaning into him. "So much from one tiny bright star!"

"The North Star isn't tiny," he said, his own voice lowering to a gruff whisper to match hers. "It's far away. Most likely it's even bigger than our own earth."

But she wasn't looking at the stars any longer. She was

looking at *him*. "'How silver-sweet sound lovers' tongues by night / Like softest music in attending ears!'"

He drew her closer. "Your words, or Mr. Shakespeare's again?"

"Romeo and Juliet." Her eyes were half-closed, her lashes throwing feathery shadows across her cheeks, and the half smile on her lips had to be the most tempting invitation he'd ever seen. "'Was there ever such a pair of star-crossed lovers?'"

And before his orderly, rational brain could tell him otherwise, he pulled her close and kissed her. She was soft and warm and willing, curling her arm around the back of his neck to steady herself. The sparkling scarf drifted from her shoulders to the grass, and neither cared. When he slanted his mouth to deepen the kiss, she parted her lips for him with a fluttering little sigh and an eagerness that matched his own. He'd never kissed another woman like this, but then he'd never met a woman as desirable as Cordelia Lyon, either.

"Oh, my lord," she whispered, breathless when at last he broke the kiss. "When you said you'd show me stars, I'd no notion *that* was what you meant."

He laughed. "I've never found stargazing so agreeable, either, nor have I—"

"No, my lord," she said, slipping free. "There can—there *must!*— be no more between us."

"Of course there can, lass." He reached for her, but she skipped backward away from him, as light as any fairy sprite across the grass.

"No, my lord," she said, the sadness in her voice a match for the unhappiness in her eyes. "No more stars, not for us."

And before he could catch her, she was gone.

Chapter Five

"**B**egin again from the start, Gwen," called Cordelia, standing on a bench so everyone could see her. "And this time try to do it from memory."

Gwen scowled, twisting the little scroll with her lines in her hands. "I am doing the best I can, Cordelia. But this is only the first day of rehearsal, and you've given me a precious lot of lines to learn."

Cordelia shrugged, unimpressed. She herself was a quick study with memorizing lines, and she'd little tolerance with those who weren't. "Goddesses always have the longest speeches, Gwen, and if you want to play those roles, you must learn the parts. Now begin again, before I give the part to someone else."

Heaving a huge breath, Gwen flung her arms toward the ballroom ceiling and plunged into the opening speech in her high-pitched, singsong voice. Ordinarily Gwen played the comic parts, saucy maids or knowing countesses, but surely the goddess of love deserved better than this.

Cordelia grimaced, rubbing her forehead. She'd have more patience with them all if she'd slept better last night, and more still if her conscience weren't haunted by that awful, magical kiss from Ross.

"I don't fancy a goddess speaking so many words, Cordelia," Gwen said halfway through her speech, giving her script a dismissive flick of the wrist. "'Tis dreadful tedious."

"Only if you keep forgetting those words." Cordelia lowered her chin, her expression hard as flint. True, this was only the first day of rehearsals, but they had less than two weeks before the wedding, and the way things were going this morning, they were going to need every minute. "Now speak the role as written, Gwen. Proceed."

As Gwen labored onward, Cordelia sighed and glanced out the window. Father was waving his arms and barking orders like a white-bearded general, hovering about the two footmen laying scraps of weary scenery out upon the lawn to air. The scenery would need refurbishing before it would play before an audience of lords and ladies, and as for the exhausted costumes in the company's trunks—oh, she'd worry about the costumes tomorrow.

"You say that's the gentleman who's to play my Weldon?" Lady Emma whispered beside Cordelia—where she'd been since the ten members of the company had dragged their groggy selves into the ballroom earlier that morning. "The tall one with the ginger hair?"

"That is Mr. Ralph Carter, an actor of the first order, my lady," Cordelia said. "As for his hair, why, a wig will make the proper transformation."

Unaware, Mr. Carter chose that moment to yawn as wide as a donkey, giving a languid scratch to the front of his breeches.

"Mr. Carter excels at portraying the most noble heroes, my lady," Cordelia said quickly, trying to turn Emma away. "Though he is not yet quite awake, I believe you will be pleased by his final interpretation."

But still Emma looked over her shoulder at the actor, pursing her lips with doubt and dismay. "Do you think him tall enough for a proper hero? He isn't close to being as large as Weldon."

"Recall that *The Triumph of Love* is meant to honor the spirit of your affections, Lady Emma, and not provide a literal depiction of them." Cordelia glanced back at Gwen, who had forgotten her lines once again and was running a desperate finger along the script to try to find her place. "Consider how little we resemble one another, my lady, and yet I'm to play the heroine."

"But both of you *are* beautiful," the earl said, suddenly behind them, "and that is likeness enough."

"Of course we are beautiful, Ross." Emma grinned at her brother, cocking her head for him to kiss her cheek. "That is why you've come to speak to us first, before anyone else."

"I came to you first, Emma, because I wanted to make certain you weren't causing mischief." He turned to Cordelia, not quite able to keep his face solemn. "Is she, Miss Lyon?"

"Yes, my lord." Cordelia curtsied to hide her confusion. She had never before been at a loss for words, either her own or another playwright's, but with Ross, she could think of absolutely nothing to say, and everything about what she was seeing: how twin dimples bracketed his smile, how his unruly hair was falling over his forehead, how he was watching her now as if there were a great secret that only they shared, which after last night in the orchard, they did.

Maybe that was what he meant by the mischief: not Emma's, but hers, letting a nobleman she scarce knew kiss her until she'd been breathless with pleasure, breathless with longing that a woman in her position had no right to feel for a man born so much further above her....

"You can stand now, Cordelia," Emma said, giggling. "My brother's not the king, you know."

"Oh, she knows," he said, and to Cordelia's surprise, he took her hand and raised her back up to her feet. His fingers felt warm around hers, his right forefinger stained with purple-blue ink much like her own. "You don't mistake me for His Majesty, do you, Miss Lyon?"

"Hardly, my lord," she said, pulling her hand free. She took a deep breath, ordering herself to stop dithering and think straight. It was only one man, one kiss, not all of England sinking into the North Sea, and besides, she could hardly blame the moonlight now. "You are the Earl of Mayne, no more, no less."

"Oh, but Ross *is* more, Cordelia!" Emma rested a proud hand on her brother's shoulder. "He is very famous as a scholar and a renowned gentleman of science, and he's written books and given papers to the Royal Navy *and* the Royal Society."

"Do your books ever include the study of apples, my lord?" If he wanted to remind her of last night, well, then, she'd remind him right back, to prove how little effect it had had on her. "Or orchards?"

His reaction was quick, his smile almost a dare. "It would be a bold scholar who'd risk following Eve into the garden orchard, Miss Lyon, even one thirsting for knowledge."

She narrowed her eyes, daring him back. "I suppose, my lord, it depends on how wickedly thirsty that scholar might be. Why, Eve might have other affairs pressing for her attention, and not be waiting in the orchard for him at all."

"A fair and just assumption, Miss Lyon," he said, the challenge in his smile making him seem less like an earl, less like a renowned scholar, and more dangerously like an ordinary man. "Though assumptions can be dangerous for scholars to make. For all we know, Eve might even have become more interested in stars than apples."

"But apples are grounded in the earth, my lord," she said, tapping her rolled script against her palm. "As such, apples are by nature more substantial and lasting than even the brightest stars in the sky."

"Yet consider, Miss Lyon, how an apple led to Eve's ruin," he said. "Wouldn't she do better for herself to turn toward the stars and the heavens?"

"Apples, Ross?" Emma frowned, suspicious, and looked from Ross to Cordelia and back again. "Orchards? Stars? How is it that Cordelia knows more than I? I thought you were studying waves."

"I am." He sighed like a schoolboy being caught out of class, and shook his tousled hair back from his forehead with a charming nonchalance—not, of course, that Cordelia was meant to notice. "In fact I should be writing now, and not dawdling here. On board the *Perseverance,* our lives were ruled by the watches, and not a moment was wasted. It's a habit I am trying to maintain here, too."

"I don't mind your dawdling," Cordelia said quickly— perhaps too quickly. "That is, now that you have agreed not to interfere in the play, you are welcome to remain and watch us rehearse. It is your right as our esteemed patron and benefactor."

She swept her arm through the air, encompassing the rest of the company, which, she now noticed, had all stopped rehearsing to eavesdrop on her and the earl, and without any shame whatsoever. Even her father stood in the garden doorway, his ears practically flapping with interest as he watched to see what happened next.

And the earl, a pox on him, did not disappoint.

"I wish that I could stay, Miss Lyon, but I only came here now to return this to you." He reached into the front of his coat and, with a conjurer's flourish, pulled out the sparkling scarf she'd worn last night. "It must have slipped from your shoulders while we were, ah, conversing. I found it on the grass after you left me last night."

"Thank you, my lord." Her cheeks flaming, Cordelia grabbed the scarf and crumpled it into a tight ball, as if hiding it in her hand could hide her embarrassment before the others, too. "Now if you can excuse us, my lord, we have much work to do here."

"I'm sure you do, Miss Lyon, as do I in my library." He was grinning at her as if he'd no intention of leaving, just as he had in the orchard before he'd taken her into his arms and whispered that folderol about the stars and the moonlight.

But the worst part for Cordelia was realizing that she didn't really want him to go at all.

"It's not only rehearsing our lines, my lord," she said in a rush, trying to convince herself as much as him. "I must still refine the play as a whole. Then we must see to the costumes, and the sets, and—"

"And I would not dream of stopping you, Miss Lyon, not for even a second. As you reminded me yesterday, a patron must know when to keep his own counsel and leave the artists to their creations. Good day, and much speed with your work." He bowed, solemn again. "Emma, I will join you later at tea."

"Yes, yes, back to our work." Briskly Cordelia turned away, refusing to let him think she'd be mooning after him when he left. She threw the incriminating scarf into her workbasket and once again unrolled her master script. "I cannot believe we've accomplished so little this morning!"

"You like my brother, don't you?" Emma asked, her arms folded across her chest and her head tilted at a thoughtful angle. "And he likes you in return. I did not think so at first, but now, after I see how you look at one another—"

"We look at one another with our eyes, Lady Emma," Cordelia said as evenly as she could. "Which is how it is usually done."

"Not with my brother, it isn't," Emma said. "The most beautiful woman in creation could walk through the door before him, and he would be too caught up in his own thoughts to notice her. I have seen it happen, and it is dreadful to watch."

"I can only imagine, my lady," Cordelia said. "Now if you please, we—"

"No, no, you must hear me." Emma gave an imperious little twist of her hand. "You see, my brother's not like that with you, Cordelia. You are different to him. He sees you, and he judges what he sees to be most agreeable."

Again Cordelia felt her cheeks growing warm—she who never blushed! "Forgive me, my lady, but perhaps you are seeing things, as well, things that do not exist."

She turned back to the other players, clapping her hands for their attention as she hurried to the front of the ballroom. "Now come, Gwen, Robert! Take your places, if you will!"

But Gwen was already in her place at center stage, her mouth twisted into the knowing half smile that audiences loved.

"Oh, aye, you know how to say 'I will,' don't you, Cordelia?" she said with a broad wink. "I will, I do, I did, and all with that handsome lord what's our patron."

Cordelia raised her chin. "The proper lines, Gwen, if you please."

Gwen swung her hips suggestively, and one of the other actresses tittered with amusement. "The lines sound proper enough for the goddess o' love to me, sweets, and if you want—"

"That's enough, Gwen," Alfred said, his voice deceptively mild. "Quite, quite enough."

"'Twas only sport, Alfred," protested Gwen. "You saw her with the lord, licking up cream like a kitten, and if she—"

"I told you that was enough, Gwen," he repeated. "If you devoted half the time to learning your part as you do to gossip, then the entire company would benefit. A word with you alone, Cordelia, if you please."

She suspected what he'd say, and she didn't want to hear it. "Can't we speak later, Father, when—"

"Now, daughter," he said, pointing to the garden door. "No more dallying."

She had no choice but to join him, scurrying out the door to the stone garden steps. "We don't have nearly enough time for staging an original production like this, Father, and now you—"

"Oh, hush, Cordelia," Alfred said, his white eyebrows coming together into a fierce thatch. "Cease being so preposterous. This production is no more original than a donkey's backside. You've cobbled together the entire Trojan War for an alderman's dinner in less time than you'll have for one silly wedding play."

"The Trojan War was easy," she said, squinting up into the sun. How like her father to choose this place to stand, with the sun around his head like a halo! "This play is fashioned on real people, which makes it much more difficult, and—"

"It's not the real people that concern me," Alfred said, interrupting again. "It's one real gentleman in particular. What exactly transpired last evening between you and the scholarly earl, eh?"

"An apology." She wished she didn't sound so defensive. "I apologized to save the play for the company, just as you told me to do."

He didn't answer at first. Instead he held the silence for an excruciatingly long moment, his hands folded across his chest and the birds singing in the garden.

Finally he sighed. "Upon my word, Cordelia. I've always judged you to be an actress of the first water, but that—that was appalling."

"It was the truth!"

"A ragtag scrap of truth, perhaps, but nothing more. The rest was there in His Lordship's face for us all to see, writ clear as morning. And as for your own—ah, daughter, if our Gwenny could read it, then so could a blind man."

She flushed but kept her head high and tried to forget the star-crossed lovers. "It—it was the moonlight. Nothing of any significance happened, I swear."

Alfred grunted, unconvinced. "It is my own fault, I suppose, for teasing you about the man. You never could resist a challenge, Cordelia, could you?"

"But I tell you, Father, His Lordship means nothing to me!"

"You know he won't marry you." This rare bluntness cut, sharp and keen. "Don't you dare delude yourself that he will. You will be an amusement, nothing more. That is the way it is with fine noblemen and theater folk like us, and why we do better to keep with our own kind."

"I no more expect to wed him than he does me!"

"That is good." Alfred's face turned hard and grim, and beyond cajoling. "And no notions of running off with him, either, or of letting him set you up in keeping, mind? No amount of gold or jewels is worth that, and I won't have your heart broken while he plays his games."

"No, Father," she said, shocked not by what he was saying, but that he'd made himself say it. "But I promise you he means nothing to me—less than nothing!"

"For your own good, I pray you'll keep that promise." Abruptly his features sagged with weariness, and he rubbed his sleeve across his face as if to clear away the memories of the past.

"I know you're half your mother's child," he said, not bothering to hide the old bitterness, "and carry her passions in your blood as well as mine. But while love can make a woman bloom like a rose, lust and greed can trample her into ruin, and so it did to your mother."

"But I'm not her, Father," she said, wanting to share the burden of his misery as she laid her hand on his arm. "I'm your Cordelia."

"True enough, lass." He put one hand over hers, and she felt the tremor of emotion in his fingers. "Which is why I fear for you so, you see. I want you to love a man who'll deserve you, who'll accept you for what you are. I want that man to treasure you as a gem, not a bauble."

She thought again of Romeo and Juliet and the tragedy that had come from their misguided passions, and then thought of how warmly the earl had smiled at her in the moonlight. In less than a fortnight, the company would give their play to the earl's guests. The day after that, they'd move on, and just as surely she, too, would vanish from the earl's thoughts.

"There now, lamb, don't be gloomy and sorrowful," he said, giving her fingers a little pat. "A wedding play calls for happy faces all around. Smile at His Lordship, beguile him, charm him all you please. But guard your heart well, Cordelia. Guard your heart, and keep it safe."

"I will, Father," she said softly, sadly, though that heart seemed to grow heavy in her chest, longing for all she could never have. "I will."

Chapter Six

Balanced on a footstool, Cordelia leaned toward him, keeping her arms outstretched behind her with her shawl draped over her wrists like fluttering wings.

"'Now has come the dreaded time when we must part,'" she said, her voice full of anguish as she gazed up into his eyes. "'Until, reunited by love, we make another glorious start!'"

From his seat on the garden wall outside the ballroom, Ross shook his head in wonder. She was too fine by half for that weasel-faced rascal, that was certain. It might only be a play that he was watching, but Cordelia Lyon was making him believe every word.

She brought her arms forward in a graceful arc, tipping her head to one side as she touched her fingers to her lips, her expressive face racked with sentiment and grief. It was, Ross decided, about the saddest, most beautiful thing he'd ever seen, even if he doubted very much such a poignant scene had ever taken place between Emma and Weldon.

"'Come back to me with the fleetness that gifts only true lovers' wings,'" she said, arching on her tiptoes up to Carter, the actor playing Weldon. "'And return with the ardency that makes my heart sing!'"

"'My heart only such endless devotion knows,'" the actor replied, placing his hand over that same devoted heart while he made sure to keep his profile seen by the audience. "'Such passion! Such yearning! Such—such'—oh, Jupiter, Cordelia, for the life of me I cannot recall what follows."

"'Such fervency that glows,'" Cordelia supplied without breaking her pose.

Carter cleared his throat. "'Such fervency that glows! Oh, dearest lady, the queen who—who'—oh, hell."

"No, no, no, Ralph!" With an impatient sigh, Cordelia folded her arms over her chest. "You've had days and days to learn these lines, Ralph, or have you caught Gwen's disease?"

Carter snorted, puffing out his chest so his belly wouldn't look as large. "How can you imply that I'd catch anything from Gwen, the ancient old sow?"

"Know your lines, Ralph," said Alfred Lyon sternly, ruling from an armchair as if it were a throne, "and she won't imply anything."

"That's all right, Father." Cordelia hopped down from her footstool. "It must be near to midnight, anyway. We'll stop for the night. But by all that's holy, Ralph, if you do not know your piece by morning—"

"But I shall, dear lady." Ralph rolled his eyes with an overwrought sigh and patted the hand still resting over his heart. "Have ever, ever I failed you, Mistress Lyon?"

"More times than I can count, Master Carter," she said wearily, turning away. "Just let this not be another."

But to Ross's surprise, she headed not to the door that led to the rest of the house, but to that which opened onto the garden wall where he was sitting. He'd barely time to scramble down before she was there, standing in the doorway staring at him with her hand on the latch.

"Miss Lyon," he said. "Good, ah, good day."

"Rather, it's good evening, my lord, nearly good midnight."

She frowned, more perplexed than surprised, as if she'd already expected to find him here. "I come out for a last breath of air, and here you are again. It would seem you wander your estates more by night than any roving tomcat."

"I wasn't roving," he said. "I'm often awake at this hour working. But tonight I was watching you rehearse."

"From here, my lord?" she asked. "Why didn't you come inside instead of peeking through the windows?"

"I didn't want to distract you." This wasn't entirely the truth. What he wanted—and had wanted the past two nights when he'd also sat here watching—was to be distracted himself, with her doing the distracting, the way she'd done in the orchard. "I imagine you've suggestions enough from Emma without having me in the audience, too."

She looked up at him through her lashes, a frank, skeptical look that he liked for being so unladylike. "That is a great change in you, my lord. Three days ago you were prepared to write, cast and direct the entire play yourself."

"I have reconsidered that position," he said, wincing inwardly at how pompous that must sound to her.

"But not the one that makes you worry about your investment?" she asked, the skepticism still there.

That was exactly the reason he'd come to watch the first night, but he wasn't going to admit that now. "My sister has decided that she wants this play very much, and so I want it for her, and the best possible version, too. Besides, I do not like intrusions upon my work, and I would imagine you feel the same."

"An intrusion would have been welcome tonight, my lord." She sighed, looking past him to the moonlit garden. "There's no use pretending otherwise. You were watching us. No one seems to be able to remember their lines, and their acting's as stiff as wooden signboards. And I agree that your sister deserves so much more."

"From what I saw, it looked fine," he said, thinking only

of Cordelia's performance. "Damned fine, and worthy of Drury Lane."

She smiled ruefully. "You are most kind, my lord, if not properly critical. I know I shouldn't be telling you this, considering that you're our patron, but it will take a Romish miracle to make *The Triumph of Love* as good as I want it to be, and as good as your sister deserves."

He hadn't expected such frankness from any actress. But then Cordelia wasn't sparkling now, either, the way she'd been in the orchard. Instead she seemed tired and discouraged, and while he felt sure he'd hear no more *Romeo and Juliet* under this night's moon, there was a new vulnerability to her that he hadn't expected. He longed to put his arm around her drooping shoulders and tell her whatever she needed to hear to feel better.

"Another day or two, and everything will be as it should," he said. "You'll see. That's the way it is with any meaningful work. The more it means to you, the more power it has to confound you at every turn."

She glanced back at him, her eyes full of challenge as she shoved a loose strand of hair away from her forehead. "You are an earl, my lord. Forgive me for speaking plainly, but what can a noble gentleman like you know of work?"

"I know a great deal about it," he declared, wounded that she'd judge him to be only one more idle nobleman. "I may not have to toil to keep a roof over my head, but I assure you that I work as hard at my scientific endeavors as any man, rich or poor, in this kingdom."

Her shoulders stiffened with wariness. "If you plan to talk to me of the heavens, my lord, using your stargazer's nonsense meant to turn my head so you can kiss me again, why, then I shall leave you directly."

"It wasn't nonsense," he said defensively. "It was purest fact."

"And was it purest fact that made you kiss me because I am a mere actress, and fair game for any gentleman?"

"I didn't kiss you because you are an actress," he said, stunned she'd assume something like that. He wasn't a calculating rake, any more than he was a boorish, undereducated wastrel. "The fact is that I kissed you because, well, because I wished to."

She frowned, her chin ducked low. "I am not certain that is a fact, my lord."

"It is," he countered, "and I am not a man who treats fact lightly. Besides, you were the one trying to confuse me by reciting Shakespeare's plays to me. That wasn't precisely fair, either, you know."

"Shakespeare isn't meant to be fair." Her sudden fierce smile caught him off guard. "'My intents are savage-wild, / More fierce and more inexorable far / Than empty tigers or the roaring sea.'"

"'The roaring sea'?" The phrase snagged in his head. "Is that Shakespeare, too?"

"You do not know?" she scoffed. "It's also from *Romeo and Juliet,* of course. The play's been much on my mind because of your sister."

"But the 'roaring sea'—you couldn't know that that is my work, what I study, described in two neat words that I'd never thought to put together. Waves and tides and currents, and the nature of oceans. These are the things that fascinate me, Miss Lyon." Caught up in his own enthusiasm, he seized her hand. "Come, come, and I'll show you!"

But she pulled away from him, taking two steps backward for good measure. "I do know the tides are guided by the moon, my lord, and I've had enough of moonlight ventures with you."

"My device for the replication of ocean waves is in my library, across the garden, there, and most assuredly free of any moonlight." He couldn't fathom why it seemed so suddenly important to him that he show her his projects, but it was. "I have seen your work, Miss Lyon. Now I should like you to see mine. My 'roaring sea,' as you called it."

She frowned, rubbing her hand where he'd held it while she considered, but it took her only a second to decide.

"Very well, then, my lord." She skipped down the steps ahead of him to the lawn, her trailing skirts catching on the grass. "I should like very much to see the proof of a working earl. It shall make for an amusing story to tell the others, such as a red calf born with two heads."

With three long strides, he caught up with her, leading the way to his library. "The waves, Miss Lyon, are infinitely more interesting than I."

She smiled, not exactly at him, but close enough to be encouraging. "I try to find interest in everything, my lord, for I never know when I might need to draw upon the experience for a role. Why, someday I may play a mermaid, frolicking in your very same waves."

"A mermaid." He gulped, imagining her all too easily as a sailor's bare-breasted delight, sinuously ducking in and out of the waves. "Are there many roles for mermaids?"

"Alas, no, my lord," she said. "There is the problem of staging. Water is the very devil to portray. Ah, I'd no notion your library was so close to our little makeshift theater!"

Opening the door for her, he saw the room through her eyes, with charts and maps and journals scattered everywhere and open books anchored by exotic seashells. At least the candles had been kept lit and replenished by the servants familiar with his nocturnal ways. He hurried to clear a chair for Cordelia, sweeping aside a basket of dried, puckered seaweed he'd gathered off the coast of Brazil.

"So this is your lair, my lord?" She ignored his offered chair to wander around the room, her curiosity unfazed by his clutter. She didn't look tired now; now, she seemed interested and full of life. "Here is where you do this great work of yours?"

"Yes." He cleared his throat, watching how gracefully she

moved, pausing to touch a shell or study a map. His "lair," she'd called it, and perhaps it was. She was the first woman he'd ever invited to see it, though, granted, she was also the first who'd ever wanted to. "I am still unpacking from the voyage, so things are not, ah, quite organized as yet."

"What is a tidy desk but the sign of a dull and empty mind, my lord?" She stopped before the long, low tank made of wood that ran the length of one wall, and carefully raised one corner of the black oilcloth covering it. "Is this the famous wave-making device that I have been promised?"

"It is." He came to stand beside her at the wooden tank, so close he could smell the heady, distinctive fragrance of her hair and skin. Her muslin gown was cut dramatically low in the bodice, giving him a glimpse of her high, round breasts pressing against the thin cotton. He remembered how warm she'd been in his arms, that body soft and yielding as he'd held her against him.

He remembered, and so did she. Sensing his interest as much as his presence, she glanced up at him from under the dark veil of her lashes.

"Remember, my lord, no stars or moonlight in here," she warned, then glided away to the far end of the tank, safely out of his reach. "No Juliet or Romeo, either."

His gaze still on her, Ross shrugged out of his coat and tossed it onto the back of the chair before he began rolling up the black tarpaulin, trying to focus his attention on explaining the tank instead of on her breasts. "Thanks to Mr. Boyle's observations, it is accepted that no single wave can rise higher than six feet from the water's surface."

She looked up sharply, her eyes wide. "Faith, you can make a wave rise six feet tall in this fish tank?"

"Oh, no," he said, smiling. "I must work on a smaller scale, and calculate the differences upward. When a single wave combines with others in a storm, you see, then the results can be twenty, thirty, even forty feet high. What makes these waves join together? Can such unions be predicted, and thereby avoided? Solving such a puzzle would make for safer voyages for ships and sailors alike."

She smiled back at him. "And for the mermaids, too, I'd fancy."

"For a mermaid, such mountainous waves would be mere sliding boards," he said, wishing she hadn't reminded him of those damned mermaids again. "But many more English sailors die each year from treacherous seas than from French guns. That is why I was granted passage on board the *Perseverance*—to study waves throughout the world's oceans."

"So you truly did sail to the Pacific Ocean?" she asked with surprise. "I thought that was only Lady Emma's invention."

"Oh, it was quite real," he said. "You've only to look around this room to see how I could not resist bringing back a memento from every last port and island."

"Fancy." She leaned over the tank's water with fresh interest, her face reflecting up at her. "So this water was brought from a faraway ocean?"

"I'm afraid it's drawn from the well in my stable yard." Leaning forward like that, she was granting him an even better view of her bosom, and making him roll the tarp more and more tightly in his fingers. "The water's changed every week, to keep it pure. If I'd imported genuine seawater clear from the Pacific, by now it would be stinking to the heavens of dead fish and stale brine."

She chuckled, smoothing her hair back behind one ear. "You know Lady Emma is particularly intrigued by the notion of you among the ladies of Tahiti."

"Is she now?" He leaned the rolled tarpaulin in the corner of the room, relieved to have even that small distraction. "It astounds me how those ladies are all anyone here in England wishes to discuss."

Her chuckle deepened, warm and rich. "I doubt I could find that island on your maps if I looked all night, yet even I have heard the stories about the navy men among the Tahitian women, like foxes set among the most willing hens."

He realized he was laughing, too, for no real reason other than that she'd started it. "Likely the stories exaggerate. True, the young women in that part of the world are astoundingly free of the constraints that bind their London counterparts. Even their emperor's daughter goes about in a…ah…a natural state, following her own tastes, I suppose."

She laughed again, most likely at his reticence, but he didn't care. "You do not think it will be the fashion in Bath next season?"

"What, in petticoats of leaves and vines, and bodices of gaudy trade cloth and flowers?" He paused, now picturing her wickedly costumed as one of those sunny island ladies. She would look fine, he decided, more than fine. "Nor would their manner of courtship find favor here. Unlike those prim English misses at Almack's who put their poor swains through more paces than a Thoroughbred nag, a Tahitian lady sees a gentleman she admires, and simply offers herself to him."

By the candlelight he could see her cheeks had turned a rosy shade of pink as she looked down at the water in the tank. "Then tell me, my lord. Did any of those Tahitian ladies admire you?"

"They admired most of us Englishmen, likely for the sake of novelty alone," he admitted. "But though those ladies are handsome little creatures, I chose not to accept their kind offers."

"Ahh." She trailed her fingertips across the water's surface, rippling through her own reflection. "So you prefer the prim young ladies at Almack's."

He shook his head. "Not at all. I don't fancy being a trophy for either group of ladies."

"No?" Cordelia looked up at him again. She was, she knew, playing with fire, the sparks ready to burst into flame as high as any of the earl's deep-sea waves. She was saying things to him she shouldn't, and he was saying them back, sharing flirtatious confidences as if they were an ordinary couple. This time she couldn't even blame it on the moonlight and stars. She wanted to be here, with him, and the more they talked, the more she wanted to stay and not leave as she should. "And here I thought it was the ladies who were considered the prizes!"

"The gentleman's always the prize when there's a title before his name," he said, tucking the cuffs of his shirtsleeves up above his elbows so they wouldn't get wet, his forearms as brown and brawny as any sailor's. "But then I'm sure Emma can tell you how badly I have confounded her every effort at matchmaking. Hopelessly particular, she calls me."

She laughed again, and thought of how it was probably a good thing that twelve feet of chilly water lay between them. "Better hopelessly particular than particularly hopeless."

"I'm afraid Emma would tell you that they're one and the same." He began adjusting the large bellows, rigged to hang from the ceiling as if in a blacksmith's shop instead of a gentleman's library. "Now, this is my wind. If I point it over the surface of the water at the correct angle, it should mimic sea waves."

He gave the foot pedal a gentle pump, squeezing a gust of air from the mouth of the bellows as the pleated leather contracted, and at once small wavelets danced across the water. She liked seeing him concentrate like this, liked seeing how the muscles in his shoulders and arms tensed and released. He hadn't lied; he *did* work. He pumped harder, increasing the next rush of air from the bellows, and the waves grew into sharper peaks.

"So you can do it, my lord," she marveled, clapping her hands with approval. "Those are the most perfect waves imaginable! Might I try it? Please?"

He hesitated. "It's not as simple as it appears."

"Oh, I could do it. I know I could. Please, my lord?" She

came around the end of the tank to stand beside him, eager to try. "All I must do is push on this pedal, isn't it?"

"Very well, but you must let me guide you. Here." She pulled up the hem of her skirt above her ankle so he could make sure her foot was properly on the pedal.

"Ha, look at that," she said, giggling at her pointed, red-striped shoe on the wide wooden pedal. "I should have worn my seven-league boots instead of slippers!"

"I'll grant you that it's scaled more for a smith than a lady," he said. "But then you are the first female ever to come into this room, let alone try the bellows."

"The first female?" she asked, amazed but flattered, too. He'd explained things in such detail to her, treating her with rare respect for her intelligence and her person, that she could scarce believe he'd never done it for anyone else. Surely no one else in the company except Father treated her half as well. Was she that special to the earl? Could he feel for her the way she was trying hard not to feel for him? "Truly?"

"Truly," he said. "I've never known anyone else who wanted to play a mermaid."

Without asking permission, he circled his arms around her so she could keep the bellows steady and at the correct angle over the water. Her back was to his chest, the hard muscles of his thighs pressing against her legs, excitement vibrating through them both as they stood so closely together.

"Now press upon the pedal and give the bellows air," he said. "Handsomely, now, handsomely!"

He felt the effort of her pressing down, concentrating hard, then the gasp of delight as the first waves ruffled across the water. She pressed again, finding the momentum, and the waves grew larger and more defined.

"There you are," Ross said. "Easy as can be."

She laughed with delight, and pushed all her weight into driving the bellows. Now the waves peaked and crested, breakers in miniature as they rolled and smacked against the far end of the tank.

"Behold, behold, I am Aeolus himself, commander of the winds!" she announced with a goddess's gleeful resonance to an invisible audience. "Behold my power!"

Caught in the glory of the moment, she swept her hand through the air and into the nose of the bellows, knocking it down toward the little waves. At once cold water gushed up and sprayed over them both, drenching them together in wet surprise.

"Oh—oh, Hades!" she cried, startled by the cold water as she stumbled to one side to escape. "Oh, my lord, look at me!"

She stood with her arms held stiffly from her sides while the water dripped and puddled at her feet. Her hair had collapsed into a sodden mass, her gown was soaked, and she struggled to blink the water from her eyes.

"Oh, lass, I am sorry!" He seized a large towel from a nearby stool—were these watery mishaps *that* common?—and hurriedly began blotting at her face and arms. His face was lined with concern, and he didn't seem to notice at all how his own linen shirt was so soaked it was nearly transparent. "I should not have let this happen, I should have—"

"Hush," she said, laughter bubbling up from deep inside her as a fat drop of water fell from his hair onto her nose. "Just—just hush."

He shook his head, flinging water like a wet spaniel. "But if I'd—"

"I told you to hush," she said through her laughter. She slipped her arms free of the towel and looped them instead around his shoulders, pulling his face down to hers. "We were going to make waves, my lord, and...we...did."

She arched up and kissed him to make him stop apologizing, and because she wanted to, and at once he was kissing her back, his urgency matching her own. His hands slid down to her hips, his fingers spreading as he drew their bodies more intimately together, their wet clothes clinging together, chilled linen over warm skin.

She turned her head just enough for him to deepen the kiss, and threaded her fingers into his wet hair to hold him. When his hand reached up and covered her breast, her nipple already taut from the cold water, she gasped into his mouth but didn't pull away. A little more, she told herself, only a little more, and she moaned as the pleasure built within her body.

But when the tall clock against the wall chimed once, she pushed away and broke the kiss. "I must go," she said, with hardly enough breath left to whisper. "Forgive me, my lord, but I must go."

"No, you don't." He curled his arm more tightly around her waist, keeping her. "Stay here with me, and we'll make more waves. And my name is Ross."

"Ross." She smiled as she said his name. "But it's after one in the morning, and Father will be looking for me to return, and if I stay awake much longer, I'll have no voice for tomorrow's rehearsal."

"Damn the rehearsal," he muttered, even as he released her. "Damn the whole infernal play, except the part with you in it."

"But the play's the only reason I'm here!"

"Then go now," he said gruffly. "And tomorrow night, after you rehearse your parts, come back here with me."

Sadly she searched his handsome face, wet hair and all, remembering what she'd promised Father. But even Father must know that some promises seemed destined to be broken; some were made too late to have a prayer of being kept.

Eleven more days until the company gave the wedding play, and eleven nights they'd have together if she dared. Eleven more nights of calling an earl by his given name, of having his smiles and his kisses and the waves all to herself.

She could choose eleven days and nights of him, or she could choose the emptiest of nothings.

"Yes, Ross," she whispered fiercely, and kissed him again. "Yes."

Chapter Seven

Cordelia sat on the sill of the tall, open window of the ball-room, sipping tea with honey and milk for her voice. Because she was not needed for the scene the others were rehearsing, she could steal these few moments to enjoy the warmth of the sun and the sweet spring air, redolent with the fragrance of new-mowed grass and early flowers.

She heard the crunch of carriage wheels on the graveled driveway, and turned with interest in the direction of the sound. Ross had told her the first of the wedding guests would begin arriving today, the ones who lived farthest away and would be staying at the hall until after the ceremony. He'd said the newcomers would make no difference in their meetings at night, but Cordelia wasn't as convinced.

Only three more days remained before the company gave the wedding play, and to her the time was slipping away faster than sand in an hourglass. As host, surely Ross must spend more time entertaining his guests and less with her. To her it seemed obvious, and inevitable, as well, but such knowledge would offer her pitifully slight comfort.

Shaded by tall trees, her window perch let her see without being noticed in return, and she tucked her red skirts more closely around her knees as she leaned forward with her cup in her lap. The glossy green coach that stopped before the white marble steps was drawn by four matched bays, and on the door was painted a coat of arms to honor its noble occupants. While footmen rushed forward to open the door for the three travelers—two elderly ladies and their maidservant—a younger gentleman from the same party drew up on horseback.

At last Ross himself appeared, tugging on his coat as he came down the steps to greet them. Cordelia knew he'd been working with his water tank, not only from the coat, but also from the large wet blotches on his trousers, and she smiled to herself, thinking of their own escapades with his wave-making device.

"Ahh, so the grandees begin to make their entrances," Alfred said, coming to stand beside her at the window with a teacup of his own. "A royal princess, d'you think, or some fantastic dowager duchess?"

"All I know is that they're guests of the Howlands." She sniffed and wrinkled her nose. "How much brandy is in that tea, Father? Faith, it isn't even noon."

He took a dainty sip from the cup. "You must know, daughter, that at my age it takes more than a libation from a honeybee to cure a ragged throat."

"Especially when you didn't return from that tavern in the village until dawn this morning." She sighed and shook her head. "It's bad enough that you mistreat yourself so, Father, but poor Ralph hasn't your stamina, and you lead him wicked places he's no business going. Look at him—he's next to worthless this morning, and he doesn't need your brandy as another excuse to mumble his lines."

Alfred glanced back at the other actor, hunched over against the wall as far from the cheerful morning sunshine as he could be, his face waxy pale and his hands jammed into his coat pockets to hide their trembling.

"Ahh, a touch of lady fever, that is all," he said. "I wouldn't worry overmuch about the lad."

"More like King Alfred's brandy fever." Cordelia set her empty cup on the floor with an empathic clatter. "Be reasonable, Father. Ralph's the play's hero, the honorable bridegroom, and I'll thank you to keep him sober and out of the Tawny Buck until after the performance."

"While you, Cordelia, are apparently playing the role of the prissy-prim goddess of misplaced virtue," her father said. "No, now don't deny it. I'm not dragging Ralph to the tavern every night. Do you think I haven't noticed what time you've been crawling into your own bed each night—or morning?"

Cordelia's chin jerked up in defense, but the guilty flush of her cheeks betrayed her. "I've done nothing to hurt the play, nor to compromise the rest of the company!"

"But you have compromised yourself a bit, haven't you, Cordelia?" He looked past her out the window to the steps and Cordelia's own gaze followed, seeking and finding Ross.

With his guests in the house, Ross had taken that same moment to pause. He looked up at the ballroom windows as if sensing Cordelia's presence, and his smile when he found her was wide and unabashed, his pleasure in just the sight of her as undeniable as another man's caress.

"You can't deny it, Cordelia, any more than you could deny him, or yourself," Alfred said, his voice leaden. "I am sorry. I am sorry."

"Oh, Father, don't be," she said softly, taking his gnarled hand in her own. "It was my wish, my own free will."

"Then I am doubly sorry." He pulled his hand away, his face closing against her. "You will be coming with us when we are done here, Cordelia. You have confounded me, aye, but I'll not abandon you to shame me more, the way I did with your mother."

"It's not like that, Father, I swear!" How could she explain that it was more than passion and desire that had brought her and Ross together, or that they'd both agreed to stop short of taking the final lover's step?

"You swore to me before, and how little weight that oath has carried."

"But it's so much more than that, Father," she said. "With him, I forget that Ralph doesn't know his lines, or that Gwen is pert to me for no reason. He talks to me, Father. He treats me as if I am every bit as clever as he is himself, and tells me tales of how the moon rules the tides, or what the queens of Fiji are called, or the difference between a narwhal's horn and a unicorn's, and—and oh, there must be a thousand other ways he has that make me feel special!"

But her father's expression didn't change. "I trust you have turned to Gwen or one of the other woman for advice in keeping yourself safe. I won't be burdened with a nobleman's bastard, another puling mouth to feed in the back of the wagon."

Tears stung her eyes as she struggled to steady her voice. "Please, Father, don't say such things—not of me, not of Ross!"

"Ross," he muttered.

She'd never heard such scorn heaped onto a single word, not from her father.

"He is the Earl of Mayne, and always will be, just as you will never be more than Cordelia Lyon, and never his equal. Have you forgotten that when we first came here, he judged us as the most disreputable gypsies, eager to steal him blind?"

"But Father, I—"

"You say you have not hurt the company by what you have done with that man," he said. "But by God, Cordelia, you have hurt me."

Deliberately he turned away from her to join the others before she could answer, his shoulders bent and his steps measured. With her hand pressed over her mouth to stifle her sob, she looked back to Ross, still on the white steps below and staring up at her window with his hand shielding his eyes against the sun.

He'd been waiting for her to look again at him, unaware of what was happening between her and Alfred, and when he saw her face turn back to him, his smile beamed, warmer than the sun itself, and he waved his whole arm at her, as if he didn't care who saw him.

Slowly she raised her hand to return the wave, her smile tremulous through her tears. But for these few days, he'd made her happy, hadn't he?

Happy…

"So tell me, cousin," said the Honorable James Kelty, lowering his voice to a more confidential level as he and Ross walked through the house on their way to James's rooms. "Exactly who was that ravishing creature in the window that I just saw you saluting?"

"You, ah, saw a lady?" Ross said, stalling. Beginning when they'd still been in school, his cousin had made it his vocation in life to cut as wide a romantic swath through young English womanhood as he could possibly manage, and Ross wanted to do his best to keep Cordelia from his path. "You must have seen Emma."

"Not unless Emma has changed from silver into purest gold." James punched Ross's upper arm. "Now be a good fellow and tell me who she is."

"She's here for the wedding."

"Another guest, and fair game," James said with relish, ready for the hunt. "Is she from this county, or perhaps one of Emma's little friends from school?"

"You won't know her, James. She's out of your circle entirely." Ross made a quick tuneless whistle, desperate to change the subject. "I say, Emma will be glad to see you again, though I should warn you that she's out of her mind over this wedding."

James stopped short, narrowing his eyes with sly suspicion. "You've staked your claim on the filly, haven't you? I know it's damned unlikely. I know you'd rather chew off your own leg than make love to a pretty girl, but even dusty old bachelors like you will change, oh, every thousand years or so."

"Well, then, yes, James, I do have a 'stake,' as you call it," Ross said with irritation, "and I'll thank you to keep your distance from her while you're here."

James held up his hands, surrendering. "I'll not poach, cousin, not on your game, if you'll but tell me the lady's name."

Ross drummed his fingers on the edge of a nearby sideboard. "She's not exactly a lady. She's, ah, an actress."

"An *actress?*" James's jaw dropped open for effect. "You're keeping an actress here at Howland Hall? Your mother would have your head for tomfoolery like that!"

"It's not like that," Ross said quickly. "She's part of the theater company that's going to perform a special wedding play in honor of Emma and Weldon."

"How deuced convenient!" James exclaimed. "You have the little darling here for your amusement for the next week or so, then off she goes before you tire of her, without any fuss or tears from her to spoil your day."

"That's enough, James." Ross's voice was so sharp that James drew back. "I won't have you speak of her in that manner."

"I said I wouldn't poach, Ross. But if she's only an actress, not a lady, and—"

"The last door on the right is yours," Ross said, that sharpness now almost a threat. "We dine at seven."

Ross turned and left before he said more. He was almost shaking with anger, and the intensity of it churning inside him shocked him. Yet all James had done was give words to what Ross already felt, and dreaded, too.

The day was fast coming when Cordelia would clamber up into the company's wagon, leave with the others and be gone from his life forever. He'd lose her as his friend, his sweet-heart, even his muse and inspiration. She was clever and passionate and unpredictable, and in a handful of days she'd filled an emptiness in his life that he hadn't realized existed. With her as an avid sounding board and critic, his work had progressed at a record pace.

But she'd made it clear from the start that there'd be no shared future for them. Fate had brought them together, she'd said, and fate would take them apart, and then she'd smiled and shrugged and spoken another piece from her Shakespeare, as if that could solve everything.

And damnation, that wasn't any solution at all.

With her ankles crossed as neatly as a dancer's and her hand resting in Ralph's, Cordelia held her pose at the back of the stage while Alfred, as the god of married bliss, delivered his blessing on the new-minted couple. This was the closing scene of the play, with only a final kiss between her and Ralph, and then a rousing fiddle tune while they all took their bows.

But while she kept her joyful bride's smile on her face, the bitter irony of Alfred's speech, preaching love and happiness, stung her to the quick. If Ross had only been another actor, then would her father be blessing their union, too? If she'd been born into a grand house like this instead of into the company, would she be in the audience, watching the play that honored her wedding?

She looked to the bench out front where Emma sat with Weldon. More precisely, Emma sat on Weldon's lap, her knees hooked over his as they kissed, with Emma making shameless cooing sounds of pleasure that Cordelia could hear clear across the room. The two seemed impossibly young to Cordelia—she doubted that Weldon could even grow a beard yet—but they also seemed impossibly in love. Without a mother to rule these past days, any scrap of propriety that would have kept them separated until after the wedding seemed to have been forgotten, and to see them together like this made Cordelia certain that Emma and Weldon had already experienced their wedding night.

What must it be like to have that joy, that freedom? How could they realize the luxury they had, to follow their hearts for life as they pleased, and the certainty that any child they might conceive between them would be welcome, loved and secure in its place in the world?

"Kiss me, Cordelia," Ralph whispered through a smile of clenched teeth. "Now who's forgetful, I ask you?"

Quickly she kissed him, barely grazing his lips with her own. Ross had spoiled her for kissing anyone else, especially stage kisses with actors like Ralph Carter.

"Fanfare and rejoicing, huzzah, huzzah, huzzah." Alfred clapped his hands, smiling at everyone in the company except, it seemed, her. "Praise yourselves, all of you. I'll grant a short respite now, and we shall gather again in an hour."

Dutifully Cordelia joined in the applause, then turned away from the others. Though no one would dare say so, she was sure they'd all overheard her earlier conversation with her father. There were precious few secrets in the company, but for now she didn't want sympathy from Gwen or any of the others. She didn't feel as if she belonged among them now. She didn't feel she belonged anywhere. All she wished was to be alone, and with her head down, she hurried for the door.

"Cordelia." Ross caught her arm, holding her back by the doorway. "What demon's chasing you, eh?"

Her smile was tight as she gave her shoulders a little shrug. "You never come to rehearsals during the day."

He closed his eyes, and placed his hand across his chest the way that Ralph was supposed to do. "'With my love to light my heart, / However canst I keep apart?'"

"I cannot believe you remembered my doggerel!"

"I've heard it enough, haven't I?" He reached out and brushed a stray curl from her forehead. "I've always been a quick study at memorizing. I was the fastest in my class to learn the first book of the *Iliad* by rote."

Purposefully she tried to keep her voice light, a match for his. She didn't want to spoil their last days together by sharing her father's tirade or her own unhappiness.

"So was it Achilles and Hector who kept you from your work today?" she asked. "Will they be the scapegoats when your paper isn't ready to be delivered?"

"No, when it comes to interruptions, those old warriors can't hold a candle—or a sword—to you." His smile faded, and he gently settled his hands on her shoulders. "I wished to see you, Cordelia, and I didn't want to wait until this evening. We must talk, you and I, before too much more—"

"Beg pardon, m'lord, but I must pass," Ralph said, trying to squeeze around them to the door. He was pale, his face gleaming with sweat, and his eyes had a strange, unfocused desperation. "I'm not feeling m'self, and I need—I need—"

But before Ralph could finish, his legs folded beneath him, and he slumped forward. Ross grabbed him around the waist, half dragging Ralph to one of the ballroom's benches.

"What is wrong, Cordelia?" Alfred demanded, leaning over the other actor with concern. "What has happened to him?"

Swiftly she loosened Ralph's collar. "I don't know, Father. He said he wasn't feeling himself and then he seemed to fold up like this. Last night you didn't go—"

"He's not had a drop, not in my company." Frowning, Alfred laid his hand on Ralph's forehead. "He's on fire with fever, the poor fellow."

"There's a good physician in the next town," Ross said. "I'll send a footman for Dr. Graham, so that Mr. Carter here can have the best care."

"Thank you, no, my lord." Alfred rose, folding his arms

over his chest. "No physicians. Your generosity is well intended, but we'll see to Ralph ourselves."

Holding Ralph's hand, Cordelia quickly looked up. "But Father, surely a surgeon would better know—"

"We always look after our own, daughter," he said. "Just because we're actors doesn't mean we take charity from fine folk like His Lordship."

Ralph groaned, turning his head from side and side, as Gwen hurried up with a cup of water.

"See now, he's better already," Alfred said. "We'll take him back to the gatehouse to rest and mend, my lord, and I promise you he'll be right as rain in time for the wedding play."

Ross frowned and Cordelia rose swiftly to stand beside him. "I do care more for the man's well-being than the play, Lyon, as difficult as that may be for you to accept," Ross said.

At first Alfred didn't answer, holding the silence, before he bowed with a rolling flourish of his hand.

"I am a man of great resiliency, my lord," he said, pointedly including Cordelia. "I can accept anything that needs accepting. But unlike others who court misfortune and sorrow, my lord, I have the sense to keep to my station in life, and I thank the Maker I can tell the difference."

Chapter Eight

Cordelia pulled her chair a little closer to Ralph's bed, striving to make out his whisper of a voice. "Your throat is no better?"

"Worse," he croaked, pushing himself higher on the pillow to slice his finger across his throat. "Like hell."

"I am most sorry to hear it." She sighed, sitting back in her chair with her hands in her lap. Alfred had insisted that Ralph would be recovered in time for the performance, continuing with rehearsals for the supporting cast and the fiddler, making the final placements of the scenery and properties, even arranging the audience's chairs in neat rows in the ballroom.

But he'd also chosen to ignore Ralph's condition, blithely leaving Cordelia behind at the gatehouse to watch over the ailing actor, and she'd sent for the village apothecary, who had diagnosed a putrid quinsy, serious but not fatal. Cordelia had watched with growing concern as the apothecary had bled Ralph, and for another shilling, he'd left a foul-smelling concoction of mallows as a purge that had left poor Ralph even weaker than before.

Now the play was scheduled to begin in less than twenty hours, the bridegroom hero was still too ill to stand or speak, and once again Alfred had gone off with Gwen and Tom and a few of the others to "feed their muse" at the Tawny Buck.

"Sorry," Ralph whispered, his face twisted with misery. "Sorry."

"It's not your fault, Ralph," she said, forcing a smile as she patted his hand. "Besides, the Lyon Company has never before canceled a performance for any reason, and I've no intention of changing that now."

He arched his brows in exaggerated surprise. "How?"

"We'll manage somehow, Ralph," she said, determined to be cheerful, if not realistic, for his sake. "We always do."

But it was past time for someone to make a responsible decision about the fate of *The Triumph of Love,* and whether Cordelia wanted to or not, that someone was going to have to be her.

"What have you heard about my wedding play, Ross?" Emma demanded, twisting her pearl bracelet around and around her wrist with growing anxiety. "I know you've heard something. Am I to have my *Triumph of Love* or not?"

Ross leaned closer to the looking glass, wincing as he ran his forefinger along the inside of his shirt collar. He knew he wasn't supposed to meddle with the black silk neck cloth once his manservant had tied it in the precise knot for the evening, but the blasted thing was near choking him.

"As far as I know the play will be shown as planned, Emma," he said. "I've no reason to believe otherwise."

"But you saw what happened yesterday to the actor playing my Weldon!" Emma was pacing now, back and forth across the carpet in Ross's bedchamber. "He was horribly ill. By now he might even have died, for all anyone is telling me!"

"I'm sure we would know if he'd died, Emma," Ross said, still trying to gain an extra half inch in his collar. "No doubt he is perfectly fine."

"But he didn't come to rehearse his parts in the ballroom today with the others!" she cried, her voice rising to a plaintive wail. "I went, and I saw with my own eyes. Neither he nor Cordelia were there, and they play us!"

"Hysterics won't help anything, Emma." Of course he'd noticed, too, that Cordelia hadn't come to the hall today, just as she hadn't come to his library last night. Here his house was full to bursting with family and guests, his only sister was going to be married, and yet all he could think of was why in blazes Cordelia Lyon had vanished just as he'd been ready to ask her to stay. "Perhaps they are simply resting their voices to make a good showing tomorrow."

"Oh, Ross, I feel so sure I'm to be disappointed!" She came to stand beside him, clutching at his sleeve as she made an especially tragic face at their joint reflection in the glass. "A wedding should be the most perfect, most glorious moment in a lady's life, and now mine is to be spoiled because I won't have my wedding play!"

"Hush, Emma, please," he said, trying to sound stern but comforting at the same time. "You're only going to make your eyes red and your nose look like a turnip, and when you go down to dinner, our guests will wonder if you're having second thoughts about marrying poor Weldon."

"My nose does not look like a turnip, Ross, and of course I wouldn't have second thoughts about my dearest Weldon!" She snuffled, rolling her eyes for extra emphasis. "It's you who promised me *The Triumph of Love,* as my special wedding present, and now everything is going to be spoiled!"

He took her by the arms, turning her away from the looking glass to make her concentrate on him instead.

"Listen to me, Emma. Everything is not going to be spoiled. Everything is going to be *fine.*"

She gave a slurpy sob, dabbing at the corners of her eyes with her lace-trimmed handkerchief. "Then you won't break your promise to me, Ross, will you? You'll make sure I'll have my *Triumph?*"

He nodded, thinking of how relieved he'd be when this wedding was done. "I've never broken a promise to you yet, have I?"

She shook her head, the tiny white flowers looped into her hair bobbing. "So you will find Cordelia and ask her what is happening?"

That was harder; that he couldn't guarantee, even to Emma.

"I'll do my best, lamb," he said, his voice gruff. "That's all any man can do. I promise I'll do my best."

And prayed that his best would be enough for Cordelia, as well.

Cordelia walked on the grass along the side of the drive as yet another coach full of well-dressed people passed by, the coaches' wheels kicking little white stones around her feet. She had not seen the hall like this before, with so many candles lit inside that it seemed to glow before her like a giant lantern. The windows had been thrown open to the warm spring evening, and through them came scattered laughter and conversation and the sounds of a small orchestra. She remembered Lady Emma speaking of a great dinner to be given as part of the wedding celebrations, but Cordelia hadn't imagined it to be quite as great as this.

Coming closer to the front door, she hung back in shadows, painfully aware of her plain yellow linen gown. She had to speak to Ross, but she'd no place among these grand folk walking up the polished steps with jewels glittering around their throats and wrists. Likely the footman would turn her away if she tried, anyway. But the door to Ross's library— that was *her* way, the one she'd shared each night with him.

She hurried around the back of the house, along the paths that led to the garden outside the library. But tonight those windows were dark, with Ross playing host to his guests else-where in the house instead of working.

She climbed up the steps anyway, pressing against the glass to peek inside. There was his desk, as disheveled as ever, the narwhal's horn, the tank for making waves and the cush-ioned bench where they'd sat and talked and kissed by the hour: it all looked like a waxwork setting now, uninhabited and frozen in time the way her memories of it were destined to be. Leaving Ross in two days would have been painful enough, but after she told him tonight that the company must cancel the play—why, likely he'd be so angry at her for dis-appointing his sister that he wouldn't even say goodbye.

She forced herself to turn away, twisting her hands forlornly in the ends of her shawl. If she went to the kitchen door, she might be able to coax one of the maids or footmen to take a note to Ross, asking him to meet her. Even so, he might not be willing to—

"Cordelia?" The glass door squeaked open behind her, and before she'd even turned all the way around Ross had gath-ered her into his arms, holding her so tightly she wondered if he'd ever let her go. "Ah, lass, I came here only to fetch a book to give to another gentleman at breakfast, but I never dreamed I'd find you here, too!"

"Oh, Ross, Ross," she whispered against his shoulder, her happiness tempered by what she must do now. "Ross, we must speak. I—I—oh, I have such bad news to tell you!"

"You do?" He set her down, his face turning somber as he went to light the candles on his desk. He was impossibly hand-some in his dark evening clothes, his waistcoat embroidered with silver and gold vines. "Then come, sit, and tell me your worst."

She took the chair across from him instead of at his side, needing the desk between them. "It *is* the worst. Ralph Car-ter has a putrid quinsy of the throat, and though the apothe-cary bled him, he is too sick to speak and too weak to stand, and—and—" She gulped. She'd put so much into this foolish play, and she hated to have it end like this. "Because of that, I—that is, the Lyon Company—regrets that I—we must cancel our performance of *The Triumph of Love*."

She held her breath, waiting for him to respond as Alfred would have in the same situation: the shouting of oaths, slamming of fists and hurling of crockery.

But Ross wasn't Alfred, and all he did was draw his brows together, more to show he was considering rather than being angry. "You have no understudy for the hero's part?"

"Father doesn't believe in them," she said. "He says we're too small a company to carry any idle players. Everyone pulls their own weight. It's always worked before."

He tapped his fingertips on the edge of the desk, the shadows from the single candle dancing over his face. "You all could simply have packed everything into your wagon and vanished in the night. Isn't that the way with some acting companies?"

"But not ours!" She gasped with indignation. "You know me better than that, Ross! I would never treat anyone so shamefully, and especially not you!"

"Instead, you have been honest with me." His smile was sudden, as brilliant as the candle's flame. "Even when I neither expected nor deserved it."

She raised her chin, still on her guard. "You should know that I cannot help it. It is how I am. But oh, Ross, I will be so sorry to disappoint Lady Emma!"

"Perhaps you won't." His smile twisted wryly to one side. "Can I be honest with you, too, sweetheart? I know all of Mr. Carter's lines from watching you rehearse. Do you trust me to say them in his place, and save my sister's wedding play?"

She stared at him, stunned. "You are an earl, a gentleman of learning and reputation. Why would you venture onto a stage with a pack of common actors to risk your good name before your guests? Why, Ross? *Why?*"

"Because I can." His shrug was sheepish, disarming. "Because I don't wish my sister to be distraught, indulged little creature that she is. But if I am being most honest, Cordelia Lyon, I am willing to make a complete ass of myself because I want to impress you."

She lifted her hand to her mouth in disbelief. "You would do that for my sake?" she asked, her voice squeaking upward. "For *me?*"

"For God's sake, sweetheart, don't cry." He hurried around the desk to take her into his arms "Save the tears for when you hear my lines."

She took the handkerchief he offered with a snuffle of emotion. "That you would do this for me—oh, Ross, I cannot believe it!"

He chuckled, pulling her closer against his chest. "'My heart only such endless devotion knows, / Such passion! Such yearning! Such fervency that glows! / Oh, dearest lady, the queen of my heart / That rules my every passion even when we're apart.'"

"Now you *will* make me cry," she said, not bothering to wipe away her tears as she turned her face up to his. It didn't matter that his delivery was as unemotional and dry as a mathematical equation. He'd done this for her, and, oh, how empty her life was going to be without him in it! "Using my own words to win me, and without any mistakes, either, like poor Ralph makes—that isn't fair, Ross, not at all."

"You told me Shakespeare wasn't supposed to be fair," he said, his voice low and gruff. "I suppose that must hold for your verses, too."

"A pox on my verses, Ross," she whispered fiercely, curling her hands around the back of his neck. "Kiss me instead."

At once his mouth found hers, as hungry as her own. His kiss was hard and demanding, as if he, too, sensed how little time was left for them together, and she gave herself freely to him, arching her body up against his. She wanted to feel him, she wanted more, and with shaking fingers, she shoved his coat from his shoulders and down his arms, and as soon as she could work the buttons on his waistcoat free, that, too, followed to the floor.

Still without breaking their kiss, she tugged his shirt free of his trousers, sliding her hands up inside the billowing white linen to find the warm skin inside. She'd already learned he'd more of a sailor's body than a scholar's, and she loved exploring the muscles of his back, the taut planes and valleys that showed the strength beneath the skin. She slid her hands lower along his spine, into the back waistband of his breeches, and he groaned, then jerked his shirt over his head.

"Who's not playing fair now?" he whispered hoarsely as he feathered kisses along her throat. With one arm he swept the top of his desk clear, papers drifting to the floor, and lifted her to perch on the edge.

He kissed her again, his lips teasing along her throat as he eased the small sleeves of her gown from her shoulders, sliding them down her arms until the soft muslin slipped from her breasts. She gasped with surprise, then gasped again with pleasure as he kissed her nipples, teasing the soft flesh into hard peaks with his tongue.

"That is so—so *wicked,* Ross," she breathed. She closed her eyes and let her head drop back, the better to feel the sensation. "What you do—what you do."

"I thought you'd left me, Cordelia," he said, his voice a rough, urgent growl as he eased her knees apart to press closer between them. "I thought you'd gone forever."

"Oh, no, Ross," she whispered, running her hands through the curling dark hair on his chest. "I would never leave you like that, with no word of farewell!"

"Then don't." His hands were warm on the bare skin of her thighs as he pushed her skirts high, higher, far above her garters and stockings, far above where they'd ever gone before. "Stay here, Cordelia, with me in this house. Stay."

"Oh, Ross, what you ask," she murmured, trying to think straight while he was doing everything in his power to make her not think at all. Higher, higher, his hand had crept, kneading her, wooing her trust, until he found a place between her legs that she'd never realized existed. When he touched her there, stroking her gently, she shuddered and opened herself to his touch, desperate for more.

"Stay with me tonight," he said again, the words burning a heated path along the side of her throat. "Please. Don't leave."

If she stayed, she would be everything that her father had accused her of being, a rich lord's plaything. She would be doomed to repeat her mother's folly, a common, low actress who'd squandered her talents on the stage for what she could earn instead on her back. She would be what every respectable person thought an actress was, and they'd be right.

But because it was Ross, her Ross, none of the rest mattered. He was offering her tonight, and tonight would be enough.

"Yes," she whimpered, nipping at the saltiness of his bare shoulder. "Oh, Ross, yes!"

He growled rather than answered, a deep, possessive sound that was so purely male that Cordelia's own desire burned hotter in response. He was making the tiniest circles with his fingertips—how could so slight a caress cause such delicious havoc in her whole body?—and she arched against him, her breath coming in quick little catches that echoed her need.

He eased her backward until she felt the leather top of his desk beneath her, kissing her still as he lowered himself over her. Suddenly his teasing fingers were replaced by something larger, thicker, blunter, pushing into her and shattering the pleasure like broken glass.

"Oh, Ross, please, wait!" She tried to wriggle free, desperate to ease the sense of invasion. "It—this cannot be right!"

"I'm sorry," he whispered, his own breathing coming in ragged gulps. "I'm—I'm sorry, but it will get better."

She swallowed hard. "You are certain?"

"I am," he said, holding her, kissing her, even as he kept himself still to let her body grow accustomed to the new sensation of his. "I—I promise."

"That—that is good." She closed her eyes, the pain lessening. It was better, better in a way that, for once, she had no words to describe. He was moving slowly against her again, and to her surprise his slow, steady strokes were beginning to bring the pleasure back, coiling the tension in her body even more tightly than before.

Instinctively she curled her legs over his hips and he groaned, driving more deeply, and just as she felt sure she'd couldn't bear it, her release came in a glorious rush, with Ross following close behind.

He pushed his weight up on his elbows to look at her, his smile so warm she wanted to weep. Too late she realized that this would make it harder, not easier, to leave him.

"Sweet lass," he said, his voice a hoarse whisper as he brushed a damp lock of her hair back from her forehead. "My own dear, sweet Cordelia. Ah, I wish I knew the perfect words to say to you now, the words you deserve."

She tried to smile. He already knew the perfect words, and so did she, carved forever into her heart:

"Was there ever such a pair of star-crossed lovers?"

Chapter Nine

❧❧❧

The dawn's mist was still low on the grass when Cordelia let herself into the gatehouse. She had never expected a night to pass so swiftly, or with such passion, and she could not keep the giddy smile from her lips as she thought of Ross, and all the wonderful, wicked explorations and experiments they'd made together in his library.

She eased the door shut after her, taking off her damp slippers before she began up the stairs. She expected the rest of the company to still be abed at such an hour, with Alfred snoring the loudest of all. But to her surprise he and Gwen and several others were gathered around Ralph's bed, the guttering candles from night still lit along the windowsill. Their bodies blocked Cordelia's view of the actor, and with a sharp stab of dread, her conscience raced to the worst conclusion.

"Why, look who the milkmaid brought with the morning cream." With his black cloak wrapped around his shoulders, Alfred looked up but didn't smile. "I trust you passed an enjoyable night away from your own bed?"

Cordelia flushed but didn't apologize as she unwrapped her shawl. "Yes, I did. How is Ralph?"

"Why, how kind of you to ask," Alfred said. "I believe you

were given the responsibility of looking after him last evening, weren't you?"

"He was better when I left," she said quickly, her fear for Ralph mushrooming. "He was sleeping, just as the apothecary ordered, and I knew you'd all be returning soon, and I—"

"I *am* better, Cordelia," croaked Ralph from behind the others. "Better, aye?"

"Ralph!" Cordelia pushed her way past Gwen to kneel on the floor beside his bed. "Oh, I'm so glad you're feeling more like yourself!"

He smiled wanly, unable to say more. No matter what Ralph claimed, the actor was still far from well, his face sheened with the fever's sweat, and though they'd propped him higher on his pillows, Cordelia doubted he'd the strength to sit upright without such support.

"Fortunate for you that he is, Cordelia." Alfred clapped his hand on Ralph's shoulder. "And fortunate for us, as well. Why, with another round of his physic, he should be right as rain for our performance at the hall tonight."

"Oh, Father, look at him!" she cried. "How can you believe he'll be fit for tonight?"

Alfred glowered, folding his cloaked arms over his chest like wings. "The Lyon Company has never canceled a performance due to weakness, Cordelia."

"And we won't now." She scrambled back to her feet, trying not to think of how creased and wrinkled her gown must look. "I've found someone to take Ralph's place tonight."

"Where, pray?" Alfred demanded. "In the hedgerow?"

"At the hall." Without thinking, she folded her arms across her chest, echoing her father's defiance as she faced him. "His Lordship himself has offered to take the role, Father."

Alfred laughed derisively, and the others followed. "An earl playing at being a player? Even as besotted as you are, Cordelia, you must see the folly in such a reckless choice!"

"What I see is a kind and generous gentleman who does not wish to disappoint his sister," she said, trying hard to keep her temper. "What I see is a man who knows all the lines from watching our rehearsals, better than Ralph himself. *And* what I see with the greatest clarity of all is us standing before the local magistrate, charged with breach of contract for failing to provide a wedding play as promised."

"But the earl is the rankest of amateurs!" Alfred protested, his voice rumbling with indignity. "Consider what his presence will do to cheapen the art of our company!"

"Then consider this, Father," she said, choosing her words with the greatest care and only the slightest tremble of emotion. "If you do not accept His Lordship as your leading man tonight, then you will not have a leading lady, either."

She had made her choice. Now Alfred and the others would, too, and with her head held as high as the queens she played, Cordelia turned away from them and left.

In the little tiring-closet off the ballroom that was serving tonight as a makeshift dressing room, Ross read his lines yet again, whispering them over and over to himself as he unfurled the white scroll with his part written out in Cordelia's tidy hand. But his hands were sweating so much that he was blurring the ink, his heart racing at such a clip that he couldn't make his eyes focus on the words. He had lectured before the learned members of the Royal Society, discussed his findings with His Majesty, and addressed the entire ship's company on the deck of the *Perseverance,* but through all that he'd never felt even a fraction as nervous as he did now.

He went to rub his handkerchief across his forehead, and at the last instant remembered he couldn't, not without smearing his paint. Gwen had first deadened his face to a ghost's white, then drawn bright red patches on each cheek and more red on his lips, and finally had ringed his eyes with thick black lines. The paint was hot and sticky on his skin, one more reason to feel damned uncomfortable, and he wondered how the devil women could put up with such nonsense.

"Oh, Ross, look at you!" Cordelia circled around him, patting at his gaudy peacock's coat and waistcoat with approval. "How vastly fine a figure you will cut on the stage!"

"What I look like is some deuced circus clown," he said, so forlornly that she laughed, her teeth too white in her bright red lips. Her lovely face was painted every bit as garishly as his, and topped by a fantastic high wig with golden yellow curls and huge paste jewels hanging from her ears.

"And I say you will have every lady in the audience sighing of love for you." She glanced down at the wilting scroll in his hand. "Are you sure of your lines? Do you wish to practice again?"

He shook his head with glum resignation. "If I do not know them now, I won't know them in a quarter hour."

"You shall be quite fine, I am sure," she said, the stiff gold curls bouncing with more conviction than she felt. "Just go slowly and calmly, and speak as you usually do, without trying to force the rhymes. And if you forget anything, simply look to me, and I shall cover it."

"Of course you'll be calm," he said. "You've done this your entire life."

"Well, yes, but what is that compared to all the useful scholarly things you know?" She reached up to smooth the silver braid on his collar. "Your work saves people from drowning and such. Mine merely amuses them."

"I like how you amuse me," he said, taking her hand and raising it to his lips. "I can't imagine any better work than that."

"Oh, my poor Ross." Her gaze softened as she looked up at him. "I know how difficult this must be for you, and I pray you realize how grateful I am that you're doing it at all."

"For you," he said gruffly. "For Emma, too, but mostly for you, and if—"

"Hush, hush, the play's begun!" she whispered, putting her hand over his mouth to silence him. "I can hear Father's prologue. Hurry, we must take our places for our entrance!"

She took his hand to lead him to the ballroom where Alfred Lyon was already speaking, his rich, deep voice likely being heard clear in the next county. There was no proper stage or curtain, but lanterns had been set in a line to light the actors, with the fiddler sitting to one side to provide suitable music. In the front row of chairs Ross could make out Emma and Weldon, his sister glowing with happiness to see her play finally beginning.

Well, let her glow away now, Ross thought with grim resignation. Once he was out there, Emma might not feel as cheery.

"Four more lines, then Father's done, and we are on," whispered Cordelia, blowing him a quick kiss that would spare their paint. "Now take a deep breath to relax, and recall your first words. And good luck, my own love!"

My own love. She'd never called him that before, or ever once spoken of love at all. Did she love him, then? Did he love her?

"Come along, Ross, now, now!" She was pulling him forward, in front of her father and into the ring of bright candlelight. Applause washed over him, and he stared out past the lanterns to the ghostly faces in the audience, row after row of them, as far as he could see. He'd never imagined he'd so many guests in his house. Who the devil were they, anyway, these scores of eyes staring at him?

The applause died away, and still he stared, as stunned as a deer caught in a hunter's sights. Someday he should write a paper on the nature of common stage fright, its effects on the general constitution and the nervous system in particular.

"Fire when ready, Ross!" his cousin James called from somewhere in the haze of faces. "We can't wait all the night long!"

Nervous laughter rippled through the audience, and Cordelia took his hand again, forcing him to look at her instead.

"'When first I rose this day with the sun,'" she began, speaking his lines as if they were her own. "'How would I guess to find my love before 'twas done?'"

"'A lady fair I'd known from birth,'" he said, the words suddenly there for him. "'But only now aware of her worth.'"

Cordelia's smile of relief was the most beautiful thing he'd ever seen. "'And I, my dearest squire, how could I see / That together our fates were destined to be?'"

The words came easily now, ready when he needed them, and so were the prompts to take Cordelia's hand, or kneel before her, or turn with her as if they were dancing. He knew compared to the others—especially to Cordelia—that he was stiff and awkward, and he couldn't make himself break the singsong recitation. But before he'd realized it, the first act was done, and she was hurrying him off to change his coat for the next scene.

"Cordelia, one moment," he said, catching her by the arm. "You said something before we began, something that I need to ask—"

"Not now, Ross, there's no time," she said, pinning a wreath of holly branches to the top of her head to signify Christmas. "Ask me whatever you please afterward. Now where's your cloak with the false snow on the shoulders? Quickly, quickly!"

He found the cloak and remembered his lines, and soon the second act was done, too, with only the third remaining. For this act Cordelia chose no fancy costume, but the same simple muslin gown she'd worn the night they'd made waves. With the end of the play in sight and only the wedding and blessing remaining, she seemed even more at ease on the stage, every gesture full of charm and grace and her eyes lighting from within each time she caught Ross's gaze. He'd heard the rest of the company discussing their plans to leave early in the morning, off to their next engagement, and he couldn't believe that Cordelia would be gone, as well. He couldn't even imagine his life then, without her in it.

She skipped lightly across the stage before him, the sparkling scarf she'd worn in the orchard drifting from her hands. She almost seemed to be performing for him alone, as if the rest of the audience didn't matter or even exist, and as he watched her, he forgot them, too.

"'My heart knows only joy when you are here,'" she said, turning in a little pirouette before him. "'To leave you ever would bring naught but tears.'"

"Then don't," he said, not written lines, but his own words. "Stay here with me, and make last night go on forever."

He saw the startled look flash across her eyes before instinctively she improvised to cover for him.

"What happened in one breathless night," she said quickly, "should not be enough to cloud wrong from right."

"What we have is right," he said, taking her by the hand. "You know it, too, else you wouldn't have called me your love."

Her eyes widened, and she swallowed hard. "What is said in haste or passion isn't always—isn't always—"

"Isn't always in the fashion?" He grinned at her. "I love you, Cordelia, and the only thing that has to rhyme with is that you love me in return."

She gasped, a tear sliding over the black painted line surrounding her eye. "I do love you, Ross, oh, so very much! But what future can that love have when we—"

"A future together," he said, drawing her against his chest with his arm around her waist. "Marry me, Cordelia. Marry me, and be my wife, and we'll make that happiness last forever."

"You are sure?" Her heart was thumping so hard he could feel it, too. "You are an earl, while I am—"

"The woman I love," he said, leaving no doubts. "I've never been more sure in my life."

Another tear slipped down her painted cheek, then another, tears of joy, not regret. "Then yes, Ross, I do love you, and I will marry you. Yes, yes, yes!"

She flung her arms around his shoulders and kissed him, and as he kissed her back, he heard the applause. He looked over Cordelia's shoulder, past the row of lanterns and into the ballroom, and saw his friends and family and other guests all on their feet, cheering and laughing and whistling and calling their names, as pleased as an audience could be.

"Oh, Ross." Cordelia smiled up at him through her tears. "I suppose we must take our bows."

"In a moment." He smiled in return and kissed her again, marveling at how impossibly dear she'd become to him. "Even if Emma's going to want my head for stealing her thunder, and her wedding play."

Cordelia grinned. "If she does, you've only to remind her that the title of this play is *The Triumph of Love.*"

"Then triumph away, my love," he said, laughing. "Triumph away, and never stop."

They were wed a month later on a midsummer's night, a date that Alfred Lyon pronounced most auspicious for a happy marriage. This time the ceremony was held not in the hall's chapel, but in the garden under the stars, with the sliver of a new moon rising above them.

The bride told everyone that her gown had been inspired by her groom's love of astronomy—a dark blue silk gauze dotted with crystals that twinkled like a thousand stars—but the guests all agreed that it was the earl's love for Miss Lyon that now ruled his life. The wedding ring Ross gave Cordelia proved it, too: a gold-and-diamond band of hearts and stars.

Alfred Lyon had offered to stage a wedding play for them, just as had been done for Lady Emma and Sir Weldon Dodd. But in the end, Ross and Cordelia had politely declined, and not just because of the prodigious display of dancing fairies and elves that Alfred had promised as part of the spectacle, either. Yet how could any play, even one staged by the Lyon Company, ever hope to top the conclusion that Ross and Cordelia themselves had improvised for *The Triumph of Love*?

And later, much, much later, after the wedding and the feast and the dancing were done, when the last of the guests had left or retired for the night, the new Lady Cordelia leaned from the window of her husband's bedchamber and gazed up at the stars overhead.

"I know one is supposed to wish on the first star of the evening," said Cordelia as Ross joined her, "but do you think it would be ill luck to wish on one now instead?"

"Not at all," he said, slipping his arms inside the coverlet she'd draped around her bare shoulders. "I don't know who concocted such baseless superstitions anyway."

"Baseless or not, I don't see the harm. I'll wish on that one, there, the brightest that's left." She pointed up at the sky, closed her eyes and whispered her wish. "Now *that* should bring us all the luck in the world!"

"Except that the star you've chosen isn't a star at all, but a planet." He pulled her closer, his hands sliding up and down along her bare skin as he kissed the nape of her neck. "But since it's the planet called Venus, I suppose I'll let you have your wish."

"Ha, as if even you have any control over wishes." She laughed softly and leaned her head back against his shoulder. "But you do know, don't you, how very, very happy you make me?"

"I've observed that, yes," he said softly. "Almost as happy as you make me, my fair thespian bride. Were there ever such star-crossed lovers, indeed?"

"Star-crossed," she said, "and now star-bound, forever and ever."

He frowned a bit, searching for a rhyme, and cleared his

throat. "Star-crossed and star-bound, forever and ever / That nothing under that heaven or on this earth will ever find a way to sever."

"That was dreadful." She laughed, and so did he, and as she twisted around to face him, she arched up to kiss him again. "Now come, My Lord, take your bow, and back to bed."

"To bed, my love," he said. "To bed."

* * * * *

Harlequin Historicals®
Historical Romantic Adventure!

CRAVING STORIES OF LOVE AND ADVENTURE SET IN THE WILD WEST? CHECK OUT THESE THRILLING TALES FROM HARLEQUIN HISTORICALS!

ON SALE APRIL 2005

THE RANGER'S WOMAN
by Carol Finch

On the run from an unwanted wedding, Piper Sullivan runs smack into the arms of Texas Ranger Quinn Callahan. On a mission to track outlaws who killed his best friend, Quinn hasn't got time to spare with the feisty lady. But he can't help but be charmed by Piper's adventurous spirit and uncommon beauty....

ABBIE'S OUTLAW
by Victoria Bylin

All hell is about to break loose when former gunslinger turned preacher John Leaf finds himself face-to-face with old love Abbie Moore. Years ago, John took her innocence and left her pregnant and alone. Now Abbie's back and needs his help. Will a marriage of convenience redeem John's tainted soul and bring love into their lives once more?

If you enjoyed what you just read,
then we've got an offer you can't resist!

Take 2 bestselling love stories FREE!

Plus get a FREE surprise gift!

Clip this page and mail it to Harlequin Reader Service®

IN U.S.A.
3010 Walden Ave.
P.O. Box 1867
Buffalo, N.Y. 14240-1867

IN CANADA
P.O. Box 609
Fort Erie, Ontario
L2A 5X3

YES! Please send me 2 free Harlequin Historicals® novels and my free surprise gift. After receiving them, if I don't wish to receive anymore, I can return the shipping statement marked cancel. If I don't cancel, I will receive 6 brand-new novels every month, before they're available in stores! In the U.S.A., bill me at the bargain price of $4.69 plus 25¢ shipping and handling per book and applicable sales tax, if any*. In Canada, bill me at the bargain price of $5.24 plus 25¢ shipping and handling per book and applicable taxes**. That's the complete price and a savings of over 10% off the cover prices—what a great deal! I understand that accepting the 2 free books and gift places me under no obligation ever to buy any books. I can always return a shipment and cancel at any time. Even if I never buy another book from Harlequin, the 2 free books and gift are mine to keep forever.

246 HDN DZ7Q
349 HDN DZ7R

Name	(PLEASE PRINT)	
Address	Apt.#	
City	State/Prov.	Zip/Postal Code

Not valid to current Harlequin Historicals® subscribers.

Want to try two free books from another series?
Call 1-800-873-8635 or visit www.morefreebooks.com.

* Terms and prices subject to change without notice. Sales tax applicable in N.Y.
** Canadian residents will be charged applicable provincial taxes and GST.
   All orders subject to approval. Offer limited to one per household.
   ® are registered trademarks owned and used by the trademark owner and or its licensee.

HIST04R   ©2004 Harlequin Enterprises Limited

Harlequin Historicals®
Historical Romantic Adventure!

**FROM KNIGHTS IN SHINING ARMOR
TO DRAWING-ROOM DRAMA
HARLEQUIN HISTORICALS OFFERS
THE BEST IN HISTORICAL ROMANCE**

ON SALE MARCH 2005

FALCON'S HONOR
by Denise Lynn

Desperate to restore his lost honor, Sir Gareth accepts a mission from the king to escort an heiress to her betrothed. Never did he figure on the lady being so beautiful—and so eager to escape her nuptials! Can the fiery Lady Rhian of Gervaise entrance an honor-bound knight to her cause—and her heart?

THE UNRULY CHAPERON
by Elizabeth Rolls

Wealthy widow Lady Tilda Winter accompanies her cousin to a house party as chaperon and finds herself face-to-face with old love Crispin, the Duke of St. Ormond. Meant to court her young cousin, how can St. Ormond forget the grand passion he once felt for Lady Tilda? Will the chaperon soon need a chaperon of her own?

Harlequin Historicals®
Historical Romantic Adventure!

PICK UP A HARLEQUIN HISTORICALS BOOK AND DISCOVER EXCITING AND EMOTIONAL LOVE STORIES SET IN THE OLD WEST!